Volume IV
The Scent of Tears

T

Tales of the Apt
(NewCon Press)

Spoils of War (2016)
A Time for Grief (2017)
For Love of Distant Shores (2018)
The Scent of Tears (2018)

The Shadows of the Apt
(Tor UK)

Empire in Black and Gold (2008)
Dragonfly Falling (2009)
Blood of the Mantis (2009)
Salute the Dark (2010)
The Scarab Path (2010)
The Sea Watch (2011)
Heirs of the Blade (2011)
The Air War (2012)
War Master's Gate (2013)
Seal of the Worm (2014)

TALES OF THE APT

Volume IV
The Scent of Tears

Adrian Tchaikovsky
and Friends

NEWCON
PRESS

NewCon Press
England

First edition, published in the UK October 2018 by
NewCon Press
41, Wheatsheaf Road, Alconbury Weston, Cambs, PE28 4LF

NCP170 Hardback
NCP171 Softback

10 9 8 7 6 5 4 3 2 1

ISBN: 978-1-910935-93-4 (hardback)
ISBN: 978-1-910935-94-1 (softback)

Cover art by Jon Sullivan
Editorial meddling by Ian Whates
Interior layout by Storm Constantine
Cover layout by Ian Whates

Contents

Old Blood

Adrian Tchaikovsky

The spreading stain of darkness gathering around Uctebri was pleasantly warm for now, but that would not last. Soon he would be shivering, heat leaching out into that growing pool and back to the world he had stolen it from. And Uctebri the Sarcad, most ambitious of his abhorred people, would die.

Lying in a pool of blood. It sounded luxurious, something his people should aspire to. *So much less fun when the blood's your own.*

The air brought the scent of smoke and engine oil, of an enemy who had no idea of the victory they had won. Above, the dark fingers of the forest sawed at each other in the wind. If he made a supreme effort and turned his head, he could see a corpse, wasted blood soaking the forest floor just as his was, and he too weak to crawl over and taste it. Past the body he could see sunlight through the last of the trees: open space and freedom. But sunlight had never been something his people prized.

Uctebri tried for tranquillity as his life seeped slowly away into the ground. It was hard, with death coming so fast on the heels of disappointment. Was he not one of the great blood magicians of the Mosquito-kinden? Was this a fit death for a power that should have shaken the world?

And might have done, in another age, but magic was no longer what it had been, nor were magicians. Now he was just the least ragged of a ragged race who had lived in shadows for so long that most thought they were just children's stories. The Mosquito-kinden's chance for power had come and gone centuries ago, back in the Days of Lore, when they challenged the Moths, greatest sorcerers of the age, for the rule of the world.

And they smashed us, Uctebri considered. *They drove us to the point of extinction. And then they fell in turn, and the busy, busy Apt rose up with their machines and their ignorance; so we are just a memory of a memory.*

He felt a deep well of frustration that he should die like this, within

7

arm's reach of a power that should have been his. A long life fighting for every scrap – food and lore both – and yet the ending the worst part of it…

Then there was movement nearby and he realised that things could still be worse. Out of the dark between the trees a figure came stumbling. It was the Moth-kinden woman and, though her grey robes were blotted liberally with dark red, she was still on her feet.

She stepped over the corpse without comment, leaning on her staff and with eyes only for the dying Mosquito. Her people had driven his to the point of destruction. He had been her reluctant accomplice, but beneath that he was her rival. Now that metal-shod staff slammed down next to his head and her face swam into view above him, drinking in his suffering. It must have eclipsed her own pain, because she could raise a smile for him. Lying helpless beneath that cold gaze, Uctebri cringed and tried to hasten his own demise for fear of the pain she was about to gift him.

Twelve days before:

Uctebri sensed the magicians as he crouched at the edge of a Wasp army camp, hoping to scavenge their leavings. Not long ago he had been darkening the dreams of superstitious Dragonfly-kinden peasantry and feeding off the richness in their veins. Now the Wasps had come with a mass-produced nightmare that Uctebri's bespoke darkness could not compete with.

Magic, his old senses told him, twitching at his concentration. The Commonweal had magic, but mostly dusty and abandoned. The Wasps had no magic, did not even believe in it. Since they came to swallow up province after province it was a rare thing to feel that touch within his mind. And a rare thing to feed well, too. The Wasps feared the dark like the Dragonfly peasants did, but when they feared something they destroyed it. Their camps were lit by burning gas and always they were buzzing in and out.

Now he was creeping too close to their sentries, because one of them had disciplined a slave an hour before and dumped the body just where their lights met the shadows, and Uctebri, great magician, was hungry. While the fighting had been fierce, there were plentiful casualties for him to slake his thirst on. Now he was behind the lines, the Wasps burned and buried the bodies and took the survivors away in chains.

He reached the body. Hunched like a shadow himself, drawing all his power about him to hide from their lamps and sharp eyes, he lapped at the wounds – cold now, but cold blood was better than no blood.

And magic was best of all. What magicians were abroad, in this wartorn and forsaken place? Magicians meant danger; magicians meant opportunity. And Uctebri had kept company only with the ignorant and the dead for a long time.

He knew then that he would seek them out, these magicians. And perhaps he would kill them, but he would at least sate his curiosity first.

He found them soon after, following that ethereal scent from shadow to shadow: two Lowlanders, southerners from a land the Empire had not conquered yet. And Lowlanders were fair game for the Slave Corps, yet the sergeant approached respectfully with a sack of loot and let the travellers paw through it. Uctebri watched, fascinated, seeing the Wasps take gold coin and hand over what must have seemed worthless trinkets to soldiers who didn't believe in magic.

They had this treasure with them all that time, he cursed himself. *And I too hungry to notice!*

Two Lowlanders: both women, both magicians, and as disreputable and worn out as Uctebri himself. One was Mantis-kinden, a tall skinny woman wearing a voluminous green robe that pooled at her feet. It had seen a few sword-thrusts, that garment, but darned more from wear than from war. Her reddish hair was long and loose, halfway to her waist; her lean face weirdly peaceful, eyes seeming to look into some other world where things were better. She leant on a long-headed spear and the Wasps gave her a wide berth.

The other magician did the talking and dispensed the gold, choosing which oddment to purchase, which to reject. She was a slight-framed woman with white, featureless eyes, grey-skinned and robed in grey. The copper band about her brow was set with the sort of stones actors used to enthral the gullible. Her open robe showed the ribs of a leather cuirass and a shortsword half-hidden at her belt. Clutching her plain, metal-shod staff, she looked more wanderer than wizard, yet Uctebri could feel the magic in her blood, speaking to his shrunken stomach. Grey skin, white eyes; Moth-kinden seldom came so far north, which was precisely why Uctebri's people had fled here centuries before, those few of them the Moths had left alive.

9

He watched the Wasps heading off and counting their coin, wondering if he dared brave the Mantis spear.

The women made camp and began to pick over the trinkets they had bought, and Uctebri decided he would try them tonight. They seemed lesser magi than he, though he was diminished by hunger and a long road. In his mind he planned his campaign, the magic he would use to baffle their own, the ancient game of power against power. Then he felt something sharp at his back and knew the moment had been taken from his hands. When he twisted about in fear and rage it jabbed harder, and he got a shove in the back for his pains, sending him staggering out into the firelight.

The Moth and Mantis showed no great surprise at his appearance. Perhaps they had been trailing their magic like a fisherman with a lure, to see what lurking magicians they might attract.

The Moth regarded him, and knew exactly what he was; he saw it in her expression. Still, no order came to send that spear through him. She only shrugged and said, "Everyone's coming out of the shadows these days."

Their third walked out from behind Uctebri: another woman, but no magician she. Uctebri stared balefully at the stocky Beetle shouldering her crossbow, and she grinned back. "What's this old monster then, mistress?"

"Monster indeed." The Moth smiled slightly. "Ruthan, let's all sit down and I'll tell you about the Mosquito-kinden."

The Beetle was Ruthan Bartrer, out of Collegium, and she was the Moth's servant. It was an eye-opening arrangement that was not explained just then, save that the Moth could speak of magic and the lost Days of Lore without Ruthan scoffing, with her hanging on the Moth's every word, in fact, desperate to understand.

The Mantis was Shonaen, and while the Moth talked she lit sticks of sickly-smelling incense and inhaled the smoke until her pupils were no more than dots. If she had ever been the death-bringer of her people's reputation, the mantle had sloughed off her long ago.

The Moth, though; when she spoke of magic, Uctebri felt something chime within himself. It made him remember how little his people had settled for, in hiding, in defeat. It made him want more.

She gave her name as Julaea, daughter of one Adguros of Tharn who had died an outcast. He had sought to rally his people to greatness, or so said Julaea. They had turned their backs on him, lacking his vision and courage. Now she was going to fulfil his dreams.

"The dreams of a dead magician are dangerous things to play with," Uctebri told her with a thin smile, but her words had their hooks in him nonetheless. And she had given him her name, which Moths were loath to do. That did more than the crossbow to keep him at their fire.

"It's time we took it back," she said simply, and laughed at his expression. "It's time for a new age of magic, Mosquito-kinden. You don't think so?"

"I have seen the greatest kingdom of magic dismantled by these machine-handed Wasps," Uctebri said quietly. "Centuries of lore put to the torch, traditions a thousand years old ground under their boots. I think an age of magicians has never been so far off. Sometimes I think we dreamt all our great days."

Julaea's smile was sharp as knives. "Old Bloodsucker, you haven't seen what I have. You think this is war, this song of slaves and slaughter? This is nothing to what the Wasps will bring. I have dreamt whole cities ablaze beneath a rain of fire. I have seen darts that pierce the strongest mail and reap soldiers like corn."

"What joyous visions," murmured Uctebri.

"Apt cities, Apt soldiers," Julaea told him. "All the artificer kinden will turn on one another and tear down everything they've built. It will be a new age of darkness, and the darkness was always ours, Old Bloodsucker. The darkness belongs to Moths and Mosquitos and Mantids."

Uctebri felt his old cynicism stir. "Prophecy," he said sourly. "If it could help us, then the Apt would never have thrown off your people's chains all those years ago. Since when has any magician been able to look into *their* future?"

"Since she was born to one," said Julaea, daughter of Adguros. "My father led a raid on the Beetle mines outside Helleron. They caught him; they chained him underground with their engines and their wheels. A year he was there, in the smoke and the scent of burning oil. When he came out under the sky he was magician no more; he had become a thing like they were, who understood the cogs and the pistons." She pronounced the Apt words carefully, learnt by rote. "He came to Tharn and tried to show them how to destroy the Beetle machines but they

11

would not listen to him. They would not trust him and they could not understand. But later I sat at his knee and listened; I dreamt of the machine future and its destruction. There is just enough of Adguros in me that I would master the world of the Apt."

"I fear you," Uctebri whispered, but he heard the longing in his own voice.

"You are right to," she told him. "I will overthrow the world. And you have seen my instrument already - the Wasp Empire will be my sword."

"An Empire has no hilt," Uctebri pointed out.

"But it does, if you know how to grasp it." He could not look at her smile now. It was too bright, too much like the fires of the Wasp machines.

A day later, on the road with the Beetle woman trotting with the sack of relics at Julaea's heels, he asked, "Why do they follow you?"

"Hope," she said, watching his eyes stray to the labouring Ruthan. "They haven't all forgotten the golden Days of Lore, the Beetles. Some of them, some few families, remember the love their kind once bore us."

A love so great they overthrew you and drove you from all your places of power, Uctebri thought, but then she gave him a sideways look and asked "And here you are. So why do *you* follow?"

"New blood is always a draw for an old man." Uctebri's grin was marred by withered lips and sharp teeth. "And your blood is very new indeed, unlike any I've sampled."

"Unlike like any you ever will, Old Bloodsucker."

"A better question is why you invited me to follow you. A frail old husk like me."

"I know power when I smell it. My people have spent centuries playing status games and ignoring the world. I will collect powerful people. I will stand on their shoulders. Even yours, old man. You're a Sarcad, a great man amongst the Mosquito."

"What little that is worth."

"Don't you want to make it mean something again?"

He stopped dead. "Am I hearing a Moth-kinden planning the return of the Mosquito? Or do you just want us out in the open so you can finish the job?"

She rounded on him, eyes flashing with a cold anger. "I will use every tool life gives me to bring down the cities of the Apt and revive the rule of magic. I will strike down anyone that stands against me, even the great lords of my own kinden. We have been in decline for half a century, all we old powers. We have retreated to our holes and forests, or traded our magic for empty ceremony or mere manipulation. It is time to fight *back*!" Her last word rang out across the countryside, a challenge to the world. "Aid me, lend me your shoulder and lift me high, and your people will share in the victory. Stand in my way and the last blood you see will be your own."

He was suddenly aware of steel brushing his wrinkled neck – the Mantis was at his back, her spear levelled to spit him.

"Well, well, then," he said softly. "Let the Wasps and the Ants and the Beetles fall upon one another. If there is no new age of magic at the end of it, at least there will be blood."

"Oh, there is always blood," she agreed.

A tenday of hard travel and buying trinkets from the Wasps saw them camping beside barren stretch of road picked clean by the war, the blackened ribs of a dead village the only landmark. That dusk he awoke to find Julaea waiting for him, her disciples gathered to her. Something had changed. For a dry-throated moment he thought they were going to kill him.

"What do you think, then, Old Bloodsucker?" she asked him. "Are you one of us?" Her gesture took in her other followers: the Beetle fussing over their supplies; the Mantis standing silent and still, a sentry whose vigilance was entirely directed at him.

Uctebri settled himself across from the Moth, sitting on the hard ground with his pale hands on his knees. His magic was stronger, out here in the wilds away from the machinations of the Apt. Julaea's company, her words and dreams, had rejuvenated him.

"You've got a good thing going on here," he remarked. "Quite a trove of Commonwealer knick-knacks in that bag of yours. Drain them all at once and you'd have quite the fistful of magic to accomplish... what? Or is it home now, for you? Going to teach your kin a lesson for slighting your father?"

"If it was?" she asked.

"Then we part company," he told her. "Let your Mantis chase me down if you will, but your people will not want a reminder that they did not quite kill all of mine when they had the chance, for all you appear not to care."

"Very wise," she said, baring that razor grin again. "Better the crossed spears of the Wasps than what my people'd do to you. But no, not home. I'm scarce more welcome there than you, Old Bloodsucker. I make my own way. When I overturn the world of the Apt, I'll make my people come to the court of the Wasps and beg."

"With that bag of trinkets you'll command the Wasp Empire?" *And is this it? Is she just the mad daughter of a cripple?* "Raise a storm, yes. Cloud a few minds or have some fearful merchant cut his own throat, but I've *seen* the Empire at work."

He had let his disdain show, and abruptly he was aware of how close Shonaen, the Mantis, was, dispassionately ready to kill him at a nod from her mistress.

Yet Julaea just smiled. "Old Bloodsucker, this is merely the gift that shall see my petition heard. This, and the power you still have in your dried-up body."

"A petition in what court?" He could no longer look at that smile. When she said, "Shonaen, tell him," it was a relief to look into the long, sallow face of the Mantis.

"I'm going home," Shonaen pronounced, as though the words were as much a surprise to her as anyone else.

"What home? The..." Uctebri tried to remember where the Lowlander Mantids even lived, "Nethyon, is it?"

Julaea sang out before Shonaen had a chance. "Not the Nethyon or the Etheryon. Not the Felyal or even Sacred Parosyal. My Shonaen is the last scion of another hold entirely. Tell me of the Darakyon, Old Bloodsucker."

Uctebri let that name lie in the dark a long while before he picked it up. "There are no Mantids of the Darakyon. Not for generations."

"Some few survived. Now, only one remains, inheritrix of all that sorrow," Julaea confirmed. "So tell me why, Uctebri."

He forced himself to meet the cutting edge of her expression. "Because your people did something terrible there. When the Apt threw you off and you had lost everything, your magi went to the Darakyon and tried to turn back history. Even my people felt it, as we hid in our holes. A ritual of fear and darkness so that none of the Apt would ever sleep soundly again. And you failed, you Moths. You overreached yourselves and poisoned the whole forest, destroyed the Mantis hold there. None walked out of that place, and only fools have walked in since."

"And what do they say of Shonaen's ancestral halls nowadays, old man?"

"That the ghosts of every Mantis and Moth still hang on the thorns there like old clothes," Uctebri told her. "That visitors are not welcomed."

"My people say the same," Julaea told him. "What they do not say is that there is *power* in the Darakyon, that they will not reach for out of guilt."

"And you know no guilt."

"No more than you, Old Bloodsucker. I will go before the twisted spirit of the Darakyon and I shall harness it to my will. I shall pluck out its heart and corrupt the very Emperor with promises of power. I shall bring ruin to all the cities of the Apt." Her white eyes gleamed with triumph. "You're smiling now, old man. It's a fearful, shrivelled thing, but I know a smile when I see it."

"With your power and mine, with the stolen relics of the Commonweal and your Mantis's birthright, you'll enslave the Darakyon?"

"Do you doubt me?"

And she was right, he was smiling.

They made tracks south, into that disputed territory that was neither Empire nor Commonweal nor Lowlands. To the east the Wasps had crushed every city to forge their gateway to the Commonweal. To the west Julaea's people kept to their mountain fastness of Tharn while the Beetles grubbed for coin in smoky Helleron. But between all these lay a stretch of forest that the roads passed north or south around; the Apt did not believe in ghosts, any more than they believed in Mosquito-kinden, but that just meant they had to invent rational reasons why they did not brave the trees.

Yet when Julaea and her tattered followers drew near forest's edge, the Black and Gold of the Imperial armies was already on display, armour gleaming in the dawn. Not some loot-fat band of slavers heading home from the Commonweal, but three score of the Light Airborne, scouts creeping past the ever-shifting borders of the Empire. Just as Julaea had said, the Wasps had their eyes on their western neighbours, whose wealth was not in old gold but in machines and industry. They were scouting out the way, seeing how far their soldiers might march before the self-involved Lowlanders took note of them.

"You can make a deal with these Wasps?" Uctebri asked the Moth.

She shook her head. "Slavers are easy to suborn. They're all in the business to make a private fortune. This lot are watching for Lowlander spies." A Moth, a Mantis and a Beetle. Whatever the Wasps might make of Uctebri, the others would fit the clothes of spies well enough. "We'll go past them at night."

"The forest will be stronger then," he noted, knowing it would not sway her.

"So will we."

The Wasps had a good watch out, but they lit few fires and had no eyes for the dark. What was plain was that more of their number had gone to scout the forest, no matter the stories they must have heard. The soldiers on the outside were growing increasingly skittish the longer their comrades were absent. Uctebri reckoned they would start burning things soon. He wondered how the Darakyon would react to that. In the harsh light of day, in these weak modern times, magic could not defeat Apt scepticism. At night, or under the shadowed canopy, a man's fears would creep up on him and poison his mind, throwing open all those doors that the old ways drew their power from. The Apt were right to fear the dark.

Julaea led them past the sentries' very noses. Uctebri had expected the Beetle, Ruthan, to tread on every stick and get herself killed, but Julaea wove the darkness and the night's silence about them. Uctebri flicked at the soldiers' minds to make them jump at all the wrong shadows, and the four of them were within the trees without the Wasps being any the wiser.

Uctebri felt the place the moment they set foot beneath its boughs. The Moths had tried their great ritual soon after the revolution. Five centuries of twisted, failed magic had festered in this place. The trees grew crooked and warty, hunched like murderers caught in the act. Overhead, the canopy layered hands of leaves until it strangled the moonlight. The forest watched them through each twig, each leaf. The night-flying insects were its spies, the ferns and moss its agents.

"How it hates us," Julaea whispered.

"It hates *you*," Uctebri corrected. The lens of the forest's attention was fixed on the Moth. *It remembers her kin, and how they ruined it. How pleasant not to be the most loathed for once.*

And yet Julaea pressed on, undaunted. She clutched the sack of Commonweal loot, and Uctebri could feel her drawing on the power that ancient magicians had stored there. Was this what those dead Dragonflies had foreseen, some renegade Moth burning their days of meditation to twist the arms of ghosts? But she spent it recklessly, treading ever deeper into the trees with Ruthan scuttling in her shadow and Shonaen striding at her side.

"You're home, Mantis," Uctebri remarked, careful not to be left behind. "Rejoice."

She stared at him. Her eyes said she had no idea who he was or where she was. Her body said she was about to kill him. Then she leant forwards, spear extended, and he heard the scrape of metal on metal. They had found what was left of the Wasp expedition.

Mostly he saw their armour. It lay between the trees with only a few white bones to evidence the wearers. Saplings grew through arm-holes and neck-holes, roots clawing through bracers and greaves and ferns springing in lurid sprays through the twisted holes that had let the blood out. The soldiers who had gone in that day had left a display looking decades old.

Uctebri felt a distinct shifting around him, physical and spiritual. The wood had not been fighting them before, not truly. Now it had them where it wanted them.

All around them, the forest shivered like the skin of a living thing. The branches overhead sawed at one another, a sudden wind keening through them like voices.

"Now," Julaea said, calm personified. "Join with me. Or die with me."

Uctebri needed no encouragement. They were in the depths of the darkness here, nothing of the Apt world outside to fetter him. He reached out against the louring wall of the forest's power and braced himself, feeling the Moth do the same, wrestling with the space around them to deny the trees their movement. A moment's slip and the trunks would close on them like teeth, the branches pierce like spears. And it was *strong!* Julaea had been right about this place. It was a great fouled well of old power neither tapped nor ebbed in centuries.

He felt the massed mind of the Darakyon try to fold the world about them, to turn its crooked trunks and withered boughs into jaws to crush them. But there was something lacking, some final force that would have cracked their mortal efforts like eggshells. They held, and then Julaea took a step forwards, and the forest swayed back around them, forced away by her iron will.

"Warriors!" Ruthan cried, squinting into the darkness. Past the stretch and twist of the tortured air, quick shapes came darting, long-limbed and bearing weapons. Caught by the forest's pressing strength, Uctebri felt a flare of panic as though their steel was at his throat already. He was an old hand at magic, though. His mind did not waver, though the forest forced fear into him through eyes and ears and nostrils.

Shonaen stepped forwards almost lazily, as though none of it was real. She took the first figure on her spear, spun about to catch another. A sword like a slice of moonlight flared at her face and she leant back no more than three inches to avoid it. The ghost warriors crowded at her, and she carved at them with her arm spines until they fell back again. No urgency touched her movements. She was like a soldier sleepwalking through weapons drill, stepping note-perfect through her forms and passes as though she was fighting dreams and shadows.

And she was, Uctebri knew. These phantasms had no more substance to them than the dark between the trees, even animated by the ghosts the forest was crawling with. It was an old magician's trick that few could master these days. Phantoms, but they could kill like real warriors, belief in them leaping from the points of their blades into the wounds they made.

And yet Julaea pressed on, a step at a time, towards the forest's centre, Uctebri bringing up the rear to prevent the forest crashing down on them as Shonaen danced her casual murders on either side.

"What are we seeking?" Uctebri demanded. "How will you rule here? It will not have you as its master." And indeed the Darakyon was showing no signs of giving up. "It hates you like poison!"

"It will have no choice," Julaea spat. "You hear me, trees? I am Julaea, daughter of Adguros. I am the voice of the Moth-kinden here, the voice you have always obeyed."

The forest shook its boughs at them in rage and the wind roared and bellowed, shredding the leaves above. And yet that final blow never fell.

"The forest has a heart," she told Uctebri. "The ritual crushed them all down, those magi and their warriors. It crushed them down and twisted off a knot of itself that they are all bound to. Hold that, and this power can be commanded, and when I can command, let it hate me as much as it likes!"

With that final word she broke through, and the whole of the Darakyon seemed to go reeling away in all directions, the trees tilting crazily, thorn-studded vines lashing as if in their death throes.

Despite it all, Uctebri felt some part of himself unconvinced. *It cannot be this easy. A trap, surely?* Yet when Julaea practically skipped forwards, he followed.

They had found her ritual site, that much was certain. The forest had ceased trying to coil itself about them and was quite still, as though marking the memory of all those who had died for the folly committed here. The trees at rest leant outwards from a central clearing, some place where perhaps the Mantids had raised one of their rotting idols, where Moth seers had stood and funnelled all their power into a ritual to return the world to the way it had once been, back when they had mattered. And they had failed, the task beyond even their united reach. Their power had got away from them and run wild through the Darakyon, and made it what it was today. Not a one of those great and wise magicians or their Mantis servants had lived.

There was no visible centre, but any magician's senses could find it. Julaea rushed forwards, hunting for the token that would allow her to make the Darakyon her plaything.

And stopped; turned, frowning, a single step back the way she had come, and then another. Her arms spread out as if for balance, but she was feeling out the topography of the magic, searching for the heart.

What will it be? A nut? A chalice? Uctebri was searching too: some small object of wood that would seem the work of human hands, but where was it? The Beetle Ruthan huddled close but Shonaen stalked farther and farther, still hunting shadows.

Julaea's blank eyes were wide, impossible to tell what she was looking at. She mouthed a word: "No..."

Uctebri came to the conclusion a moment after. "It's not here," he said. "How can it not be here?"

The wind rustled the leaves around them. The forest was laughing at them.

"Mistress," Ruthan called, voice trembling. She had ventured past the focus of the wood, that mocking absence. The moon shone down obligingly; the forest wanted them to know the sacrilege it had enacted on itself.

Uctebri spotted a camp, overgrown, the fire long cold. The intruders had not escaped freely, for the brambles and vines writhed amongst the ruin of tents, the splintered cages of ribs. At least one of them had lived, though; lived, and carried away the Darakyon's heart.

"Who dared…?" Julaea hissed, coming to the Beetle's shoulder to stare. Uctebri knew she would be naming every magician she ever knew, wondering which of them had the guile to creep in here and thwart her.

Ruthan, crouching by the ruined tents, held up some broken metal thing. Uctebri studied it a long time with his dark-adapted eyes before he could understand its purpose.

It was a crossbow, and what could be seen of the other personal effects looked Beetle-made – turned out in some faceless factory somewhere, not the work of a craftsman's hands. Oh, perhaps these had been some magician's servants, as Ruthan was, but Uctebri already knew it was not so. No sorcerer had come here to steal Julaea's prize, but only the ignorant – only the Apt.

"It knew someone like you would come to command it," he whispered. "And so it gave its heart to those who could never use it, could never even understand what they had discovered. Some Beetle-kinden has it on their mantelpiece even now, or on their desk as a paperweight."

Julaea hissed in pure frustration. Her white gaze fixed on Ruthan. "This is you."

The Beetle woman shrank from her. "Mistress, no!"

"Your people. Not content with driving mine into obscurity, now you steal our last scraps."

Ruthan started, "I only served you –" but Julaea cut her off.

"I cast you out. I withhold my protection from you. You are none of mine any more."

"No!" Ruthan reached out an imploring hand, but the moon was gone with shocking suddenness. Darkness clawed in from all around, bristling with the spiny arms of praying mantids, the hooked thorns of briars. The Darakyon swallowed Ruthan Bartrer without hesitation, one more set of bones to moulder on the forest floor.

Julaea turned her despairing gaze on Uctebri. By then he had closed the distance, and with a convulsive gesture he drove his knife hilt-deep into her side.

Her look was equal parts bafflement and outrage, no room for the pain at all. "What?"

"You're not the only one who remembers the wrongs done to their people," he snapped. He had the full intention of using the blade again, but he had forgotten Shonaen, and now the Mantis came leaping out of the wood with her spear levelled.

Even here in this Moth-made ruin, the Mantids still defend them. Uctebri had little magic left after testing himself against the Darakyon, so he let go the hilt and fled, as his people had always fled.

He made his magic a knife-blade to pierce the forest; not the grand siege that Julaea had brought, but a slinking escape route that wound under branch and over root, worming through the darkness as he twisted his way towards where the moon still shone. He closed the path behind him. Shonaen had to cut her own, assailed by shadows and not half the magician he was. Yet she was younger and stronger, and enraged. She gained a step at a time, as he cut desperately for the forest's edge. Briars plucked at his sleeves, nettles burned his skin and the ground knotted beneath his feet, yet somehow he stumbled on in his headlong flight, never looking at the enemy behind until he saw the enemy before him.

The first glint of dawn was in his eyes then, and he threw up a hand to shade them, seeing too late that some of the shapes cutting across the light were men, not trees. The Wasps had come to look for their missing scouts, a line of them wading into the forest verge with levelled crossbows and threats.

Uctebri skidded to a halt, realizing they had already seen movement and would be on him in a moment. He turned to find some last shade that might endure the dawn, but Shonaen was closer behind than he thought and her spear-point lanced through his side in a shock of pain and wasted blood.

Then he was on the ground, rolling over in agony so he could see the thrust that would kill him. Shonaen stared down at him, her eyes barely focusing on him, and he wondered if she knew she was killing a flesh and blood man, and not another shadow.

The first crossbow bolt winged wide of her, but close enough to catch her notice. She saw the Wasps and shrilled at them, challenging all the armies of the Empire to single combat. Uctebri laughed, though each chuckle cost him dear.

The bolts skipped past her, and she even spun one aside with her spear-haft, but this addled creature was no Mantis Weaponsmaster from song or story. She rushed them, her darned robe catching on the thorns, and the first shot landed, buried to the fletchings in her shoulder. Another three followed, and two blasts of stingshot from the Wasps' hands. Shonaen dropped her spear, clutching at the air as though she saw the glorious history of her people there, just out of reach. The Wasps took no chances and shot her another half-dozen times before they were sure she was dead. Thus perished the last scion of the Darakyon.

They did not find Uctebri as he lay there bleeding. The shadows were too deep.

Sometime later, after the Empire's finest had called off the search and retreated from the Darakyon's bounds to their camp, Uctebri saw Julaea come limping from the forest's heart, and knew that his time was up.

She shuffled over to him, leaning heavily on her staff. Its metal-shod end rammed the ground beside his face and he shuddered. She would not survive him for long, but he found that was remarkably little consolation.

"It… was a good plan," he whispered. The forest had fallen obligingly silent.

"It still is," she hissed around her pain. "The heart is out there. As you say, some Beetle, a paperweight or ornament. But it is there."

"You won't be fetching it…" His words were inviting that staff to smash his pointed teeth, but he could not keep them back.

"No." She sighed and dropped to her knees, and her hand found the hilt of Uctebri's dagger where it jutted from her side. "Would you?"

"If your Mantis had not finished me." He let out a long, wheezing breath. "It was a good plan. I am not so proud that I wouldn't have stolen it."

"Someone should." She leant on his chest as she dragged the dagger out, so that black spots wheeled before Uctebri's red eyes. "There's none but you."

"I'm done."

"I know your kind," and she spat real venom about that. "You can heal. If fed." She stared down at him with fascinated loathing. "We should have exterminated you vermin centuries ago. I should have cut your throat before using your power."

"Yes."

"But here we are, and someone needs to make the plan happen. Someone needs to destroy the Apt."

Uctebri stared up at her as she raised the smeared dagger blade and contemplated it.

"For my father," she said, and inserted it almost gently under her chin, opening her throat up with a flourish of her wrist that would have done a conjurer proud.

Uctebri was weak for days, but Julaea's blood had been enough to replace the vigour that he had lost. The Wasp patrol was long departed by then, and the forest had recovered Shonaen's body. Of their intrepid little band, only he survived.

We will meet again, he told the Darakyon, as it brooded and watched him. *I will hold your heart in my hands.* And he would need other power: relics, artifacts, the blood of magicians. He would need to inveigle himself into the counsels of the Wasps and tempt them with the impossible. Before hearing Julaea speak, he would not have believed it himself. Now her blood was in his veins and her purpose in his mind.

By dusk he was already limping away, the forest receding at his back. The sunset was red with the blood of Empire.

The Scent of Tears

Keris McDonald

I was sold to Colonel Sigurt to cover a racing debt. Not the normal sort of gambling debt, you understand – I came from a family of good standing, and Father was not the sort of fool to squander the wealth he'd won in military campaigns upon idle bets. But he owned, as many Wasp-kinden men of good family do, a mews of racing wasps, and he had long ago entered into a rivalry with Sigurt, for reasons that were never made entirely clear to me. Shared time in the Imperial Army, I understood, and some bitterness from their youth. Both men were loyal servants of the Empire, needless to say, but their rivalry was not an amiable one and it was conducted, among other means, by way of their racing teams.

So, as the long war with the Dragonfly Commonweal dragged on, the battles played out back home in the skies over Capitas grew more intense. My father's mews grew to over forty of the finest racing wasps including the breeding queen and they were not cheap to maintain. What with riders and handlers and food to provide for – wasp grubs eat an enormous amount of meat and feed the adults with their sticky secretions, but racing beasts need expensive specialist nectars too for that extra edge – it became expedient for Father to accept sponsorship from other parties. This was on the understanding that his wasps would win races, of course. When we accepted the Royal patronage and fielded a racer in the Emperor's own escutcheon it was a proud day for the Family Gunthar.

Then it all went wrong. There was suddenly something – a parasite, a fungal infection, we were never certain – in the nest, and the grubs withered like raisins in the sun. Without the young to feed them the adults went hungry; Father spent a fortune buying in gallons of feed, but it was inferior stuff at that quantity and our racing form dropped alarmingly. Prestigious races were lost. Two of our best free-born riders were lured away to join other mews. Our sponsors were suddenly demanding their money back. The Emperor himself expressed disappointment to my father's face. Our family went almost overnight from wealth to disgrace and near-ruin.

Then our breeding queen, who was several decades old and worn out replacing the dying grubs, succumbed to the sickness too.

Of course my father had to sell family assets. The wasps themselves were worthless because of the infection; nobody would touch our surviving racing-stock so he sold off household slaves and heirlooms of his military campaigns.

And finally he sold me.

I think it was enormously offensive to him that Colonel Sigurt should be the one to take his only daughter, but at the price offered he could not refuse: it was enough to allow him the possibility of starting afresh with new racers, though on a smaller scale. And there were few enough other offers; the bedchambers of the Wasp-kinden are awash with slave women from every nation we've conquered: elegant Dragonfly-kinden, nimble Fly-maidens, curvaceous Bee-women. Flesh is cheap in Capitas since the War began. But the sale was humiliating for him in the extreme. He could not bid me farewell the day they put a slave-collar about my neck and led me from the house where I had once been an honoured chattelaine.

As to my own feelings, I will not dwell upon them. We of the Wasp-kinden are proud, the women no less than the warriors. I shall not be seen to weep.

I was taken on foot through the streets of the city to the grand house of the family Sigurt, and then made to wait in the servants' porch until evening before I was admitted. I bit my lip and refused to beg for water, even after hours on my feet. With only the wrought iron gate between me and the street, I could look back out at the world I had lost, at the caleches drawn by beetles with painted carapaces rumbling past and the view over Capitas down to the grand ziggurats by the river, at servants pausing to gossip as they passed one another and off-duty soldiers strolling about enjoying their time away from barracks. It seemed infinitely strange to me that the world could still look as it did the day before, yet suddenly I was no longer a part of it.

Of course I could be seen there too, waiting in such a visible place, tethered to a wall-ring. My family's humiliation was very public. Throughout the day respectable Wasp faces peered at me from within the caleches that passed. Some I recognised as women I had once counted as family friends.

It was hard to enter that house, so similar to the one I had left, with its flat roofs clustered with flowering vines and its terraced gardens tended by Bee-kinden slaves. Back home I had everything I could desire. My father had been generous and indulgent of his family. Here I had nothing except by another's leave.

Colonel Sigurt rejoiced in my humiliation. That was the point of his purchase; certainly he wasn't extending aid to his rival from any kindly impulse. I was familiar with his face from social gatherings in the past; his sharp blue eyes and the nearly invisible brows; the grey-blond hair, shorn close at the nape of the neck, that flopped over his forehead. I soon grew familiar with his tastes and his habits. He was most appreciative of his purchase.

"Do you think your father's picturing this?" he would hiss in my ear as he pinned me to his bed. "Do you think it haunts him?"

You know what? I *enjoyed* sex with Sigurt. It was the only time I got to hurt him. He hurt me worse, of course. But at least it felt like I was fighting when I gouged my nails into his skin or struck at his face or bit down on momentarily unguarded flesh. It was the only time I didn't feel like a slave.

He liked that too. With his weight crushing down upon my back and my face pressed to the rumpled sheet, he would draw his lips softly across my shoulders and whisper, "You have such spirit, daughter of Gunthar." And once, "Not like that cold husk of a wife upstairs."

Ah: his wife, Fyrtha. Her first words to me, spoken quietly in passing, were; "Fall pregnant, and I shall cut you open myself." She was the artificer of my excruciation. More so than Sigurt himself – for at least he was frequently away from home, attending the Emperor or his military superiors in the Tactical Corps. Fyrtha was always there. She was a tall, elegant woman with a mane of golden hair that I think was the last remnant of a great beauty. She had borne Sigurt children, certainly – there was mention of two sons in the Army, a daughter married to one of the magnates in the Consortium of the Honest. But these days Fyrtha had no children to care for and Wasp women rest no more easily under the yoke of idleness than do their men. Her luxurious life had turned wearisome upon her, I think, and a fall in the past that had hurt her back prevented her spending her energy in the traditional leisure pursuit of

Wasp-kinden women; flying to the hunt. Her mind dwelt too much on little slights and grievances; she was a dangerous friend to her social equals and a terror to her household.

Given that I was one of the slaves Sigurt had purchased especially for his own entertainment – all of us Wasp-kinden, by-the-by, for he was blood-proud and wouldn't soil himself with lesser women – I was in a curious position. She could not destroy me or obviously mar my looks for fear of angering him, but I was one who incurred her particular contempt because I distracted her husband from her bed. When he was away from home she would make me sweat and labour alongside the Beetle-kinden slaves in the laundry house. And for the slightest infraction – a glance that was not humble enough, a sheet that the wind had blown off the line into the yard – she would have me whipped by Lars the doorkeeper, but only across the back. The food she let me have in Sigurt's absence was of the worst kind, often spoiled by damp or weevils, and though this persecution sounds petty I discovered how hard it is to remember one's pride when one is hungry day after day.

The only source of relief from Fyrtha's attentions came from her fondness for gem-wasps. It was a fashion that had spread among the wealthier families over the last few years, but she was particularly susceptible. Some people are. The sting of the tiny iridescent insects – worn tethered to a broach at the shoulder, where their black and green markings may be seen to shimmer pleasingly as they crawl about – is no more than a pin-prick and induces a temporary sense of euphoria. I'd regarded the habit as an entertaining distraction, but for Fyrtha it was solace and necessity. She would lie by the fountains on the terrace for hours in a haze of contentment.

There were times I envied her, and wished for the burn and the glow of the gem-wasps' poison.

One day I crawled into the sunny patch under the orchard wall to recover from my latest beating. My back was burning, my dress sticking to it where Lars' cane had broken the skin. Only the sun on my limbs felt good, and I cradled my head in my arms to cut off the outside world. My ears so muffled, I saw feet in the dust before I realised that anyone had come up upon me; brown feet in artisan's sandals, not soldiers' boots. I uncurled quickly, fearful of the weakness I was displaying.

It was a man. One glance at those warm brown eyes, that solid build and the fuzz of cropped hair haloing his skull identified him as Bee-kinden.

"Chattelaine Dagmar?"

My first reaction was of tremulous rage that he should creep up on me like that, but I swallowed the anger that burned in my throat. "Chattelaine?" I sneered, my voice hoarse. "Not any more."

"Do you remember me?"

I stared at him. For what should I remember a Bee-kinden slave? He was dressed plainly, with a collar bearing the Sigurt crest as did my own, but wearing no other clue to his identity. Yet he did look familiar.

"Should I?" Bee-kinden slaves are everywhere in the Empire. They tended our gardens and furnished our houses and decorated our public places. Let Beetle-kinden do their artificing with metal and grease and steam; they have given our Empire machinery and firepower. But for beauty in creativity, for sculpture and painting and the gentler arts, we turn to the Bee-kinden. Upon the very wall surrounding the Imperial Palace the mile-long mural *The Triumph of the Wasps* records all our achievements and glories and aspirations, yet is the work of Bee-kinden hands.

"I used to belong to your family." He stood with his hands knotted together, a look of trepidation on his face. "Before I was sold to Colonel Sigurt."

"Ah." Suddenly he seemed to me not just a clumsy intruder but a friend, as I placed him in my memory. My voice softened. "You were my mother's perfumer, weren't you?"

He perked up. "That's right."

"Effer…"

"Everel."

"Everel." I thought how foolish it was of me, a slave myself, to take offence at being approached by him, and it was a thought I was not used to. "I'm sorry," I said, tasting the awkward words on my lips. This man had been around all my young life, and I'd had no conscious memory of him.

He flushed a bit. "Not to worry, Chattelaine Dagmar."

"Don't call me that, or she'll have you beaten too."

He nodded. "Are you badly hurt… Dagmar?"

I prickled. "No worse than usual." I was lying, as I happened; this was the worst whipping I'd received yet. I'd dropped a pitcher of wine and splashed Fyrtha's dress.

"Shall I take a look?" He drew from his pouch a pot with a wax seal.

29

"I have a salve here that's good for healing without scars. It's honeycomb and yarrow and –"

"I thought you were a perfumer?"

"Well. You know. I make myself useful where I can. Poultices and tinctures of all kinds."

"Why?" I fixed him with a glare. "Why are you doing this for me?"

He looked away, abashed. "You're hurt. I don't like to see anyone hurt."

Which was, I thought, why the Bee-kinden are now our vassals. The Empire is not afraid of hurting anyone, its own citizens included. I smiled weakly.

"Besides, I remember… your family… with…" He seemed to be having problems choosing his words. Eventually he settled for, "I was not mistreated there, for a slave."

"Are you treated badly now?"

He shrugged. "She's not the easiest of women to please. But she appreciates the skills I bring to her household. Including some small medicinal knowledge." He held out the pot of salve again. "Will you let me?"

Warily, I nodded. As he moved behind me I loosened the knots of my neckline.

His hands were so gentle I had to bite my lip to stop myself crying.

Moments of kindliness were rare in my life now, and I mistrusted them when they came. Even Sigurt could be perversely generous at times, though. One afternoon when we were lying back at opposite ends of his big carved bed – Bee-kinden work that, too – he ran his fingers through the sweat on his chest, picked up the trickle of blood from the bite-mark I'd left on his collar-bone and laughed.

"I think you like this as much as I do, Dagmar. Or else you wouldn't put so much effort into it."

I glared at him sullenly. I was saying nothing. The hand not on his chest lay with fingers loosely curled over the palm – relaxed, not threatening, but ready with a sting should I launch an attack. My very silence made him grin.

"I have something for you, Gunthar's daughter."

I raised my eyebrows and touched fingertips gingerly to my swollen and split lip. I could still taste blood. "I doubt I want it, Colonel."

"It's a present."

"I'm sure."

"Look under the bed." The jerk of his chin made it an order. I slid my aching limbs off the mattress onto the rug and looked. There was a box there, fairly small and plain. "Go on," he urged.

Cautiously I brought the box up into the light. The wood was undecorated except for a row of holes in the lid. It was big enough to hold a severed head, it occurred to me, and I braced myself inwardly.

"You'll like it, I promise."

"Your word means everything to me," I whispered, but he took no offence at the undisguised insult, for once. Sitting up straight and telling myself not to cry out, whatever it should be, I opened the box. Inside was a jet black wasp longer than my hand, which twitched its antennae.

"He's yours," said Sigurt. He sounded pleased with himself. "Male; don't worry: no sting. Go on, lift him out."

I scooped the insect from its container. It seemed almost torpid, but clung to my wrist and fanned its wings experimentally. Like all insects it was lighter than it looked. Its abdomen pulsed, glittering like polished jet.

"He's been starved down. If you go to the mews and get him some nectar, he'll bond with you soon enough. You don't have the Art of Speech, do you?"

I shook my head slowly. Then I looked over at Sigurt, who lay smiling, eyebrows raised in anticipation, watching me with pleasure and curiosity. I think now he might have been wondering if I'd just kill the little wasp out of hand to spite him. If I hadn't been so sore and tired I might have thought of it at the time myself. "Why?" I asked.

"I thought you'd like him."

This made no sense to me at all. "What?"

"Don't you? He cost quite a bit. Black is the fashionable colour right now."

I gaped. "But I'm a slave."

"I can give you a present, can't I?" He was sounding a little irritated. "I can have you dress how I like, and look how I like, and if I want you to have a pet you can have one."

"I see." I didn't. Not really. He'd completely thrown me this time.

"Don't you like him?"

"He's beautiful," I allowed. The wasp had climbed onto my forearm and I could feel its legs pricking my skin. He was a pet suitable for a real lady. My heart, which had been turning over in confusion, sank at the thought. "Your wife won't let me keep him."

He waved a hand dismissively. "Don't worry about Fyrtha. I'll have a word."

I bit the inside of my cheek and nodded, almost forgetting myself for a moment.

"You're pleased?"

"Yes."

"Now say 'Thank you'."

I remembered my place in an instant. My eyes met his. "Thank you, master," I said grudgingly. It was the first time I'd ever uttered those words to him without being forced to surrender by pain first.

"No." He lay back. "Come over here and say 'Thank you' *properly.*"

Colonel Sigurt got his chance to show off both me and my pet in public. He took us to the races as part of his entourage for the Vespasian Trophy. Fyrtha was there, of course, as were all the men and women of the great families of Capitas. She wore drapes of black and gold – Wasp-kinden women are keen to show support for their menfolk in the Imperial Army. I, being a slave, wore blue, but it was Spider-kinden silk and no cheap linen shift I'd been put in. I must have presented a strange, contradictory sight in my fine dress, with a tame wrist-wasp to hand and my Wasp-kinden features made up and my fair hair in an elegant coiffure: very much the daughter of Empire, except for the slave-collar about my neck and the bruise about my left eye which the make-up did not disguise. I know that many of the people that came to greet Sigurt and his wife stared at me, their glances sliding ineluctably despite Fyrtha's obvious irritation.

"Yes, that is Dagmar of the family Gunthar," Sigurt would say with a smooth smile. He was delighted to parade my father's shame.

I did not look anyone in the eye. How could I, when these people had once been my equals, my neighbours, some even my friends? Now they looked at me as if judging some racing animal for form and comportment. I kept my eyes on Lissi, my little wasp. Greedy by nature, he had tamed easily and no longer needed to be tethered to my wrist, but would sit at my shoulder and dart out to investigate brightly-coloured objects and other pets. He was a fine source of distraction.

Then the event began properly, with the parade of the day's racers in their family colours. Racing wasps are not like the big black-and-gold beasts of the Heavy Airborne, which need to take the weight of a fully-grown man. They are smaller and faster, their streamlined abdomens tending to a dark brown in colour, and they are ridden by undersized women and boys too young for military service. But the animals are just as skittish and aggressive as the Army wasps, and though their jockeys all possess the Art of Speech they have a hard time controlling their mounts. That is part of the skill, of course. Wasps of different families, being bred in separate nests, have a distinct desire to fight each other and we saw many a feint with venom-dripping sting come close to stabbing home.

I could not help looking for the silks of the family Gunthar, but couldn't see them on any rider. In all probability, I knew, my father had not managed to raise a team in time for this year's competition; entering for the Vespasian Trophy requires considerable investment. Certainly some of the mews owners were making their money back; people were betting freely and large sums of money were changing hands about us. The wasps tore back and forth over our heads buzzing, like scores of Beetle-kinden orthopters.

Colonel Sigurt's own team placed third overall, up a place from the previous year. He was satisfied, if not delighted. It was as he was leading us down the marble steps of the arena that he all but ran into my father who was hurrying the opposite way, talking intently to an irritable-looking Fly-kinden man.

"Gunthar!"

We all stopped, letting the crowd part around us. Sigurt and my father locked gazes, one with an expression of pleasure, the other with dismay. The Fly-kinden took the opportunity to slip away and I wished I could follow his example.

"Sigurt." My father's voice was heavy. He wore, I could not help noting, the same robe he'd had on last year, the gold-thread trim looking a little worn. He'd lost weight, I thought, and his face was more lined than I remembered. Sigurt, standing two steps higher up and accompanied by his wife and assorted relatives along with an entourage of guards and household slaves, had all the advantages.

"A profitable day for you, I trust, Gunthar?"

"Not so profitable as yours."

Sigurt nodded smugly. "Ah – Have you seen your daughter recently?" He grabbed my arm and pulled me to the front. "Give greeting to your father, Dagmar."

All the blood had drained from my face. My father looked ashen. "I wish you health, my sire," I rasped. "Is my mother well?"

He did not answer. He stared at me as if I were a ghost.

"She's looking well, don't you think?" said Sigurt breezily. "She's come on well under my care, Gunthar. Learned a number of new skills. Shown a surprising aptitude for some activities." He patted my shoulder and my skin crawled. "In fact I'm thinking of putting her on the entertainment rosta for the Regimental Reunion this year. Do you think she'll go down well with the junior officers? Or perhaps the lower ranks? Just think how well your family name will be known after that. You'll be quite famous."

My vision started to go blurry at the edges.

"I have no daughter," said my father quietly, his eyes flat. Then he walked away.

I made it all the way back to the house without throwing up. It was the only pride I had left to cling to. As soon as I was alone I ran out into the gardens, fled behind the box hedge down to the orchard terrace and scrambled behind the wall, where I spewed into the dust and then sat digging my fingers into my belly as if I could eviscerate myself. Lissi crawled over my shoulders and head, agitated, and nibbled at the exposed skin of my neck to try and get my attention. I barely felt it.

Everel found me there. He has an instinct.

"Dagmar. I heard –"

"Keep off me!" I sat up and thrust my palm out at him in naked threat, and he flinched. Lissi took to the air and buzzed around anxiously.

"Dagmar…"

"I said don't *touch* me!" I was coiled up like some scorpion disturbed under a stone, my arm raised and shaking. "You're just Bee-kinden – how dare you even *talk* to me like you know –" The utter stupidity of my own words struck me dumb mid-sentence. My face was going all awry, my throat knotting up.

Everel knelt, lifted his closed fist and slowly put it into my open palm, looking nowhere but my eyes. My fingers closed over his hand. "Don't cry, Dagmar."

I swallowed hard and managed to rasp out, "I'm not going to cry."

"Don't cry yet. I have something to help you."

"Help me?"

"Come to my workshop. Come on."

It took some persuasion, but eventually I let him turn his fist over, palm to palm, and raise me to my feet. He gave me a piece of lemongrass from his pouch to chew, to take away the bitter taste, as if I were a child being comforted with a sweet. Then he led me back through the terraces and the servants' courtyards, avoiding anyone else, to a small stone room with louvered shutters.

I held on to my pain all the way.

"Your wasp has to stay outside, Dagmar."

"Lissi? Why?" My voice sounded dull and hoarse.

"This is a perfume workshop and wasps are very sensitive to smells. It could get confused, angry…"

"He doesn't have a sting."

"He could fly into a wall and hurt himself. Believe me."

So I told Lissi to wait outside and left him with a dab of syrup from my nectar bottle, before following Everel into his workshop. The door didn't even have a lock, and if you know anything about the habits of slaves that will tell you how much Fyrtha was feared by hers. Inside the room was lined with racks of glass bottles, each holding an oily-looking yellow or brown liquid. There were bottles of seedpods and berries and petals and dried leaves too, waxy-looking resins and powdery spices and curls of bark. By the hearth in the corner was a stack of copper pans and funnels of varying sizes and peculiar shapes.

The smell, a riotous combination of scents, was almost overwhelming. My swollen eyes stung.

"This is all yours?" I was surprised enough to forget my own woes for the moment: I'd never seen anything like this because Wasp-kinden women of good repute do not wear perfume until they are married. "Why do you need so much stuff?"

Everel, opening a shutter to let in fresher air, said a little stiffly, "I was a member of the Perfumer's Guild of Szar before I was captured. This is all I brought with me. All a perfumer could ever need."

I looked at a flask of juniper berries and then moved over to the racks of liquid. *Bergamot* read the first label I glanced at. Next along were *Clove* then *Rosemary* then *Lavender*. Some were unfamiliar, however.

"What's *Liquid Storax*?"

"It's the resin bled from the Liquidambar tree. Have you seen one? In autumn the leaves turn to brilliant red and gold – quite beautiful. Most of the groves we know of were in Beetle-kinden lands, and they've been felled now. For firewood. To feed the charcoal kilns of Helleron. And thus the world is advanced."

I didn't miss the edge in his voice.

"And *Velvetbloom*?"

"Ah. That's from a flower that blooms in the woods of Felyal. It has racemes of soft, velvety petals."

"Is it a poison?" I could see the barbed sting symbol inked on the corner of the label.

Everel pulled a face. "At this concentration they are all poisons, to some extent. But velvetbloom is rather more dangerous... I wouldn't want to pull the stopper from that one, not here. The flower is pollinated by little wasps, in the wild, you see. It has a scent that to us humans is unremarkable, but to the insects it is meant for it smells like a dying wasp."

I looked at him questioningly.

"Have you ever watched a nest of small wasps going about its business? They usually forbear to attack humans and bigger animals unless the nest is trodden on or directly threatened, or unless some of the guard wasps are swatted. We think they give off a scent as they die – a signal that they have been attacked. The others rush to defend the nest from anything they can see, driven by this alarm. So this flower gives off a similar alarm, and wasps cluster all about the flowers to sting them over and over again, and in doing so they pick up pollen and spread it from flower to flower."

"But why would you want to wear that as a perfume?"

"Well, they don't here in the Empire. Obviously. But velvetbloom is an ingredient in a very old Moth-kinden perfume, according to our records. And..." His face tightened. He looked at his hands. 'And I've known it used. In concentrate. There is..." He swallowed. "There was a Bee-kinden stronghold outside Szar called Scop, and when the Empire attacked it one of our princesses of the royal blood holed up there with her loyal troops. It was well fortified, and high up, and difficult to get siege machinery to the walls. The losses the airborne Wasps were taking as they tried to attack from above were untenable. So the officer in charge of the attack ordered that bundles soaked in velvetbloom oil be dropped in over the walls of Scop. Then they released all the cavalry wasps, riderless, to attack. Drawn by the scent, they went into a frenzy. There were no Bee-kinden survivors. At all."

I looked at his blunt, patient face, the down-drawn corners of his mouth. "Did you…?"

"My family came from Scop."

"I'm sorry."

"That your Empire conquered my people?"

I hesitated. "That you are sorrowing."

"All slaves live in sorrow."

Blinking, I turned to look at the racks of bottles, the hard fist of pain and fear under my breastbone clenching momentarily.

"It's like a secret language. Or a library of the world," said I softly after a while. "I didn't know there were so many perfumes in existence."

Everel relaxed a shade. "You've probably smelled very few. You Wasp-kinden are mad for the sweet ones, all loaded down with vanilla." He waved his hand at the bottles. "But there are recipes here dating back centuries, for all the kindens. Even ones we have no contact with now. It's the legacy of my guild."

"What does a Spider-kinden woman wear?" I asked. I'd seen a Spider diplomat at a party once, and had been intrigued by the knowing, humorous glitter in her eyes.

"Spider-kinden tend to like woody-based scents. Ant-kinden like them spicy, Mantis-kinden prefer variations on citrus notes." Everel reached out and plucked a bottle to show me. "This is a Spider-kinden scent."

It was labelled in meticulous handwriting *Webs of Cedar*. I began to unstopper the bottle but Everel pulled it from my hands hurriedly.

"Wait. These are concentrated essences – if you splashed some on your skin it would blister you. To be worn they have to be diluted with purest alcohol at least ten times over. That way the scent comes properly alive. To be used in a fountain, say, you'd have to dilute it fifty times over in spirit, and then again in the water." He brushed my hand with his. "Wait a moment. I'll show you how to sample a little."

Opening a chest that stood beneath his workbench he extracted the topmost of a heap of small raw silk squares. He unstoppered the bottle, holding it at arm's length, then dabbed the handkerchief briefly with the oil. Re-stoppering the bottle immediately, he waved the cloth in the air a few times then passed it to me, holding it by the corner. "Don't touch it to your nose."

I bent my head over the fabric. The scent was warm, heavy and a little disturbing. Not unpleasant, but not a scent I could imagine wanting to wear. It did not compare with the alluring sweetness that had surrounded my mother like an aura and lingered in every room she passed through.

The memory of my mother made my heart sink again. "So what has any of this to do with me?" I asked dully.

"Ah." He sat down on a tall stool, hands on his knees. His eyes were wide and earnest. "Scents affect us all, in ways we don't realise. They bring the past to life. They change our moods and our hearts. Rain on dust makes us nostalgic. The air of spring makes us restless. Dagmar, I want to make you a perfume."

"You think," I whispered, "that you can make me feel better?"

He shook his head. "I think I may be able to make Sigurt feel differently about you. To need you more than he does now."

I laughed harshly.

"I mean – in a different way. There are scents that evoke tenderness, the instinct to protect; like the smell of a baby's skin. Scents that remind us of home, of good food, of satisfaction. They're smells that make us comfortable. We like to keep them around us. Ask yourself why some couples bond forever, and other fall apart no matter the initial attraction – the masters of my guild would have said that the secret lies in *scent*. The aromas of two individuals that, without either of them knowing it, blend into one harmoniously or clash irredeemably."

Wide-eyed, I shook my head. Everel pressed on.

"I could, with luck and Art, devise a scent that worked upon Sigurt to make him content in your presence. To make him not want to lose you to any other man, not even for a moment."

"You'll make him love me?" I laughed, my voice ragged.

"If it will save you."

I walked round the worktable, running my hand over the grain distractedly. "Why?" I asked at last. "Why? – after Scop, and being enslaved? I'm Wasp-kinden. Why would you want to help me?"

He sat with his mouth open, just a little, as if his words were still buzzing round inside his head and refusing to emerge. He even flushed a shade darker. Then he took a deep breath. "There are forests to the north of here, on the hills above Lake Limnia –"

"Is this another perfume story?"

He just smiled sadly. "The wasps there are big, armoured hornets, twice the size of a honey-bee. In fact, if they discover a honey-farm they can destroy a farmer's entire livelihood. The hornet flies into the hive and the guardian workers meet it at the doorway and try to sting it to death. But the hornet has such thick plating that the stings cannot sink in far enough, and the bees tear themselves apart and die for nothing, while the hornets bite their smaller foes in half. So a few scout wasps can kill a whole hive of bees and bring their brethren in to steal the honey and grubs.

"But," he continued, the ghost of a smile on his face, "there are wild bees in the hills too: an older breed than the farmers' honey-makers. When a hornet finds their nest, the wild bees do not try to fight it. They let it enter deep within the nest. They do not sting it. They surround it instead, and cover it with their bodies many bees deep. The wasp cannot move easily, but it isn't alarmed. Then the bees begin to vibrate their wings and bodies, and their vibration creates heat. And with countless patient tiny movements, they heat the hornet up so much that it cooks to death."

I almost laughed, but I was a little shocked.

He spread his hands. "Do you know what I believe, Dagmar? I believe you Wasp-kinden are a young culture. Like youths armed with sticks and intoxicated by your first sip of beer you run riot, wanting to fight anyone you meet. Well, that cannot last. It may take many years, but having an Empire will change you. Living with other kinden will change you, even though they are your slaves. Letting Beetle- and Fly-kinden become citizens will change you, and you will not see it happening and you will welcome it.

"You learnt artificing from the Beetle-kinden. From us Bee-kinden you will learn beauty. Already you have gardens and painting and music: we will teach you to love beauty so much that you can't live without it, so that war becomes unbearable. We will teach you luxury and civilisation and peace. It may take centuries of slavery and suffering, but in the end we will smother your cruel Empire with contentment." His smile was sad, full of the knowledge of how much this was going to cost him and his kinden. "So, where I can, I will change things. I will even teach Sigurt to love, if that can be done."

We looked at each other for a long time. Everel's vision, encompassing so many years, had left me dizzy. Then I nodded. "How do you make this perfume?"

"I'll need something from you. I need your tears. Can you cry, Dagmar?"

"Not in front of you," I whispered.

He looked pained, but he fetched a glass bowl from a drawer and laid it on the table for me. "I'll wait outside."

Alone, I sat on his stool and looked down into the milky glass of the dish. Not for the first time I considered my other course of escape: it would be easy enough to sting out my own throat. But self-murder was an act of cowardice that would besmirch my family's honour worse than anything Sigurt or his regiment could do to me.

Crumpling my head in my hands, I let go and began to weep, my tears splashing one by one into the bowl.

And perhaps Everel's perfume did work. It's hard to say. I know that the first night I wore it, Sigurt lay behind me and traced his fingertip down my spine, through the beads of sweat, gently over the unhealed welts.

"I didn't mean what I said, about the Regimental Reunion," he murmured. "You know that. It was a joke."

I stiffened, my breath seizing in my throat.

"I mean – I said it to provoke your father. You don't have anything to worry about."

For a moment I felt as if I'd forgotten how to breathe and could not start again. I rolled over onto my back, ignoring the burning of my broken skin, and stared at the ceiling. "Why do you resent him that much?"

Sigurt sat up, reaching for the wine-cup by the bed. He shrugged. "He scorched me over that jockey a few years back."

"And before that you won that disputed finish on a coin-toss. And before that he beat you to the bloodline Queen... It goes back years, one then the other. What started it?"

He looked into the depths of his goblet. "Army stuff. When we were junior officers."

"What happened?"

"You don't need to know."

"Who started it?"

Sigurt looked irritated. "He did. During the attack on Myna."

"The Beetle-kinden city? My father was only a junior officer then."

"We both were. We both led squads over the walls. Street-fighting then; dirty stuff. The city was a maze, and the bloody Mynans... even the ones that couldn't fight wouldn't surrender. It was pathetic... Children with sticks. After a while just the endless effort became exhausting." He took a mouthful of wine. "We were just hacking our way round corner after corner, and it all looked the same. Then I took my squad into this little courtyard, and before I knew it they'd pulled a net over at roof-level, and this squad of Mynans appeared out of nowhere behind us. They were taking us apart. Eventually it was only me on my feet. Then Gunthar showed up at roof-level."

Sigurt's eyes were like stones.

"What did he do?" I asked.

"He rescued me." He cast a sour glance at my face, but I'm not sure he even saw me. "He blasted a hole through the netting and lifted me out by the scruff of my neck."

I pushed myself up onto one elbow. "He saved your life?"

"And the weevil boasted about it in the mess that night."

I felt nauseous at his ingratitude. Was this what all my humiliation and pain was all about, after all? "That's what you're angry about? That he saved your *life?*"

Sigurt seemed to register my existence properly, with a scowl. "Don't you have any idea about honour, girl? Do you think it's something to be proud of, to be overwhelmed by a mob of cripples and old women, and to be hoiked out of there like a sack of laundry? To be laughed at by all your peers?"

"Would it have been better to die there?"

"Yes!" he shouted. "Of course it would, you fool – I thought our women knew better than that!" His scowl became a sneer as he bared his teeth. "Maybe you've started to think like a slave after all."

Sick with anger, I raised my open hand to him. He reacted fast, backhanding me so hard that he knocked me half off the bed. I nearly blacked out; the room was spinning, my head ringing. I slithered to the floor.

"Don't you think of trying that!" Sigurt growled.

Everel would have understood what happened next. Lissi, who had been resting quietly on a post of the bed, flew up and buzzed around Sigurt, his motions jerky with agitation. My tame, gentle, loyal Lissi, frightened by my distress. He couldn't sting, but he dashed into the Colonel's face, his wings a blur. Sigurt recoiled with an oath, batting him away, and lifted his right hand.

"No!" I screamed, but the bright flash of energy was followed by the hiss of burning juices and Lissi exploded into fragments of blackened chitin. His transparent wings helioptered to the rug slowest of all.

The smell of burned wasp was enough to turn stomachs.

"What?" demanded Sigurt, his voice rising. "Why are you looking at me like that? I can buy you another one!"

But I kept on looking at him like that.

"Get out!" he exploded. "Get out of here! And send someone to clear this mess up!"

He forgave me, though. The next day was set aside for a family reunion: Sigurt's eldest son was visiting on leave from the military front in the Commonweal. A grand dinner was laid on and members of the extended family invited. Lanterns were strung in the trees of the terraces in preparation for the long summer evening. The fountains were perfumed with rosewater and Grasshopper-kinden slaves with voices of exceptional sweetness sang from a balcony as the guests strolled about. Of course Sigurt would not miss the opportunity to show off his racing team, so as the sun set they were scheduled to fly past in formation and show their paces.

I caught only glimpses of Sigurt's son as the festivities wore on; my role was to wait quietly in the garden with a tray of gilded marchpane fancies and look decorative as the Wasp-kinden guests strolled about admiring the work of the gardeners. From what I saw, the younger man seemed to be cast from his father's mould. I wore my newest gift; a thick necklace of plaited gold thread that rested snug and heavy around my throat. Sigurt had put it on me personally that afternoon.

"There," he'd said, his fingers stroking the nape of my neck. "That suits you better than the old one."

What could I answer to that? It was costly doubtless, but it was still unmistakably a slave-collar.

"You are…" he'd mumbled, "precious, like this gold. To me. You know that."

I'd lowered my eyes obediently and said nothing. Perhaps there was tenderness in Sigurt's heart. But not enough of it.

The family Sigurt were relaxed and convivial, and the younger children chasing each other shrieking around the topiary, when Everel came up to me, his eyes averted diffidently from his masters. Of course they would not notice one more scurrying slave, regardless of the worried look in his eye.

"Dagmar…"

I took a deep breath as he touched my arm.

"Dagmar, talk to me. There's a bottle of scent essence missing from my workroom." His voice was very low. "Do you know anything about it?"

"Velvetbloom."

"Yes, that's the one – Dagmar!"

"You should leave."

"What have you *done?*"

I looked deliberately over his shoulder and he followed my gaze to where the ornamental fountains plashed and murmured, filling the air with a haze of perfumed water droplets that turned to rainbows in the afternoon sun. The scent of roses was glorious. Every squeeze of the pump sent atomies of rose-laden spirituous liquor into the warm air. It would have taken a keen nose to detect the smell of velvetbloom in that rich mix, though I'd poured the distilled oil into all five of the pre-prepared rosewater demijons.

"Oh no," said Everel as he understood.

"Run and hide," I whispered. "Pick a room with no windows and a heavy door. Though wasps will chew through wood."

He locked my gaze with his own, horror in his wide brown eyes. "You can't have…"

"Hurry," I warned. "They're nearly here." A flick of my chin indicated the ranks of racing wasps sweeping down toward us. Their dark bodies swooped in perfect formation, describing circles and loops to display the skills of their riders, skeins of mounted insects interweaving. There were maybe fifty of the beasts in all; the entire mews. Everel cast them one look, then his gaze swept the people on the terrace all about us: Wasp-kinden and slaves. Men and women and children.

"Oh Dagmar –"

"Run."

His hand closed around my wrist. I turned my palm over, opening it toward his chest. For a heartbeat he did not react. He looked stunned.

I hoped he could see the sorrow behind the implacable intent in my eyes. I did not desire to hurt the one man who'd showed me kindness.

Numbly, he let go of my wrist. Then he hurried away toward the buildings, stumbling, nearly falling over his feet

And now they are here. It is nearly done. The deep drone of the wasp

43

wings has lifted to a higher, more frantic burr. Precision is lost, the formations fall apart. Wasps jag about, ignoring the riders trying to control them. The first jockey is thrown in mid-air. Sigurt gets to his feet, aware that something is badly wrong. The smile has vanished from his face. He knows wasps, and these are moving fast and erratic, their abdomens curled so their stings are fully unsheathed. Even before the venom, the strikes of those stings are going to be like the stabs of rapiers.

We stand in an invisible aura of death. It fills the air about us.

And I wait, proudly. This is my moment. This is the revenge of the Family Gunthar. It hangs on translucent wings over our heads, about to fall; a whirlwind of glossy chitin and elegantly curved needles.

It is beautiful.

Wonder

Frances Hardinge

Gebri noticed her at once, or so he told himself later.

He saw the Collegium crowds part reflexively to let through a dozen or so Ant-Kinden. They were moving with the slow, informal gait enforced by the busy street, but they were unmistakably a military body. They wore swords, they held formation and there was a measured tension in every step.

He could not see them well past the throng of taller figures. Even with his artfully raised heels, he was scarcely four foot one. However he glimpsed bleached-white faces, and cropped, dark hair.

"Tarkesh Free Army," somebody muttered. Some of the tension went out of the crowd, but only some. During the darkest moments of the recent siege of Collegium, the arrival of the Tarkesh force on Spiderland ships had turned the tide of the battle. They had driven out the Vekken invaders who had forced their way past the broken walls, and earned some trust. However, there was still an uncomfortable feeling that there were a lot of armed foreigners on Collegium's rubble-strewn streets. Occasionally they almost felt like an occupying force.

Gebri's contribution to Collegium's defence had been rather less dramatic. He had been training as an artificer, but the ornate musical automata he favoured were as much use in a war as a soap bubble doorstop. Instead, like a lot of other Fly-kinden, he had found himself hastily recruited as a messenger. In practice this had meant long, hazy hours of flying in search of this or that person while things exploded around him. He was not sure that he had actually helped at all.

So he was curious to see the Tarkesh heroes, and employed a little sputter of wing power, raising himself just high enough for a better look. He was borne aloft just long enough to glimpse the face of one of the Ant women.

She was staring out across the busy thoroughfare, with a stony patience and alertness. There was a brute pragmatism about her, but also a stillness. Gebri could almost imagine her gazing out beyond the broken walls of Collegium, to defy some distant foe. Or perhaps she was looking into the past, and remembering walls that had already fallen, the once-invincible bastion of Tark.

There was no softness in her, no delicacy. She was fascinating. Her face was a stubborn and unyielding white cliff, and Gebri's heart broke against it like a little blue wave.

Later he found out, through his usual maddening persistence, that her name was Ansida. At least, he was *almost* certain that Ansida was the woman whose face had struck him like a lightning bolt. To his disquiet, he quickly discovered that most of the Tarkesh women looked surprisingly similar. At the back of his mind there was always the creeping worry that he might have settled on the wrong one.

"It's not courtship unless you talk to her," one of Gebri's fellow students told him bluntly at last. "What you're doing is 'stalking'. She hasn't even noticed you. I'm surprised she hasn't trodden on you."

None of Gebri's usual strategies were of any use. Normally he would gain an introduction through mutual friends (they had none), or find out where she let her hair down (she never did), or discover what made her laugh (nothing did). Furthermore, she never seemed to be alone. The Tarkesh visitors moved around in groups, wary and synchronised, occasionally glancing at one another as they conversed silently over their mind-link.

"There's no way to join in their conversation!" Gebri protested to his friends. "What am I supposed to do, laugh uproariously every time I think one of them has made a joke? It's impossible!"

And as with all situations that he had declared impossible, Gebri persisted.

He was astute enough to see that his own mechanical creations were unlikely to appeal to Ansida's practical temperament. So instead he guiltily dipped into his funds and bought her a new crossbow, to replace the damaged one at her belt. Back when Gebri first set out for Collegium, his uncle had unexpectedly revealed hidden reserves of cash and social aspiration. He had insisted on Gebri taking some money for 'tools and books and gentlemanly pursuits and posh clothes and whatnot'. This was a misuse of the money, but Gebri was living in a strange and dangerous new world, and old promises seemed less important than they had.

When he approached Ansida and presented her with the bow, she spent a while staring at it, and then at him.

"This isn't mine," she said carefully.

"It is now." Gebri swallowed. "This is... a token of my esteem." She still seemed to be waiting for an explanation, now with a hint of uncertainty in her gaze. In desperation, he reached for poetry. "It means... that I will follow you the ends of the Earth."

"I'm not going to the ends of the Earth," she said.

"Well. Then I suppose I'll... follow you to and fro. Unless you tell me to go away." Gebri was getting the distinct impression that he was in a conversational boat where nobody had any oars.

"Mm," she said, still staring at the bow as if she thought it might be booby-trapped. But she took it from him, sighted down it and tested its weight in her hand.

She did not tell him to go away that day, or the next, or the next. One day, after she had spent hours working a street clearance crew, with Gebri dogging her steps and trying to help, she heaved her bag onto her shoulder, and then hooked a finger through Gebri's lapel buttonhole to pull him along with her.

There was nothing coy about the gesture. As she led him back to her lodgings, Gebri had to run to keep pace.

For the next week, Gebri was utterly delirious. He had a lover. And there was something exciting about being seen with *this* lover. Her practicality and strength made him feel less flimsy. He walked taller with her at his side. She was twenty-five, a good seven years older than him, which made him feel worldly by association.

It was only as time went by that unease and dissatisfaction started to nag at him. He had supposed, in his youthful, idealistic way that physical intimacy would demolish every door between them. Sometimes she would share an anecdote unprompted, and he would feel that they were getting closer. But conversation was still hard.

"What was Tark like?" he asked once, as they lay watching the moon dip past his chamber window.

"Peaceful," Ansida said, after a little thought.

"Peaceful?" Gebri could not quite keep incredulity out of his voice. The Ant cities were notorious for their wars against each other, and the Ant-Kinden for their prowess as soldiers. How could anywhere peaceful have produced Ansida?

"Quiet," Ansida clarified. "Much less... chatter."

47

Gebri swallowed, uncertain whether this was a gibe, or a request for him to shut up and let her sleep. A moment later, Ansida sat up, got out of bed and started dressing.

"I've upset you." Amid his anxiety, he felt a sting of annoyance. *If you're angry, why can't you just tell me?* "If you'd rather I didn't ask about Tark —"

"I'm not upset." Ansida pulled on her tunic. "I'm needed somewhere, that's all."

After she had left, Gebri lay alone, feeling cold. A message through the mind-link had called her away. Perhaps her comrades needed her to break up a fight or investigate something. They had reached into his little sanctum and plucked her out without effort.

Even when we're alone together, at any moment she might get a mental knock at the door.

No, it's worse than that. They don't need to knock. They're already inside the door. Her mind is linked to theirs all the time.

I'm never, ever alone with her.

That thought opened great cracks in his happiness and his thoughts, and a host of doubts crept into them like spiders. He started to wonder.

Day and night, Gebri could not stop himself wondering.

When Ansida sat or lay beside him, was her mind really in the room with him? Or was she discussing military formations with other Tarkesh in another part of the city? Was he being enjoyed absent-mindedly like a sandwich, while her mind was busy with more important matters?

Worse, was there an audience for his every word, gift, and caress? Did Ansida's comrades discuss his efforts, and give him marks out of ten? Had the entire Tarkesh Free Army seen his bare knees?

He became obsessive, collecting fragments of evidence that fed his paranoia. One of the Tarkesh recognised him, and greeted him in an offhand way as "Ansida's pet". That little barb bit deep into his mind. Did they all call him over the mind-link? Did *she* call him that?

Did she laugh at him? He had never seen her laugh at all, but perhaps she was a different person in the silent world of Ant-Kinden communion. Perhaps she was renowned for her warmth and wit. Perhaps she was the joker of the army. How would he know?

"What do Ant women want in a romance, anyway?" he asked one of his Fly-kinden friends, who seemed to be an expert on sex despite having a face like a crumpled dish-cloth. The answer was not reassuring.

"From what I hear, they're not so big on *romance* at all. They'll mate, but they're usually pretty level-headed about it. Not many legends about Ant maidens throwing themselves into the sea with broken hearts, that's all I'm saying."

The wondering was exhausting. It gnawed away at Gebri's concentration, his sleep, his ability to work.

He was jealous. Bitterly, desperately jealous of a communion that he could not share. He was still a forlorn little wave breaking against a cliff that would never yield, and could never let him in.

And like many unhappy people in love he began to convince himself that it was the *situation* that was an unhappy one. It was bad for everyone. His beloved needed to be saved from it.

So he sought out Vyssa.

Hardly anybody admitted to consulting Vyssa, and yet the services she offered were surprisingly well-known amongst the students of Gebri's acquaintance. It was understood that if you had love troubles, and if your case or your payment piqued her interest, she would intervene on your behalf, in her own inscrutable Spider-kinden way. Of course, a Spider who was a true master of such subtle arts would not be selling their cunning by the quart in a run-down room above a shop, but Gebri was willing to settle for one within the reach of his purse.

She was older than Gebri expected, wearing her years as if they were a silver shawl she had donned on a whim. Embroidered hangings hid the faded walls of her rooms, but not the smell of damp. Her smile quietly drew Gebri's story from him, loop by loop, like silk from a bobbin.

"Well," she said at last, "to be *quite* honest, you don't sound like an obvious match. What is it about her that you find so compelling?"

"Everything! She's so strong, she could tear me apart, nothing dents her, but… it's as if I can *hear* something inside her. Like the sad note you sometimes hear inside a storm. And I like… everything… the way she places her feet when she's sparring… eyes… even her knuckles…"

"Well, that was splendidly inarticulate, so you're probably sincere, at least." Somehow Vyssa's kindly smile was an anaesthetic, and Gebri could not even feel the barbs of her comments going in. "And you feel that while she has a mind-link with her comrades, your relationship is doomed?"

"She's locked into that mind-hive, and she doesn't even realise it," Gebri answered promptly. "Like a cog in a machine."

"I thought you liked machines."

"I do! But people aren't machine parts! She's so much more than that! She's different from the other Tarkesh! She's special!" Over time, Gebri's feverishly thoughts had settled into conclusions that he could bear. "I want to rescue her," he said with quiet pride and conviction. "I want to show her that she doesn't need them."

Vyssa took a very long while to stir her tea, watching the little red blossom petals eddy and whirl.

"I see," she said at last.

"Can you do it?" he asked eagerly.

"Of course. If that's what you want. But if I take this case, there's something *you* must do. It will be a shock for her, you know, losing that perpetual connection. So you must soften the blow. You must be ready to bring it home to her that she has never really fitted in with her fellows."

"I... How?"

"Oh, not with words. But machines are your real language, aren't they? So take one of your contraptions, and change one part inside it, just a little. Not enough to stop the device," she traced small, disdainful circles in the air, "doing whatever it does. But enough that the part clearly does not fit there any more."

Gebri stared at her. "How is that supposed to prove anything to anyone?"

"You need to trust me," said Vyssa. And of course Gebri found that he did.

It should be easy, Gebri told himself. *After all, getting a delicate machine to run perfectly is the real challenge. Any idiot can create an imperfect mechanism.*

One of his musical boxes had a hinged front so that the inner workings could be admired. He carefully dismantled the mechanism, and selected one of the larger cogs. With great care he engraved fine patterns into it, so that it was more beautiful than its fellows.

Now all he needed to do was to file one of its teeth half a hair's breadth, or perhaps enlarge its central hole so that it sat more loosely on its axle. Just enough for a rattle, a wobble... The thought of tiny cog teeth catching and jarring set his own teeth on edge.

The cog was so flawless, its efficacy so extraordinary. His artificer's soul recoiled from the thought of maiming it. One stroke with the file, one gentle abrasion, and it would become imperfect. Ordinary.

He had to clench his hands to stop them shaking, as he prepared to mar the beautiful thing he had made.

Vyssa opened her casement after Gebri's first pebble rattled against her shutters, and came down to let him in.

"I couldn't do it," he blurted out. "I can't do it! I've changed my mind. You haven't… done anything yet, have you?"

Vyssa settled herself in a chair. She was still dressed, and seemed unsurprised by his midnight visit, but he was too flustered to wonder at this.

"One likes to start quickly with this sort of task," she said mildly. "It's never an easy matter getting an Ant thrown out of their community. Framing them isn't straight forward – they live in each other's heads, so you have years of solidarity, trust and intimate familiarity to overcome. But here in Collegium, things are more complicated – so many interesting tensions right now! If enough *locals* believed that your fair Ant was guilty of something, and politics came into play, an example might have to be made of her to prevent a little crisis. If she's honourable enough, she might even volunteer to be a sacrificial lamb…"

"Don't!" Gebri was aghast. "You can't! This wasn't what I wanted!"

"Of *course* it was!" Without her smile, Vyssa's face seemed narrower and less kindly. "You wanted her to leave her comrades, but deep down you knew that she would never do so of her own free will. You wanted me to take that decision away from her. Yes, that would leave her in an aching solitude, more terrible than if she'd been buried a thousand feet deep. But never mind, she'd have *you*, wouldn't she?"

He wanted to protest, but could not.

"All right!" he erupted. "Yes, maybe I have been lying to myself. But whatever you've done, I need you to undo it! I'll double your commission – I'll owe you anything you like."

The Spider sighed.

"You need to learn that there are times when you cannot take back your decisions. Sometimes the die is cast. The arrow is loosed. The avalanche is descending, and cannot be halted by apologies or arm-waving.

"Fortunately – very fortunately – this is not one of those times. I accept your new offer."

Gebri slumped with relief into the armchair. Due to the height of the seat and the shortness of his legs, this was a fairly short slump. It was only after a few minutes of listening to his heart slow that he realised that Vyssa was quietly engaged in some darning.

"Shouldn't you be...?" He swallowed, not wanting to be rude, but fighting a sense of panic. "Don't you need to act quickly? Talk to people and un-frame Ansida?"

"Mmm? Oh no, not really. I never actually *did* pull any strings, you know. After you left me last time, I did precisely nothing."

"What?" Gebri sat bolt upright. "You tricked me! You... you just wanted me to be in debt to you! For nothing!"

"Oh, you owe me and you know it." Carefully, Vyssa pushed her long needle through the fabric, and glanced at him, eyebrow raised. Gebri wilted beneath her frost-grey gaze. "I've opened your eyes, and not a moment too soon. Count yourself lucky that you came to me, and that I was feeling charitable rather than playful.

"But perhaps you had better leave for now. My sense of whimsy has been known to return unexpectedly."

The next morning, Gebri found Ansida in a secluded square, preparing to train with some of her comrades. When he handed her the musical box, she handled it gingerly and with unease, as if somebody had handed her a sick pet and asked her to take care of it.

"It was supposed to be a metaphor." Gebri was pink with shame. "That cog – that's you. I wanted to show that you didn't really fit in with the other Tarkesh... but you do. Beautifully.

"I'm disgustingly jealous." He had thrown himself into self-loathing with youthful enthusiasm, hoping of course that if he reproached himself enough nobody else would need to. "I'm a horrible, selfish person. It's just that... you and your friends, you're so self-sufficient. Sometimes I don't feel you need me at all."

"Self-sufficient." Ansida raised her eyebrows and let out a long breath. "Gebri... we're like ship-wrecked mariners. Tark was our ship. It sank. The captain died. Those of us who are left, we're all adrift, clinging to the same timber." She frowned, then corrected herself. "No, we *are* each other's timber."

"I wish I could be your timber," said Gebri in a very small voice.

Ansida gave him a sidelong glance, tinged with affection.

"You're something else," she said. "You're... a puzzle. I can't hear your thoughts, so I have to piece you together. And I can never know if I got it right. I'm always watching – guessing – wondering. It's very..."

"Tiring?"

She frowned in thought.

"It *is* tiring," she admitted, with her usual brutal frankness. "And annoying." She gave him a small, grim smile. "But I was going to say 'exciting'. I have to stay alert all the time. Reading you. The way I do when I'm facing an enemy."

These were not the words Gebri wanted to hear, but they were strangely warming. He was never half-forgotten or ludicrous, then. He was as troublesome and mysterious to her as she was to him.

Ansida stared out across the little square with the same expression he had first seen on her face, and now he felt he understood it a little better. If he was a mystery, then what was this crowd, this street, this city? She was adrift indeed in a sea of eternal strangers, a cacophony of unwanted, incomprehensible voices.

"Tark fell," she said, with a shrug. "There is no certainty any more. No safety."

Perhaps that was what Gebri had been scrabbling after all along, some kind of certainty to cling to. *Perhaps if I can secure this woman, if I can be sure of her, then I will be safe. My world will not collapse. The Wasps will not come. Collegium will not fall.*

But she was right. Safety had died a long time ago, and everybody at the Collegium had been stepping over its corpse for years and pretending not to notice.

"I know," said Gebri. He gave her hand a squeeze, and somehow his small hand seemed to fit hers better than before.

"But living in fear is still living, isn't it?" she said, and gave him one of her fleeting smiles.

After a few minutes, of course, Ansida left him to train with her comrades. The group moved and parried with a practiced precision, readying themselves for blows and foes that would inevitably come.

And Gebri watched her in wonder.

The Promise of a Threat

David Tallerman

Wasps did not threaten, they promised.

Or so they claimed; and what reason did Meyr have to disbelieve them? After all, Wasps were no strangers to atrocity. Even if he could somehow ignore their steady yet inexorable effort to stain every corner of the map in black and gold, how many Mole Cricket-kinden had died at their hands? Whether beneath the lash or by the steady regime of starvation and mistreatment which characterised the Wasp occupation of Tzeina, they had ended ample Mole lives for the possibility of wholesale slaughter to seem utterly plausible.

So what was this insidious mistrust Meyr felt, as he listened for a time beyond count to the Captain named Temmen, whose glowering, thin-boned face and bitter gaze represented the Wasp Empire in this small corner of the occupation?

"I need not remind you what will happen should you attempt an escape," Temmen pronounced, though of course he was about to. "Whatsoever village you were brought here from, it will be razed to the ground. Your family, everyone and everything you knew, that will be the price of your disobedience." Temmen's eyes roved over them, full of hatred, as if what he warned them against was a crime they'd already committed. "This is not a threat but a pledge," he concluded – as he always did.

And though Meyr had no reason to question, he could not quite still that worm of suspicion crawling around the edges of his thoughts.

It was Hoyl who gave Meyr's doubts concrete form. "I just don't believe him," he said softly.

They were walking from the cavern the Wasps had made their centre of operations, back towards the westerly seam that was the current focus of their efforts. All of this – the broad passage, the lamps that burned continuously, the occasional signs affixed at junctions – was for the Wasps' own benefit. They were not natural miners, that much was certain, nor were they suited to a life underground. It was clear, in fact, that the handful of Wasps assigned to these depths as overseers and wardens despised their task – clear, if nothing else, from the purposeless brutality with which they went about it.

No surprise then that there were a goodly number of Auxilians assigned to Tzeina, mostly Ant-kinden and the occasional Bee, both races no more inclined to bemoan a lack of daylight than the Moles themselves. In the early days, the Wasps had tried using Mole-kinden to guard their own, but that had never worked well; it was difficult to train a Mole to cruelty, no matter the effort applied. The Wasps seemed gravely puzzled by these giants who could kill with a blow and yet were disinclined to do so, regardless of reward or grievance; such sentiments clashed with their entire perception of the world. Even Meyr himself pondered sometimes – another creeping worm of dangerous speculation – why Moles were so reluctant to put their strength to service in their own defence.

Meyr wanted to look at Hoyl, to see what was in his friend's face. He found that he didn't dare. Anyway, surely he knew, as he knew also what was coming. He desired no part of this; merely to listen was too great a risk.

"If there's one thing you can trust in," Meyr muttered from the corner of his mouth, "it's Wasp cruelty. Suspect the stars in the sky and the rock underfoot, but that Wasps will kill at the slightest provocation... only a fool would question that, Hoyl."

Hoyl harrumphed through his massive nostrils – though whether he was disagreeing or conceding the point Meyr couldn't say. Nor was he soon to find out. Ahead in the flickering shadows, a Wasp sentry was peering their way with altogether too much attention, misery and loathing etched into each line of his face. Meyr dropped his head, became the enslaved Mole he was expected to be, the passive giant so easily overborne by a more determined race. Mole-kinden history was one tale of peonage after another, or at best of gainful exploitation; there were times when Meyr wondered if it wasn't something ingrained in their nature, this will to suffer and labour with such meagre reward.

Hoyl, at least, found subservience onerous. Still, he bowed his head as they passed the Wasp – sufficiently to avoid comment – and he held his tongue until they'd reached the work face. It was as close to a safe place as they had, and paradoxically as close as they ever were to freedom, for the Wasps didn't come here. There were a scattering of Ants supervising, but Moles didn't need much supervision to make them mine; doing so was precisely as hard, Meyr thought, as persuading a Wasp to sting. Every creature acted according to its nature.

But again, there was Hoyl – and on that day as others, he evidently wasn't committed to his labour. Meyr knew what was on his mind, knew that sooner or later those doubts would bubble to the surface, and that then he would have no choice except to listen. And it occurred to him that he knew this because Hoyl's thoughts so intimately mirrored his own; the sole difference being that Hoyl was a little braver or a little foolhardier than Meyr himself.

Nonetheless, he couldn't but flinch when Hoyl spoke up once more, the whispered words drifting from the near darkness like the scent of stink damp rising from a deep working. "Consider the logistics. Aren't Wasps all about logistics? What idiot would kill hundreds to punish one, or even to keep a few dozen in line? And consider the manpower required. No, Meyr, Temmen's is an empty threat, and we all know that in our hearts."

"I'll tell you what isn't," Meyr hissed back, louder than he'd intended. "If they hear you talking that way, it will be the crossed pikes for us both. Maybe they won't kill hundreds to prove a point, but they wouldn't hesitate to sacrifice two. Pits, Hoyl, they'd be grateful for the excuse."

Meyr sensed rather than saw Hoyl shrug his shoulders. "Then let's not talk," he murmured, in a tone that made quite evident he didn't mean, *let's forget about it.*

Meyr was shocked by how tempted he found himself. Surely the reason Hoyl made no further effort to convince him was not fear of discovery but that any arguments he might make were too obvious to waste words on. This, here and now, was the entirety of their future, slaving to appease a race who despised them for everything except their usefulness. There was scarce cause for hope; only that the Wasps might someday be turned back in their interminable war. And, from what snatches of news reached them here in the depths of Tzeina, there was no great likelihood of that.

Yet Meyr's fear was great. Appreciating that it had been trained into him, built over months and years by stubborn repetition, did little to diminish what he felt. Behind his eyelids he could envisage the corpses of his parents, whom he hadn't seen in five years, bleeding out their last upon the crossed pikes – or, more plausibly, shot down amidst the mass of their neighbours.

"You're like a brother to me, Hoyl," Meyr rumbled. "I barely remember a time when we didn't know each other. So believe me when I tell you that this is for your profit as much as my own: forget these ideas, and never speak to me of them again. Or I promise you, the Wasps won't be your only worry."

And Meyr turned his full attention to the rock beneath his claws, willing Hoyl with all his strength of mind to do the same.

That night, Hoyl went.

Meyr heard him leave. He had not been able to sleep, despite the weariness of his body. He'd lain awake, staring at the close ceiling. They slept underground, so as to be nearer to their work, and even a Mole grew claustrophobic eventually when the sun was a distant memory. Perhaps the Wasps didn't understand that this was not how Moles would choose to live; perhaps they regarded them as a wholly subterranean race, without need of sunlight or of fresh air upon their faces.

Hoyl would prove them wrong on that count – or else he'd die trying. He trod quietly for one of his size, but there was no disguising the soft slap of his feet against the stone. Meyr listened until the noise diminished, until it was gone.

Perhaps, also, the Wasps had really persuaded themselves that Mole-kinden were too inured to slavery ever to conceive of flight. Again, Hoyl would challenge their preconceptions this night. With no locks to keep them, escape was as simple as walking out. Oh, there would be sentries, and Moles were hardly equipped for stealth, but these mines were vast, threading into regions the Wasps were altogether ignorant of. Meyr had no doubt that his friend could find a way to the surface, and from there he need only lose himself amid the desolation surrounding Tzeina, the tracts of debris the mine had vomited up over the years.

Hoyl was resourceful. He was clever and quick-witted. He stood, at any rate, a chance. However, there were a great many Wasps, and a great many Wasp allies. Meyr hearkened to the darkness, with ears attuned to the rhythms of his underworld home. Somewhere water dripped with a steady pulse; the earth shivered softly, alive in a fashion the Wasps could never hope to comprehend. Meyr heard no sounds of violence. That didn't mean Hoyl had survived. A single sword blow or the brief sizzle of a sting was all that would be required. Hoyl might dwarf the Imperials, but he was still flesh and blood.

As the minutes wore by, Meyr could no longer separate out the two possibilities, or grant one precedence: in his imagination, Hoyl gazed at a star-spread sky, Hoyl crashed to his knees with half of his long, lean face scorched away. In Meyr's thoughts, his friend gained his long-dreamed-of freedom and died over and over, and Meyr wondered dimly if sleep would ever come for him again.

Yet Meyr must have slept, for how else could he wake to such paroxysms of fear? He opened his eyes with a jolt, but then could hardly bring himself to move further – as though to rouse was to invite disaster. He wanted badly to believe that everything he remembered as having occurred in the night was a dream, that Hoyl's resting place was empty because he was prematurely up and about.

It wasn't true. Hoyl was gone. Now it fell upon those who remained to suffer the consequences.

Meyr persuaded his body into action. He felt painfully self-conscious, for the others would be noting Hoyl's absence, and they all knew Meyr and he were friends. He felt guilt too, as though it was he who had abandoned Hoyl and not the other way around. Both emotions built in him a fierce tension, a certainty that soon a confrontation must come – whether it be the Wasps arriving to drag him away or his fellow kinden making enquiries he dare not answer.

Meyr fell into step in the procession towards what the Wasps referred to as the hall, the sole cavern large enough to hold all of the Tzeinan Moles. He tried to judge whether there were more Wasps than usual guarding their passage, while keeping his view set strictly forward, lest he draw attention. Did *they* know Hoyl was his friend? It might not matter. If they picked out one in ten for execution, as he'd heard they sometimes did, his odds were the same as anyone's.

In the hall, Captain Temmen already waited upon the platform. Amid the half-light allowed by the scant lanterns, his expression seemed grim to Meyr – but then he had never seen Temmen look otherwise.

"I need not remind you of what would happen should one of you attempt escape," the Wasp captain rasped.

Meyr felt melded to the stone beneath his feet. Here it came, the awful consequence of his friend's infraction.

"Whatsoever village you were brought from, it will be razed to the ground. There will be no restraint shown, and no mercy; such is the cost of even the smallest act of rebellion. Your family, everyone you knew, will suffer for your disobedience."

But... this was just the speech. These were the words Meyr had listened to so many, many times before – and though he kept anticipating a deviation, like a twist in an oft-told tale, it didn't come. The threats were the old threats. Temmen's showmanship was the same familiar, threadbare act.

The Wasps were being circumspect, Meyr decided, as Temmen drew to a close. They must have realised from the head count that Hoyl was gone, but not even Wasps were savage enough to conduct executions without first establishing a few rudimentary facts. There would be interrogation, of that particular kind the Wasps so favoured, and the next day would bring its inevitable repercussions.

However, the next day was the same. There were no executions. No one had vanished in the intervening hours. There was no change in Temmen's speech, beyond the typical variations he inserted. If anything, the only detectable difference was a note of ambivalence, or maybe a lack of conviction.

Finally, on the third day, Meyr understood. What he was witnessing was not some aberration of Wasp policy. This was all Temmen, and Temmen's cowardice. Knowing how easily he might cover up the desertion of one single Mole, he had chosen to do precisely that. He hadn't carried out his threat because he couldn't. He was merely a provincial captain, hardly able to erase villages with the wave of a hand. Nor did he dare punish the Moles of Tzeina. To do so was to harm their tenuous productivity; brutality and neglect had already thinned their numbers dangerously. Most likely, Temmen considered his position under threat – which, for a Wasp, meant much worse than the threat of demotion – and dared not admit even one more failure.

That was the truth. Meyr was convinced. It had all come down to Temmen, and he had made a decision, the only decision he could make. He'd been caught in a lie, just as Hoyl had claimed he would be. Hoyl had called the man's bluff, and Temmen had no answer.

Understanding left Meyr's mind awhirl. He felt as if the earth had crumbled beneath his feet; as if he'd dared to meet the Wasps' gaze and they had blinked. Their entire, vast Empire was a sham, built on lies and empty threats. If one cowardly officer could undermine it simply to save face, how solid could the edifice really be?

But following unavoidably from that revelation there came a question. If Hoyl's vanishment had caused barely a ripple, what was keeping Meyr himself here?

Nothing. There was nothing. His freedom was within his grasp, and all Meyr had to do was find the courage to reach for it.

A week had passed since Hoyl's departure. Meyr judged, without real evidence, that if there were to be repercussions, they would have been enacted by now. It was as though Hoyl had faded from the world, as though the walls had opened up and claimed him. Had he been disposed of by the Wasps, dragged away to some isolated cell for them to make their inquiries upon his body, the effect would have been exactly the same. Indeed, that would be what most assumed had happened. There was another miscomprehension in Temmen's favour: people would always fear the worst when it came to Wasps. Given a choice between hope and fear they would, through habit, infallibly opt for the latter.

Only Meyr knew the reality. If Hoyl had been caught, if he'd been killed in his escape attempt, they would not have kept that a secret. Therefore he was free and his success could be replicated.

Not by the same means, though. Since Hoyl's disappearance there had been one change: the Mole-kinden mineworkers were now kept under guard by night. There was invariably a Wasp warden, with an Ant accompanying to offer the benefit of their night vision. No one else would be walking out as Hoyl had, and there was no possibility of fighting free; those two were in easy shouting range of others. It would have taken every Mole-kinden there to battle a way out, and for all his anger at the Wasps, Meyr was no rebel leader, ready to talk his people into a frenzy. He doubted anyone was capable of such a thing.

Or so Meyr told himself. The truth was, he'd already accepted in his heart that if he left he would do so alone. For the sentries meant nothing to him; those two might have been twenty. Meyr's escape plan was as uncomplicated as any could be, simpler even than Hoyl's. The solitary difference was the path he'd chosen.

Assuredly the Wasps knew there were a few like him, possessed of the rarest of Mole-kinden arts. They must be aware that there were those among their captive workforce to whom the very walls were no obstruction. But what could they do? Mining was skilled work, at least the way Moles approached it, and could not be done in shackles. Nor were there Wasps enough to keep every Mole under constant scrutiny. Anyway, doing so would have made no difference. It was impossible to discover just who might have the art. Certainly no one knew about Meyr himself; he had guarded what made him rare and special with uncharacteristic jealousy. Perhaps he had intuited, deep down, that this day might eventually come.

If only he'd reached that insight sooner and had gone with Hoyl. Now Meyr was alone. For two nights he had lain in the deep darkness, wondering if the time had come, finding always at the last that his nerve wasn't ample to the task.

This night was different. He'd sensed it immediately. Some process had been working itself out in his consciousness, like an acid corroding all resistance, and abruptly his final misgivings were gone. There was no reason to stay, and so he would leave.

Still, he had to be cautious. If they should hunt for him, his art might not avail to save him. So Meyr patiently observed the dim forms of the two sentries. The smaller one concerned him most, the Ant. So long as he was here and watching, Meyr dare not slip away. Therefore he waited and waited – until after a while the man began to resemble a statue, immune to frailties of the flesh. *Curse you*, Meyr thought, *don't Ants ever need to piss?*

Apparently they didn't. But untold hours later, the pair did change shifts. Meyr was beginning to drift by then and almost missed his chance. Yet when his sleep-heavy eyes caught that glint of motion, he snapped to wakefulness so complete and vivid that time seemed temporarily to have grown sluggish. The guards' backs were turned, as they spoke in hushed whispers with their replacements; even the cursed Ant was diverted.

Meyr rolled from his bed, as lightly as a being of his size could, and slid into the stone of the wall.

This was Meyr's art, a trait unique to Mole-kinden – and one extraordinary by any measure. What was a Wasp's sting compared to this? Or the Ants and their mind-link? What Meyr did now defied all nature, and to him seemed as ordinary as traversing empty air. He could feel the consistency of the earth about him, could recognise seams of ore, fissures, stripes of crystallisation, with a subtlety that outmatched his habitual five senses.

Having taken a moment to steady himself, Meyr began to ascend, his motion something between climbing and swimming – for the rock around him felt both solid and liquid at once. What his mind couldn't altogether comprehend, his body accepted without complaint. There was an impression of freedom, too, that had nothing to do with his current business: it wasn't the possibility of escape that thrilled Meyr but the joy of being, literally, in his element. He was a Mole, and he gave himself over to a deeper nature, one that centuries of slavery had failed to erase.

Nevertheless, as he moved gradually onward, sliding through this matter that should have crushed his flesh and bones, Meyr couldn't deny that there was a thrill, as well, in defiance. He had rebelled, was even now rebelling. He had rejected his masters, as so few Moles had ever done, and that knowledge was intoxicating.

Meyr was dimly conscious of the passages threaded about him, though which of his faculties imparted that knowledge he couldn't have said. At first, he was careful to avoid them, lest he appear beside a patrolling Wasp. But it was a long time since he'd made use of his art, and doing so required more of his strength than he remembered. He could no longer judge where he was – though somehow, however disorientated he became, he was always aware of the surface above him.

Finally that need to get his bearings, not to mention the growing lassitude slowing his strokes, got the better of him. Meyr dove for the nearest wall and slid through, stepping easily into the hollow of a wide passageway. Had there been anyone to see, they would have received the shock of their life; but there was no one and the tunnel was dark. Meyr hurried to one junction and another, stopping at each to read the symbols scratched there by his fellows. By the time he'd run his broad fingers over the second set of glyphs, he knew where he was – and that he was almost free.

He had recovered much of his strength by then. In the next passage, Meyr returned to the rock and to his upward swimming. A minute later and, with a gasp, he was breaching the surface.

This time there was light. Meyr wanted to shy away; instead, with his head and shoulders protruding and the rest of his body encased in solid earth, he forced himself to look. There was a bonfire close by, and dark shapes round about. There were torches too, bobbing out there amid the darkness. But the figures surrounding the fire had their backs to Meyr, and as his eyes began to adjust, he saw that the patrolling scouts were nowhere near his position either. Here was as good a chance as any.

Meyr drew himself the last distance. The sense of space was nigh on overwhelming; he had been so long underground. He picked the direction farthest from all of the numerous fires, though he had no idea if it would lead anywhere he wished to be. Hunched, he crept into the deeper darkness, braced with anticipation for the moment when the alarm was called and a dozen Wasps descended, palms spitting fire.

They didn't see him. Wasp eyes were worthless in the dark, and there were not so many of them. This was only one small mine, their duty to guard a few passive slaves. Even with Hoyl gone, they hadn't learned to adapt expectations founded upon years of habit. In their minds, Moles did not rebel, did not escape. Moles did not slip away in the night.

Yet here I am, Meyr thought, with a rush of exhilaration such as he'd never felt, *doing just that.*

When he'd travelled far enough to be out of hearing range, Meyr settled into a lumbering run. Mole-kinden were not exactly built for speed, but they had stamina in abundance. He knew he could keep his pace up all night – and so he did. He ran until a grey dawn tinged the promontories, and later the plains of dull stone, the scrub grass, the crooked trees. Only then did he start to consider the need to hide himself. While settlements were scarce in these parts, that didn't negate the risks of a Wasp convoy, a scout party, or a low-flying ornithopter with an overly curious pilot.

Meyr hadn't thought his plan through. Indeed, it struck him that he had nothing deserving of the term. What was he to eat? Where would he rest? He was in his own lands, lands his people had walked for ages beyond memory, but he was also in enemy territory. However he might despise the fact, every step he took merely carried him from one portion of the Empire to another.

In the end, he decided to keep walking. Likely he'd detect any potential threat before they spotted him, and so long as he had at least a modicum of strength left he would always be able to drop into the earth and conceal himself.

The question became, then, what was to be his course. If he'd wanted only to lose himself, Meyr would have turned west, towards the Delve. But though he had lived there long enough to regard the city a home, it wasn't *home* – and that wouldn't be the destination Hoyl had chosen. No, Meyr's heart told him that, if he was truly a free man now, it must be Span he returned to: the village of his childhood, and the place where the Wasps had made him their own.

Yet Span was three days walk away, with little hope of finding food in-between.

It didn't matter. He was free. What was three days walking compared to years of slavery? Meyr chose his bearing and adopted a steady trudge, one he felt confident was sufficient to the task.

On the second day, Meyr nearly blundered into a small Wasp caravan: a dozen men and two laden pack beetles, travelling who knew where. After that, he realised he was too weak to resume his former pace – and that if he didn't eat soon he'd be too weak to continue at all. He had overestimated his own strength, sapped over the long years by Wasp misuse.

A centipede, caught off guard and squashed half flat by the rock Meyr was wielding, provided his first meal in two days, and his first as a free man. The leathery meat tasted indescribably good. In an adjacent hollow, Meyr found a small pool and drank his fill, then washed the dust from his skin. He spent that night huddled beneath an outcrop of rock, calmer and more at ease than perhaps he had any right to be.

For the remaining two days, Meyr travelled steadily, taking time to hunt and in general to attend to his body's demands. It had dawned on him that there was no great need for haste, and that he would prefer to return home looking something like a free Mole-kinden rather than an escaped slave.

By the afternoon of the fourth day, he'd concluded that he was near. Though years had passed since he'd last seen this landscape, aspects were familiar: a copse of trees here, a particular slope of red-tainted stone there. Meyr's steps slowed – began to drag. So much might have changed in his absence. For all he knew, his parents were no longer alive.

As he drew closer, however, Meyr recognised that it wasn't only such doubts that were slowing him. The source of his resistance was worse even than that. And as the sentiment of acquaintance grew stronger, so did his craving to turn away – to go anywhere but forward, no matter if that meant back to Tzeina.

Sure enough, when he reached it, Meyr found Span empty.

Maybe what he'd sensed had in fact been the absence of sound: of those constant, small noises that should have announced the presence of life. Yet as Meyr descended towards the village, Span's lack of habitation was easy to see. Every street was bare of traffic. The windows of the low-set houses stared vacantly. Moles, of course, did not build wholly or even mostly on the surface, but Meyr knew that the abandonment was total.

The Wasps had carried out their threat. To punish one escapee, they had erased an entire community.

Or so he initially thought, with a horrified numbness that obliterated almost everything else from his mind. As the minutes passed, as he explored streets made alien by their desolation, the truth dawned on him by degrees. This had not been a slaughter; the signs of disruption were too few. Most homes had been left open, and in the ones he dared to probe, any essential belongings were largely vanished, whereas trivial possessions and heavy furnishings remained.

So Span had not been expunged by violence. The village had simply been evacuated. Its inhabitants, every last one, had been sent to slave elsewhere in the Wasp Empire, swapped around like cogs in a machine. Meyr's parents, his sister, might be anywhere, and he could conceive of no way to find them. To all intents and purposes, they were vanished from his world.

At that admission, Meyr wanted to break down and weep. But his body refused to stop. So instead he trudged on, in the direction of the far outskirts. He felt as emptied as his surroundings – and for precisely the same reason.

The Wasps. They'd taken everything from him, and had done so unthinkingly, without ever once seeing Meyr the Mole-kinden. He was a resource, and they had used him absolutely.

Then Meyr turned a final corner, into a street that broke from the edge of the village, and the last strength went out of him. His legs would no longer hold him upright. He crumpled to the dust of the road.

From that lower angle, the spectacle before him was yet worse. The seven figures suspended at the street's end seemed to tower over him. A detached part of Meyr's mind pointed out that the Wasps couldn't possibly have used standard pikes, not for Mole-kinden. These would have had to be manufactured especially – and the cold logic of that more than the scene itself made him want to retch.

Six of them Meyr didn't recognise. The seventh he did, though decay had made familiar features strange. But Hoyl had borne a scar across his brow, where a Wasp overseer had lashed him, and even with his flesh as flabby and rot-worn as it was now, that slash of white stood out proudly.

Something else moved in Meyr's thoughts then, another increment in his growing understanding of how Wasps worked and of how they'd built an empire spanning such tracts of the known world. One Mole meant nothing to them, no more than a lone rivet or a single head of grain. But if Temmen had turned a blind eye to one escapee, surely he couldn't do so for two. Hoyl's escape might not have exacted punishment upon his kin, but Meyr's would. He had barely considered the possibility, yet now he saw with leaden certainty that the blood of other Moles was on his great, clawed hands. Back in Tzeina there would be just such a display as this.

Meyr hauled himself to his feet. His body felt curiously heavy and distant, as if it were some construct his mind was manipulating into action. He walked with weighty steps towards the seven bodies, the seven sets of crossed pikes. He had a dim notion that perhaps he should take them down, should try and bury them, though the earth was dry and hard.

"You!"

The cry came from somewhere to his left. It didn't take the accent to tell him the speaker was a Wasp, for who else would be here in the remnants of Span? Nor did it require any leap of imagination to assume that they were one of those who'd done this to his friend.

"Who are you? Wait there."

Meyr could hear the rumble of hurrying feet. When he looked round, there were seven men approaching, all Wasps and in the black and gold. Meyr allowed them to spread out in a loose half circle about him. He was unacquainted with the weapons they were pointing his way. They didn't appear especially dangerous, but Meyr knew better than to underestimate Wasps and their capacity for violence.

Their officer took a position at the centre of the crescent his men had formed. "A runaway, is it?" He chuckled. "We see none in years and then two in a week." He motioned nonchalantly at the enormous corpse suspended before them. "Or was that a friend of yours? Did you two cook this up together?"

"He was my friend," Meyr agreed.

"Then you should have chosen your friends more wisely," the Wasp officer proposed.

Meyr pondered this. It was true that Hoyl had been overhasty and something of a troublemaker; by Mole standards, he'd been a strange one. Nevertheless, he had been kind and brave and sharp-witted. He had deserved much better than the torturous death they'd given him. Better slave-masters would have found a use for such a man; but to the Wasps Hoyl had been only a faulty gear in their immense machine, and so they had broken him utterly.

"I think," Meyr said slowly, "that he was the best friend I could have hoped to find."

"Ah. Well." The Wasp officer smirked. "If that's the case, I suppose you'll be glad to end up next to him." And he raised a hand towards Meyr.

Then the Wasp was screaming, a raw shriek that grated upon Meyr's nerves. Meyr had had no thought of hurting the man. He simply did not wish to be touched. Yet the Wasp's arm from below the elbow was at an impossible angle, and there was blood spreading across his sleeve.

Meyr nearly let him go. But the remaining six were aiming those weapons of theirs, training overcoming their immediate shock and horror. So instead, Meyr hoisted the Wasp officer – in time for half a dozen projectiles to thunder into his back.

The Wasp made an imperfect shield. Whatever ammunition those weapons fired, apparently mere meat and bone, or even armour, weren't fit to stop it. One shot at least passed straight through and grazed Meyr's bare torso. He scarcely felt the impact, but rather than wait for another round to strike, he hefted the officer and flung him, knocking two of his men to the dirt.

Stingshot scorched Meyr's shoulder. He ignored it. The man who'd fired still had his palm upraised, so Meyr leapt towards him, caught the hand, and wrenched. There was an audible crack as his shoulder dislocated, and the man screamed – until Meyr's fist shattered his jaw.

The Wasp had had his sword drawn in his other hand; as he lost consciousness, the hilt slid from limp fingers. Meyr snatched it up. There were three Wasps left standing. They had their weapons aimed, but there was fear and doubt in their eyes. One fired and missed, and in the time that took, Meyr had closed the gap between them.

Rather than try and wield his acquired blade as it was meant to be used, he treated it as an extension of his reach. The Wasps, rapidly dropping their ranged weapons in favour of clutching for their own swords, had no defence against such inelegant violence. Meyr hacked and hacked, and barely cared if they struck back. They slashed at his arm, his thigh, but glancing blows wouldn't suffice to stop him. By then he had sliced clean through one Wasp, almost halving him about the middle, had cleaved the hand from another. The last turned to run, and since Meyr wasn't convinced he could outpace him, he flung his blade. Skewered through the ribs, the Wasp skidded into the dirt and lay still.

Meyr took up one of their dropped swords and methodically finished off the wounded. He had never killed before, and now he'd taken seven lives and felt nothing. He wasn't angry, though perhaps anger would come. He wasn't afraid of retribution, though retribution seemed likely.

He knew he should take Hoyl's body down, and set to work on burying the dead Wasps. It would be quick work to a Mole. Yet he couldn't find the strength. Meyr sat in the stripe of dirt where village met wilderness, his back to the suspended corpses. His body was profoundly listless, as were his thoughts. He shut his eyes.

Time passed. Meyr had no way to measure how long. Then he heard a noise, distant but approaching. After a while, it occurred to him that what he was hearing was the whirr of a propeller. So it was to be the Wasps after all. The prospect hardly troubled him. He would put up enough of a fight that they'd have no choice except to kill him; he was capable of that much.

The craft drew nearer, and descended. Judging by sound alone, Meyr imagined it to be of considerable size. He only stirred when the propellers had been silenced, and when he discerned voices. Some note in their tones, or their accents, had roused his curiosity.

Four figures were approaching, with their craft – a small airship – settled farther off in the distance. They were certainly not Wasps. The man in front was a stocky half-breed with Beetle blood in him, there were a couple of Ants, and a woman of some kinden Meyr didn't recognise. Nor was he familiar with their emblem: a grey glove against a background of subtly different shade and texture.

The half-Beetle was assessing the scene with a dispassionate gaze. "I fear that's our sale gone up in smoke," he observed.

"Dead Wasps make for even poorer customers than live ones," the woman agreed good-humouredly.

The half-Beetle came over to Meyr, stopping just out of his reach.

"What's your name?" he asked.

The earnestness of the query surprised Meyr, and then the fact that anyone should think to care. "I'm Meyr," he said.

"And you did this?" the man inquired, indicating the fallen Wasps with a tilt of the head.

Meyr nodded.

"What risk is there that you'll try and do the same to us?"

Meyr considered. "Are you with the Wasps?"

"As occasional business partners," the half-Beetle confirmed, evidently picking his words with exactness. "The Iron Glove is an independent organisation, with no allegiances to anything other than itself."

"Then," Meyr said, "you've no reason to fear me."

The half-breed shuffled his feet. He was young, Meyr realised, younger than he'd originally taken him for, and seemed ill-fitted to leadership. "My name's Totho," the man announced. "And as I say, we represent the Iron Glove. Manufacturers and traders of the finest armaments and related mechanisms."

His brow creased with thought. "Since it appears our customers won't be spending any coin today," he added, "we'll be leaving now. Would you care to come with us? If you've nothing pressing, I mean. We're heading well away from here... there's no risk of you being found. And we can always use a pair of strong arms."

Somehow, the offer didn't surprise Meyr as much as he felt it should have. Something about this ragtag assembly suggested that this was how they did the bulk of their recruitment; despite their smart and matching uniforms, he deduced instinctively that they were organised in very different fashion to the Wasps. This half-Beetle clearly hadn't gained his position through physical prowess, or even strength of personality, and yet he exuded an impression of focus and of sharp intelligence.

Meyr considered. But there was little to contemplate. All of his old life was gone – had been taken. His choices were to go with this strange half-breed and his allies or to stay here and die, and he wasn't quite ready for the latter.

Meyr got to his feet. "I'll come with you," he decided. "Only, first I must bury my friend."

The Unforeseen Path

Juliet E. McKenna

Tesk's world ended in a single day. Though the end had been some while in coming. His city of Strave had been under siege by the rival Ant-kinden of Neme for nearly three ten-days by now.

Not that the men and women of Strave anticipated defeat. Far from it. They shared their resolve through unspoken thought, each and every one bolstering the others, whether they stood guard on the walls, cooked the meals that sustained the soldiers or went about the myriad routine tasks of non-combatant lives. The city was well supplied with stores of both food and weaponry. It was the Ant-kinden way.

The ochre-hued army of Neme would batter itself on Strave's remorseless walls until they could no longer stand their losses to the crossbows, nailbows and other weapons assailing them from the ramparts. Then they would retreat.

Then the silent communion of thought which united Strave's population would consider whether or not they should open their gates and send vengeful forces in pursuit, to turn that retreat into a rout. Or would their city be better served by tending their own injured and assessing the damage inflicted on their walls by Neme's siege engines? Those best placed to gauge such costs to the city would share their knowledge with the rest. Consensus would arise among the population and their Queen would give her orders accordingly. It was the Ant-kinden way.

Tesk was undecided, as yet at least. Strave's resistance hadn't been without grievous loss. Neme's army had trebuchets and repeating ballistas. They had launched massive stones to batter the walls and blazing bales of oil-soaked rags to burst on impact and scatter the ramparts' defenders. Successive showers of black iron bolts had pierced arms, legs, chests, heads. As Tesk took his post above the East Gate just after dawn, he could feel the pain of the wounded lying in the nearest

71

hospital several streets away. Close enough for the stretcher-bearers to get casualties to the nurses and surgeons quickly enough to save their lives. Not so close that their suffering demoralised the city's defenders.

He drew a breath of the cold, clean air as he assessed the distant line of Neme's forces. Faint threads of smoke from cook fires rose into the pale sky, far enough beyond the reach of Strave's catapults for Neme men and women to eat their breakfast in peace. There was no sign of any more purposeful activity; no sounds of weapons being readied, carried to the silent watchers on the walls by the carefree morning breeze.

Tesk concentrated on the refreshing chill of the morning. He flexed strong muscles beneath the dusky blue carapace of his armour in a practised sequence from head to feet and back again. He dwelled for a moment on the savour of the fruit and meat porridge that he had so recently enjoyed, before exchanging a silent glance with Gep on his right hand and Lyk on his left. They joined him in focusing their minds on their own health and strength.

Sharing a nod of accord, all three turned their thoughts to those suffering in the nearby hospital. Tesk endured a measure of wordless pain, offering his own sense of well-being in return, to help some unknown fellow-soldier resist the agony of his wounds. He could feel the other men and women of the gate watch doing the same, as they lined the ramparts beyond Gep and Lyk. Everyone knew that if they were to be injured, when they found themselves on the other side of this exchange, they would heal all the faster for it. This was the Ant-kinden way.

Later, and far too late, Tesk realised how subtle hints of disaster had wormed their way into Strave minds at the very start of the battle. That had happened precisely because this custom of offering solace left the city's defenders distantly conscious of the painful possibilities of injury. If only that unforeseen consequence had been more easily recognised, like a faint rumble of thunder, however far away. But it was more akin to those shifts in air pressure that see people turn irritable and argumentative without quite knowing why. A tension that's only relieved when the storm breaks over their heads.

The first apprehension shot through the Strave kinden consciousness from the westward battlements. As the daylight strengthened, Neme forces launched a bombardment. Unwelcome but not unexpected. Tesk blinked and saw the oncoming rain of missiles through some unknown other's eyes, before that prudent soldier ducked down, crouching behind the solid protection of the walls. Another blink and he looked out from the East Gate's heights, scanning the Neme ranks ahead of his own post for any sign of movement. Was their enemy going to try an all-encircling attack?

Apparently not. Tesk felt a frisson of anticipation surge through the city. The westward defenders could see the Nene soldiers advancing. The foremost held up great shields of woven wicker to foil the oncoming hail of missiles from crossbows and nailbows.

Let's see how well those things hold up against stones as big as a man's head.

Some unknown trebuchet master's scorn shot through Tesk's mind, swift and deadly as lightening. He caught a glimpse of a great weapon's sling being loaded with a basket of lumps of flint, murderously sharp-edged.

Another blink and different eyes showed him that the Neme second rank was carrying ladders. These were the troops determined to scale the wall before all those defenders who had taken shelter could return to their posts.

Soldiers alongside the ladder troops would carry ropes and grapnels. Everybody knew that, even if no one could yet see them. Those were weapons in themselves. Previous attempts to scale the walls had seen more than one of Strave's resolute defenders hooked and dragged to fall screaming from the wall in a welter of blood.

Far away, at the very edge of the thoughts that were reaching Tesk, someone's memory of a friend's death tainted the soldiers' united resolve with dread. Whoever might be fearing such a fate was instantly answered by a rush of reassurance from comrades close at hand. Others offered defiance, some calm assessment of the odds, the rest whatever they hoped might counter that fearful recollection.

The Neme advance picked up its pace. The rhythmic thud of marching feet was accelerating now, ominous, inexorable. The dark mass of the rest of the army was pressing close behind the assault troops, all in perfect step. Once they had a foothold on the walls, these were the killers who would sweep through every street, every alley and house in Strave. Whomsoever they didn't slaughter, they would brutally enslave.

Once more, trepidation shivered through those defending the far side of the city. Where would the first attack come? How many on this stretch of wall would be lost or wounded today? Yet again, those further along the walls shared their courage to reassure any doubters. Strave resolution would win this day.

Along with Gep and Lyk and every other soldier looking east, Tesk let all those whom his mind was touching see the empty field of battle before them. An instant later, swift as thought, they all glimpsed the plain around the city as seen from a full circuit of the walls. The Neme advance was limited to a narrow front striking at the westward gate.

Which doesn't make it any less deadly.

Whoever thought that was merely cautious though, not cowardly. The west's defenders braced themselves. As those unseen soldiers gripped their weapons, Tesk's hand closed around empty air in unison with the rest of his own troop looking east.

What's that?

The first thought was bemused. Puzzlement swiftly spread along the ramparts from the West Gate. With the sun rising in the east, long shadows were spilling westwards from Strave's towers to obscure a clear view of the attackers. What was that shifting, blurring darkness clustered behind the Neme army?

The enemy advanced. There was some allied force there; that much was obvious. But the unknown threat became no clearer. Who was backing Neme? Some other rival city in these fertile lands? That was not the Ant-kinden way.

Strave missiles rained down on the attackers. Here and there, Neme soldiers fell, dropping their wide wicker shields to leave the ladder men exposed. Only for an instant. There were more than enough willing hands to pick up the woven-branch panels which were more than serving their purpose. The Neme assault marched closer.

Away to one side of the West Gate, a Strave trebuchet captain's inspiration prompted a flurry of activity. His was the first weapon to fling a shower of blazing acid but others quickly followed. Moments later, wicker shields were ablaze all across the advancing Neme front.

Why wait to use the lethal concoction on enemies huddled at the base of the walls? Better to use it to stop the Neme forces getting so close in the first place.

Tesk glanced around, involuntarily, to reassure himself that the trebuchets close by had their own supplies of Strave's most closely guarded secret. That blend of chemicals and incendiaries clung wherever it struck, consuming steel, wood and flesh alike in an inferno of flames and corrosion.

Now Neme's vanguard were throwing their wicker shields aside. The front rank was in disarray. A fresh volley of bolts from Strave's walls compounded the spreading chaos.

What's that?

Searing agony lanced through the West Gate's defenders. Even so far away, Tesk flinched. Though that distance meant he could rally his wits to wonder where the pain had come from.

Has someone mishandled a fire acid jar?

No one had an answer. The unknown torment pierced the West Gate soldiers time and again. Their minds were a turmoil of panic and pain. Tesk was only one of countless Strave soldiers trying to rip through that confusion.

WHAT IS GOING ON?

Those further along the walls could see a little more clearly. Teske caught glimpses through the gazes of ten men and women, maybe twenty of them, all aghast. Lean, lithe warriors rose above the Neme kinden's heads on shimmering wings of inborn art. They were armoured in black and gold. Blinding light shot from the outstretched palms of their empty hands.

Wasp-kinden!

Strave defenders recoiled from those murderous stings. Men toppled from the gate's battlements, and from the walls on either side. Most were dead before they hit the ground. Those who survived the fall to land outside the city died fighting the Neme vanguard. Those who fell within the ramparts struggled to drag themselves clear of the reserves now hurrying up the narrow stairs and walkways to reinforce the city's defence.

Meantime, the Wasps were darting towards every break in the Strave line. Deadly, coruscating light lanced from their empty hands, and every flying soldier gripped a sword in his other fist. As soon as they were within arm's reach, they stabbed and slashed, swift and practised. More Strave defenders died.

Now the Wasps were landing on the battlements. At first they stood back to back. They quickly began pressing outwards, forcing Strave's soldiers back. Neme ladders clattered against the gaps that were opening up. Ant-kinden armoured in ochre-coloured steel swarmed up to overwhelm the West Gate's guard. Rear-echelon troops with axes followed to break through the bastion's doors.

Wood splintered and metal buckled. Within moments, Neme troops were inside the tower. Strave soldiers fought to protect their comrades now trying to disable the great gate's mechanisms. Neme fists punched and blades hacked as the attackers redoubled their efforts to open the way into the city. Bruises bloomed purple, highlighting the faint blue sheen of Strave skin. Blood flowed red on both sides.

Down on the ground, outside the walls, more troops from the Neme rear echelon were attacking the gates. Prybars were thrust into axe-gouges, into every joint and crack to splinter the iron-studded wood. Heave after heave of Neme shoulders strained the hinges. There was no fire acid left aloft to pour down their heads. The baulks of timber thrust through the great gates' hasps groaned.

Help us!

Tesk half-turned and took a step. He couldn't help himself. All along the eastward rampart, men and women stirred. Fear and frustration clawed at their minds.

The gate gave way. Neme soldiers rushed through. Strave troops were cut down and trampled underfoot. The Neme forces swiftly fanned out. Squads marched down every street. Detachments darted along back alleys. Doors were kicked in and windows smashed with the butts and hilts of weapons.

HELP US!

Tesk's head snapped from left to right. He saw his struggle reflected in Gep's eyes and Lyk's, and in every face beyond them. A soldier gripping a nailbow bared her teeth in a snarl. Tesk felt his own lips curl.

We must stand fast.

Did he think that for himself first or did his mind echo those around him? No matter. Their shared resolve muted the desperate cry from the West. Everyone knew beyond doubting that the Neme ranks all around the rest of these walls would be poised to attack at once, if any of Strave's defenders deserted their post.

Besides, detachments of reinforcements were spread throughout the city, ready to converge on any breach. Armed men and women were already hurrying to answer the West Gate's call.

All is not lost.

Strave will not be taken.

Then the rapes began.

Tesk staggered under the onslaught. Frantic, he fought to ward off the assault. Like all adult Ant-kinden, he was used to confining his thoughts to his immediate partner during sex. That was only common courtesy, as well as a wonderful source of heightened, mutual pleasure. But inevitably, in the throes of ecstasy, everyone dropped their guard from time to time. Ant-kinden learned to turn such thoughts aside, to deflect such unconscious intrusion, to shield those adolescents still exploring the scope of their awakening Art.

This was different. This was impossible to ignore. This was pain. This was outrage. This was terror. This was men and women alike stripped naked, viciously beaten and brutalised. This was split lips and broken teeth and eyes swollen shut. This was wrenched joints, twisted limbs and torn, bleeding flesh.

Rape is not unknown among Ant-kinden. It is vanishingly rare. A victim thrusts their own anguish straight back into a rapist's mind. Only the irredeemably corrupted can withstand that. Regardless, an attacker will be caught. Their identity is known within moments. There is no way to hide it. Every hand will be raised to exact retribution, so formal justice is rarely required.

This was different. These aggressors were Wasp-kinden. Their minds were impervious to Ant-kinden pain. They might just as well have been deaf to their victims' screams.

This was worse. This wasn't indiscipline or lust, as captives were tossed from one attacker to the next. This was calculated violation. Victim after victim saw the cold truth in every assailant's eyes. Wasp pleasure wasn't in their bodily release, however momentarily gratifying. Their swell of satisfaction came from knowing that all of Strave shared in this abuse. As suffering ripped through the city, this was rape as an act of war.

SURRENDER!

Better slaves to Neme than this!

Glimpse after glimpse of the carnage to the west showed Tesk Strave soldiers throwing down their weapons, empty hands raised as they dropped to their knees. Neme troopers beat them bloody regardless, leaving them senseless on the cobbles.

"No!"

Tesk's shout tore through the silence before he realised he'd cried out aloud.

Consternation rippled along the wall. He saw the silent question in

Gep's eyes, felt it echoed in myriad minds.

What do we do now?

Answers came thick and fast, coloured with fear and fury.

We fight!

We die.

We sue for terms.

We gather to make a stand.

We fight? Then we will die.

We fight to save our city.

We will suffer beyond imagining before we die.

We run.

We run to save our people.

We run.

We run to save ourselves

We run.

Despair threatened to overwhelm him. Desolation splintered his mind. Smoke was rising in the west now. Strave burned. The breeze carried the stink of it towards them. The utter devastation of defeat followed close behind. There was no resisting.

Tesk's throat closed as he struggled to swallow. His eyes stung with tears provoked by the grief of countless numbers weeping, all hope abandoned.

If we survive, Strave survives.

That defiance came from closer at hand. Tesk looked wildly around, desperate to find an ally.

Dead, we cannot save our kinden. Alive we can retake our city.

We retreat and we regroup.

It was no good. Tesk couldn't identify the source of these thoughts. This new resolve was spreading, though. Spreading too fast? Men and women were deserting the East Gate, heading down from the battlements. Any notion that this might be treason was immediately, violently quashed.

"No." Tesk whispered.

Gep didn't even turn to acknowledge his forlorn plea. Lyk was on Gep's heels. Tesk could taste their resolve like bile in his mouth as they vanished down the steps with the rest. Below, he heard the rumbling rasp of the gate being unbarred. Ahead, he saw the Neme ranks stirring.

If we hold close together and hit them hard, we can break through their lines.

Their lines are thinner here than anywhere else.

They've moved so many troops around to the west, ready to follow the vanguard through that breach.

Defiance blazed in the Strave soldiers now gathered inside the gate, strengthening their common purpose. Somehow Tesk found himself on the stairs hurrying down to join them. More and more of the East Watch pressed close behind him. The ranks waiting below greeted each new arrival with heartfelt relief.

Their force was over a hundred strong. No one needed to take charge. They fell into step, every weapon at the ready. Each soldier marched close enough to the next for mutual defence, far enough apart not to hinder each other when it came to the fight.

Neme forces promptly brought the fight to them. Whoever was in charge of the siege engines on this side of the walls didn't waste ammunition on such a small detachment. That commander preferred to rain missiles into the already demoralised city. Instead two companies of foot-soldiers were sent to embrace these deserters in a murderous pincer movement. No one needed to read Neme kinden minds to see that intention. It was as plain as the strengthening daylight.

The Strave company held true to its purpose. They could all see a point of weakness in the enemy lines ahead. For whatever reason, these particular troops were shifting and shuffling, betraying insidious indiscipline. Why were they so eager to advance? For what purpose? To claim their share of spoils as the city was ransacked? Keen to seize slaves from the surrendered populace?

Sharing a rush of venomous hatred for those lusting to plunder his home, Tesk picked up speed with the rest of his kinden. Now they were running rather than marching, still in perfect step, all in heartfelt accord.

I will not die today. I will live to have my vengeance.

Safety and time to plot their return lay on the far side of Neme's army. Now they were close enough to see the youthful faces of the wavering troops. Novices. No wonder they were easily swayed by the prospect of loot.

The forces sent to intercept them were veterans. No matter. Whoever had given those orders had miscalculated. That commander had not realised just how fast Strave's last hope could run. They would reach the Neme lines before that claw closed around them. Just barely.

Tesk was in the forefront, sword in hand. They hit Neme's wavering contingent like a hammer blow. A lifetime's training was amplified by co-ordinated purpose all around him.

Hit the weak points in armour at elbow and knee.

Go for the neck, the armpits, the wrists.

Go for the eyes.

Down is as good as dead.

We're here to escape, not to kill them all.

Blood flowed. Bones broke. Men died. Neme's novices could not withstand such single-minded ferocity. They barely inflicted a handful of wounds. Strave's last company broke through with devastating swiftness. They did not break stride or slow their advance, pressing on to leave the ground behind them littered with wounded and dying.

Someone snatched a glance over her shoulder. Tesk saw that the veterans' pursuit was frustrated by the novices trying to succour their wounded or clamouring to attack the city. No doubt plenty of the veterans wanted their chance at pillage now that their prey had escaped. Tesk might not be able to read their thoughts but he recognised Ant-kinden ensnared in indecision.

Whatever consensus prevailed, it wasn't pursuit. Strave's men and women turned their attention to the path ahead. Wherever it might lead, they wouldn't stop running until they found sanctuary.

The days and miles passed by. Food was scarce and water still harder to come by out on the treeless summer plains.

The Ant-kinden of the city of Vore refused them entry, even for a few days' respite from their travels. They would only accept those willing to yield to indentured servitude. Slavery in all but name. A proportion of the Strave refugees were weary and desperate enough to accept such conditions. The rest pressed on.

Without adequate medical supplies and proper rest, even minor wounds festered and worsened. Men and women died. The rest pressed on.

The Ant-kinden of Stal saw them coming and laid a cunning ambush. That was when Lyk died. The rest pressed on.

Tesk was ripped from a fitful sleep one morning by furious disagreement. Brae proposed that their ragged company turn mercenary.

Why cling to the dream of restoring Strave?

We must look to the future and how best to survive.

Treason.

Plenty of other kinden pay handsomely for proven soldiers' services.

Treachery.

Tesk's head rang with these conflicting convictions. He could barely gather his wits to consider these questions himself. When the clamour settled, more than half agreed with Brae. They decided to strike south towards the Spiderlands. Tesk stayed with the rest. They pressed on.

One moonless night, a little less than half of the remainder departed while those they had not trusted slept. These men and women had reached their decision more circumspectly, more covertly. All they left behind was an impression that they would seek some salvation in the Commonweal. Gep was among them.

The rest pressed on. Tesk could recognise every individual's thoughts by now. The vast silence beyond their group consciousness became more and more apparent. More and more oppressive. He grew to dread being the last one to fall asleep, the first to wake in the morning. To find himself so utterly alone in that emptiness, without another mind to touch his own.

Sleep came hard and fitfully, trying to rest without shelter on the barren ground, perpetually hungry and thirsty. As the days passed, some slept never to wake again, when the morning came. The rest pressed on. The only prospect more terrifying than death was being left as the last one alive, condemned to die wholly alone.

They reached a range of low hills. Tesk had no idea where he and his last handful of companions might be. No one had chosen this path. This sorry remnant had no one to call a leader. They made the simplest choices as and when they must. Now they were merely surviving, living hand to mouth, and barely clad in the remnants of their uniforms and armour.

They took a turn into a shallow valley, for whatever reason must have seemed best to most of them. Tesk saw houses ahead, tilled fields, tended orchards. A small contingent of the inhabitants gathered together as they approached. They were all stocky and broad-shouldered.

Beetle-kinden. Makers, not soldiers. Though these men and women gripped their hoes and scythes and looked ready to make a fight of it, and they outnumbered Strave's sorry stragglers more than five to one.

A tall woman strode forward. There was a greenish hue to her sun-bronzed skin and in the braids of pale hair coiled high on her head. "Who are you and what do you want?"

Tesk halted, and realised, bemused, that the three other men and two women were looking to him to speak for them all. He cleared his throat and tried to speak. His mouth was too dry, his tongue too unpractised. He coughed convulsively.

"Here." The Beetle woman offered him a leather-wrapped bottle. She was no warrior. No soldier would come within arm's reach of a potential enemy. Strave's survivors consoled themselves with that thought.

Tesk uncapped the bottle and found it full of sweet water. As he drank, he felt the sensations of his own quenched thirst burning in the others' parched throats.

"Please –" he gestured to his companions.

Several of the villagers looked to the woman. She nodded permission and they offered the water they'd brought for their day's work in the fields to these ragged strangers.

"Where are you from?" the woman demanded.

"Strave." Tesk grimaced. The barest mention of their lost home still provoked intense pain in all the Ant-kinden's minds. "Our city fell to the Wasps. Do you know of them?"

The woman nodded. "Their Empire sent envoys to the villages east of here some while ago. They offer an alliance that they promise will fill everyone's hands with gold."

Tesk choked on the horror shuddering through his companions.

Have we come so far, at such cost, only to find our enemy waiting?

One of the Beetle men snorted his derision. "They offer the black earth of an open grave for those who won't kneel to them."

"Yet you hope to fight?" Tesk couldn't hide his despair.

"Hardly." The Beetle woman smiled. "We know where our kinden's strengths lie. We intend to hide. We've already asked those settlements east of here never to speak of us."

They place such faith in those whose minds they cannot share?

"You trust –?" He couldn't think how to continue without insulting her.

"You think we're fools?" She challenged him with a sardonic look. "As soon as we've gathered enough of our harvest to see us through the winter, we're leaving. The Wasps and their allies can find empty houses with enough loot for them to carry away, satisfied. There are other valleys for us in these hills, places only reached by secret routes which intruders will never find. Even ones who can fly."

She offered him her hand. "My name is Passia. If you and yours are willing to work, to help us build our defences, you are welcome to share what we have."

Belatedly, Tesk recalled the customs of envoys he's seen coming to Strave from Beetle-kinden and other cities. Those who could not read another's true intentions offered an empty hand as a sign of good faith. He took it, hesitant, and was surprised by the strength of her grasp.

The relief flooding through the men and women who flanked him nearly dropped him to his knees.

Good food, clean water, fresh clothing. All these things put new heart in Tesk surprisingly swiftly. As he felt his own spirits rising, so he was buoyed up still further by his companions' renewal in both body and mind.

Within days, the Strave men and women joined those Beetle villagers scouting out remote hollows in these hills where they might find refuge from the expanding Wasp Empire.

Before the leaves on the trees burned with autumn's colours, Passia and the other Beetle elders had chosen three suitable locations that would comprise the new settlement. They would be close enough together for easy communication between the divided community, far enough apart for the loss of one not to compromise the other two's defences. Strave's survivors made certain of that, just as they directed the labouring villagers to disguise their hidden paths still further and to create overlooks and choke points where any invaders could be slowed and slaughtered.

By the time the first frosts silvered the grass, the Beetle community had left their old village behind.

There was still a great deal of work to be done, building storehouses and homes. Tesk was glad of it. He could labour all day, concentrating on nothing but the work in hand, and then he'd fall into his bed so exhausted that he slept unaware of the emptiness all around him.

Even surrounded by amiable, labouring Beetle-kinden, he was utterly alone. He was the only one of the Strave Ant-kinden in this particular hollow of new settlement and it took conscious effort to reach the others with his thoughts.

When he had last done so, he found Nas and Ock locked in a tight new pairing; a refuge and a bulwark against the unwelcome sensations of life amid men and women with silent minds despite all their chatter and laughter.

Tesk felt a stab of jealousy swiftly followed by the shame-faced realisation that brushing against the pleasure Nas and Ock took in each other's bodies did at least dull the lingering recollection of Strave's violation by Wasps.

Dyn, Vort and Jond had taken to spending as much time as they could away in the hills. Hunting won them friends when they returned with deer meat for the villagers. Scouting reassured them all that the Wasp Empire's advance had indeed passed them by.

Opening his eyes to see another dawn, Tesk forced himself out of bed, threw some wood onto the embers in the small iron stove and visited the out-house. Bringing a pail of water back from the well, he washed, shivering in the cold as he dragged on his loose, coarse labouring clothes. He grimaced as he stretched. All his muscles protested. Whatever these Beetles might lack when it came to warfare, no one could match their stamina.

Was there anything left to eat? He looked around his single-roomed house, gritting his teeth against his aches and pains.

A hand rat-tatted the door knocker. Tesk took a step back. He couldn't help it. He was still unused to this reality of people approaching while he remained unawares. He took a deep breath, fists clenched. Then he forced himself to open the door.

"Good morning." Passia held up a loaf of bread, fragrant and still warm from the communal oven at the heart of the village. "I brought your breakfast."

"Thank you," he managed to say, haltingly. He cleared his throat. "Please, come in, and welcome."

She looked around as she entered. Tesk tried not to resent the frank curiosity on her face as she took in the bare table, its single stool and the straw mattress with its blankets on the far side of the room.

"Did you hear several of our potters have set up a new kiln?" As she set the bread down, she gestured towards the far side of the settlement. "I'm sure they'd trade a day of you hauling clay for some bowls and plates to brighten this place up."

"I'll –" Tesk broke off, hissing with pain as he reached for a knife on the far side of the table. Unexpected agony locked him in place.

"What's the matter?" Passia was at his side in an instant, her eyes searching his face.

"My back," he said through gritted teeth.

"Where?" Her hands were already probing through the loose tunic. She found a viciously knotted muscle. "Here?"

Tesk could barely nod for fear of making things worse. "Yes."

"Lie down." Passia stripped his tunic off over his head before he could object. "On your belly."

He did as he was told, dropping onto the mattress. Anything to ease this pain.

Passia knelt beside him, her strong hands already at work. "You need to take things a little easier."

"I –" Tesk couldn't think what to say. He turned his head to face in the other direction, away from her concern. "Ah..."

"How long has your back been hurting?" Passia demanded as she drove merciless fingers into the muscles below his shoulder blades. "This hasn't come on overnight."

"A day or so," Tesk lied. That was one thing about this place. It was possible to lie. Sometimes anyway. From the way Passia snorted, he didn't think she believed him.

"You need to stop labouring for a few days," she said firmly, her hands moving down his spine.

"I can't. I –" Tesk couldn't think how to explain.

Passia's response surprised him. "You can learn." She worked her way back up to his shoulders and began to massage the stiff muscles on either side of his neck. "You need to spend less time inside your own head."

"What –?" Tesk tried to turn over but that brought on another spasm.

"Don't think. Feel." Passia's insistent hands forced him down onto the mattress. "Relax."

At the moment, all Tesk could feel was stabbing sensations from his abused muscles and nerves. Little by little, though, Passia's practised massage loosened the tensions racking him.

"Don't think. Feel," she repeated.

He gave himself over to her ministrations. Gradually, the pain eased. He began to breathe more deeply. As straw crackled in the mattress beneath him, he smelled the scent of the dried herbs mingled with it. He felt the growing warmth in the room as the firewood in the stove burned down.

"Stay where you are." Passia's hands left his back.

Tesk heard her cross the room. The stove's door clanged as she opened it to throw on more fuel. She returned and he heard the rustle of cloth.

"Don't think. Feel."

Her hands were on his back again, but this time her touch was different. Still firm, her hands caressed him, explored him. Tesk had never experienced anything like this wordless intimacy. Confused, he tried to formulate some thought –

"Don't think. Feel."

He felt the pressure of Passia's breasts against his back as she leaned over to kiss the nape of his neck. She did it a second time, and a third, then her lips traced the line of his spine down his back. All his attempts to make sense of what was happening dissolved in a rush of physical sensation.

Straw rustled as Passia withdrew. "Shall we continue?"

Tesk rolled over and opened his eyes to see her kneeling beside the mattress, her own tunic on the ground beside them.

He didn't know what to think but he did know what he was feeling. His mind might be in turmoil but his body had no doubts what he wanted. His urgent flesh pressed against the fabric of his trousers. His gaze met hers.

"Yes."

Passia smiled as she leaned forward, laying a hand on his muscular belly. She caressed him in circles, edging ever lower. As their lips met, as Tesk's hands cupped her breasts, she loosened the drawstring of his trousers. She slid her hand within to grasp him with an appreciative murmur.

Shedding the rest of their clothing took a moment. Tesk lay back as

Passia straddled him and slowly eased the two of them together. A shiver ran through him and through her in the same moment. He realised some things needed neither words nor any mental link. She leaned forwards and began to move, gently, rhythmically.

Tesk teased her nipples with his thumbs and began to move beneath her, harder, swifter. Once he was sure of her release, he rolled them both over and lost himself in pursuit of his own orgasm. She moved her hips to play her part in securing his ecstasy. With no need to shield his thoughts from Ant-kinden neighbours, it was like no sex Tesk had ever known.

At last, he lay spent and sweating, his hips between her thighs, his head between her breasts as she gently stroked his hair.

Tesk drew a breath. "I should thank you –"

"You think this is all about you?" Her stroking hand caught his earlobe between finger and thumb, pinching gently. "I told you. Spend more time outside your own head."

Her hand returned to caressing the back of his neck. "Where else am I going to find a lover without causing some argument or jealousy among my own kinden? We're a small community and we've all known each other lifelong. Before the Wasps came, I found lovers among the other villages. I imagined that's where I'd find a husband, but now, such travel risks betraying us all."

"Then this –" Tesk didn't know what to say.

Passia shifted so he rolled onto the mattress. She propped herself on one elbow, looking unblinking into his eyes. "This was as pleasurable for me as it was for you, and we're friends, aren't we? We've worked together often enough. I trust you. I admire your courage through all that you must have endured, even though you never speak of it. I value your hard work and your skills. I'm grateful for the knowledge you've shared with me and my kinden that will help keep us safe from the Wasps. I've found you attractive since the first day I saw you, and since then I've come to know you for a good and honest man. I've been looking for an opportunity to let you know you'd be welcome in my bed. But –" she tapped his forehead with her forefinger "– you can be incredibly dense when it comes to taking a hint."

These matters were so much less complicated among his own kinden, Tesk reflected. He didn't know what to say, though he knew for certain he didn't want to say the wrong thing. He settled for drawing

Passia close and kissing her. That seemed to answer.

As winter passed with fewer and fewer tasks to be done outdoors, they spent more and more time together.

In bed, Tesk drew on his memories of those things previous lovers had found most erotic. To his growing delight, he learned to read Passia's responses and gained a new appreciation for the pleasures of the unexpected from her.

Outside, among the other villagers, he watched and listened and learned. As he grew to understand them more fully, so they accepted him as one of their own.

By the time the spring leaves unfurled, Passia had moved into his little house. As soon as the last frosts were past, they would be building more rooms. They would have plenty of help from the rest of the village. After all, Passia's belly was swelling with each passing ten-day, so she could hardly undertake such toil. They weren't the only ones bringing new life to the settlement, so Tesk knew he'd be able to return the favour.

Their child was born on a night fragrant with the scent of dusk flowers. The midwife's lamp showed the infant's skin was shot with two colours, like silk. With the light at one angle, the baby's face had the faint green sheen of Beetle-kinden heritage. Swaddled and in Passia's arms, the subtle blue gloss of Strave blood was apparent.

Tesk sat close on the edge of the bed and smiled at those tiny fingers grasping his own. Then the baby's wandering gaze met his and all that had gone before was lost in this single moment. Tesk didn't care how many years it would be before that wondering mind met his. The promise of this unlooked-for marvel was enough. He would never be alone again.

The Message

John Gwynne

Malrec stood at the edge of camp, leaning against a wide-boled pine. He was sweating, despite the cold, but it had been a long, hard day's climb to get here.

One of many, and not the last.

He wiped sweat from his face and rubbed his greying, short-cropped hair, squinting as he stared into the distance. Before him the ground rose steadily, the sinking sun bright upon a patchwork of woodland and green pasture that rolled up to a sheer cliff face, towering dark and brooding over the world around it. East and west the cliff stretched, as far as Malrec's eyes could see.

The Great Barrier Ridge. And with it, the end of our journey.

Behind him were the familiar sounds of his crew making camp. Two men and one woman who had saved his life more times than he could remember.

Though I've returned the favour for each of them more than a few times, myself.

A speck of movement ahead of him, hugging the shadows as it emerged from a stand of pine, then darting across a space of open grassland. Out of habit Malrec's hand twitched, palm open, ready to use his sting. In heartbeats he saw it was Strakus, returning from his scouting mission. Malrec sucked in a deep breath of cold mountain air and relaxed his hand.

"It's there, chief," Strakus said when he reached Malrec. A young Ant-kinden, newest member of Malrec's crew. "A path, up into the ridge. Just like you said."

Just like Drephos told me, Malrec thought. *And good job, too, or we'd have walked all the long way from Chasme and the Exalsee to here for nothing.*

"Good lad," Malrec grunted, patting Strakus' shoulder. "You've done well." As a rule, Malrec didn't show much emotion. In his line of business, it didn't pay to get too attached to your crew-members, but

Strakus' youthful, earnest enthusiasm was endearing. There was something vulnerable about the lad, which reminded Malrec of his own son. He pushed that thought away, into a dark corner of his mind. Something glinted in Strakus' hair, catching the last rays of the sinking sun. Malrec reached out and brushed it away, held his fingertips close to examine it.

"What is it?" Strakus asked.

"Nothing. Just a cobweb," Malrec said, rubbing his fingertips together. "Come, put some food in your belly, you've earned it." He turned his back on Strakus and strode back towards the rest of his crew and their small camp.

Moonlight broke through the canopy above and silvered the ground, the flames of their cook-fire long since stamped out. Malrec sat a little way from the fire, an ember or two still glowing, watching the others. Strakus was already snoring, curled up with a thick cloak wrapped about him. His snap-bow hung from a cord around one shoulder. Drae was on first watch, and trying to spot her amidst the darkness was a futile exercise. That was a comfort, though, as, if he couldn't see or hear her, then neither would anyone fool enough to sneak up on them. Drae was Mantis-kinden, as much a weapon as any living thing could be, and as elegant and silent as morning mist.

It felt to Malrec that they were the only people alive in all of the Lowlands, but you could never be too careful. Half the world seemed to be going to war as they'd made their journey northwards from Chasme in the south-east to the rim of the Great Barrier Ridge. They had crossed in the wake of one Wasp army, Tynan's Gears, as they ground their way inexorably towards Collegium; and then, only twelve days gone, they had seen the evidence of another Wasp army marching westwards upon Sarn. Strakus had just stood and stared at the furrowed tracks and detritus that marked the army's trail. He had once been a citizen of Sarn, exiled for who knows what reason. Malrec didn't know why, only knew that once an Ant-kinden was exiled from their city they could never go back. Perhaps that was why the lad worked so hard to fit into Malrec's crew, because he needed to belong somewhere.

And what better place than my band of misfits, exiles and deserters?

Vargen, his oldest friend in all the world, was tending to his weapons, a small arsenal of knives and short-swords. He looked up, somehow sensing Malrec's eyes on him, stood and strode over, his passage little more than a whisper on the thick carpet of pine-needles, even if he did limp a little, favouring one hip over the other. Vargen was a year or two younger than Malrec, but physically Vargen was the older of the two.

Old wounds and cold weather are a poor mix.

"So," Vargen said as he sat beside Malrec, a belt of knives slung over one shoulder. "Tomorrow see's the job done."

"It should," agreed Malrec. They had served together, stood in the wall of shields and guarded each other's backs against the Dragonfly armies of the once-proud Commonweal. If Malrec trusted his life in anybody's hands, it was Vargen. He already had, more times than Malrec could count, or even remember. "If all goes to plan."

They shared a look, both knowing how rare a thing that was.

"If all else fails, we've always got him," Vargen said, nodding towards the bulk of ox-muscled Ralken, who was methodically rasping a whetstone over his collection of axes. Two smaller and single-headed, built for throwing, and one long-shafted, double-bladed weapon, built for destroying anything that had the misfortune of being in its way.

"Indeed," Malrec grunted. "Even so, I'll be glad when this job is over."

"One of those feelings?" Vargen asked.

"Huh," Malrec nodded.

"Good job I sharpened my knives, then."

"Better to be ready than dead," Malrec muttered their old squad's motto.

He was remembering where this job had started, as he had been handed a sealed scroll by the artificer Dariandrephos, founder of the Iron Glove, the world's foremost expert on all things mechanical and weapons-like. Malrec had first met him when the man had gone by the title of Colonel-Auxilian Drephos, and he had been Captain Malrec, but that had been another time. Another life, it felt like.

'There should be little risk,' Drephos had said.

'Then why are you paying me to do this?' Malrec replied, not even trying to keep the disbelief from his voice. His mercenary crew had a certain reputation, one for getting the job done, and usually leaving a pile of bodies behind them in the process.

'It is important to me that this package is delivered. The Lowlands are wracked with war, and your destination is a long way; you'll be travelling through the heart of

that war-torn world. Investing in you gives me the confidence that my package will at least reach its intended destination."

"*And there'll be a warm greeting for us at the end of our journey, no doubt?*" Malrec had asked.

Dariandrephos had just shrugged at that. "*I can only hope that it will not be too warm,*" he'd said, and then leaned forwards and whispered something in Malrec's ear. "*Only if things aren't going well, you understand,*" the Artificer had said as he stepped away.

"Better to be ready than dead," Malrec muttered to himself.

Malrec woke with a start. It was still dark, and there was a pain in his neck where he'd slept with his back against a tree and his chin on his chest. The basal rumble of Ralken's snoring set a rhythmic time.

Another sound, a grunt, something scraping. Malrec looked around, one fist going to the hilt of his short-sword, the other hand raised, palm bared, ready to use his art. The grunt again, and then he saw him.

Strakus, slumped against the base of a tree. There was a tremor in his body, head scraping against the bark. Malrec was on his feet, shrugging off his bee-fur cloak, sleep banished in an instant as he padded towards Strakus. He saw the three shapes of the rest of his crew curled around the long-dead fire.

Strakus on guard, then, must be close to dawn.

He muttered a word as he passed them and Vargen stirred, Drae rising. Ralken continued snoring.

"What's wrong, lad?" Malrec whispered as he drew near to the Ant-kinden. He crouched, Strakus cloaked in shadow. Then the breeze shifted the canopy above and moonlight filtered through, bathing Strakus in pale light. He was awake, eyes wide, staring at Malrec. His lips moved, slurred words, his tongue dark and swollen.

"What is it?" Malrec hissed, his senses screaming that something was wrong, his flesh goose-bumping though he didn't know why. Then he saw it. A lump on the side of Strakus' head, from his crown to below one ear, making his short hair stick out at all angles. No, more like a cluster of lumps, shining fluid-dark in the moonlight. And they were moving, like porridge that bubbles when it's over-cooked.

"What the...?"

There was a wet, tearing sound, as of ripe fruit bursting, and one of the clusters erupted. Long-legged creatures spilled out, translucent spiders, bodies smaller than a fingernail, scuttling out of the lumps, over Strakus' face, down his neck. More and more of the clusters tore and vomited out their many-legged inhabitants, shining silver in the moonlight. Malrec stared, frozen, over thirty-five years of experience in the field of battle not preparing him for this. Some of the spiders were pausing after their initial rush of freedom, sinking tiny fangs into Strakus, piercing his skin. And they were growing. Malrec felt something bubbling up in his throat – bile, a scream? – as he saw the spiders' bodies expand and bloat, their silver-translucent exoskeletons growing darker, gorged with blood, then fraying and splitting as the spiders outgrew them, shedding their first skin for another as a month's growth took place in less than a few score heartbeats.

"Help…me," Strakus whispered, a bubbling, terror-laden hiss. Footsteps behind Malrec, a grunt of horror from Ralken as Malrec slapped at the spiders swarming on Strakus' face, squashing some, scattering others, but there were so many, more still emerging from what Malrec now realised were egg-sacs laid beneath Strakus' skin.

"What in the seven hells?" Vargen cursed behind him, Malrec swiping another handful of the rapidly growing spiders from Strakus' face. One of them clung to Malrec's hand, a sharp pain and Malrec saw it bite into his thumb. Without thinking he summoned his art, a glow and then his sting was loosed, vaporizing the spider in a heartbeat, the sting arcing high, sizzling into a branch somewhere above. A flare of sparks and the stink of pine resin as something ignited. Two pin-pricks of blood welled on Malrec's thumb, one dripping down into his calloused palm. His hand began to go numb.

Many of the spiders were fist-sized, now, Strakus littered with their cast-off husks. Strakus was pale, his skin drawn and emaciated as the spiders continued to literally drain the life from him. His eyes were wide, full of terror, pleading with Malrec for help, though he had no strength left to voice it. Malrec looked on futilely. Then a shape loomed over his shoulder and a rapier stabbed down into Strakus' chest, Drae's razor-sharp blade slipping between ribs to pierce Strakus' heart. A shuddering sigh and Strakus slumped. The spiders continued to gorge on him, though some were starting to scuttle away.

Malrec stood and took a few steps back, a branch bursting into flame above them, sending shadows and light dancing. Within moments most of the spiders had disappeared, scuttling into the darkness.

An incoherent grunt from Ralken, the huge Scorpion-kinden stamping violently on a spider, a small explosion of green-black fluid.

"What?" he said with a shrug to Malrec's questioning look. "I don't like spiders."

Malrec looked back over his shoulder as they left the cover of the trees and swore under his breath, not for the first time that morning. Strakus and the tree he'd died against were little more than charred, blackened stumps, but much of the glade was still burning, smoke billowing in thick black clouds.

So much for arriving unannounced.

He sucked in a deep breath and readjusted the weight of the pack upon his back. *Nothing I can do about that, now, and we can't just walk away, so it's on with the job.*

At least the feeling in his thumb had returned, which had come as a great relief. He remembered the creeping paralysis as it spread through his hand, and how Strakus had been unable to move, a torpefied meal for a thousand scuttling beasts.

He clenched and unclenched his fist, just to make sure it was still working, whispered a warrior's eulogy for Strakus as he gave a final shudder at the memory of how the poor lad had died, and led his crew on towards the Great Barrier Ridge.

Drea's slender form was just a shadow in the ravine ahead, Vargen plodding steadfastly along beside Malrec, Ralken remarkably quiet for his bulk as he took rear-guard behind them. They'd found the entrance to the ravine where Strakus had described, hidden behind what appeared to be a rock-fall. Since then, they had wound their way ever higher into the granite cliffs of the Barrier Ridge. Malrec was mindful of the uneven ground and Vargen's stiff limbs, setting the pace at steady, rather than fast. His old friend hadn't said a word since they'd left camp and the charred remains of Strakus behind them. It was playing on all of their minds.

Malrec paused and looked up, wiping sweat from his eyes. Slate-grey clouds were bunching high above, cloaking the peaks of the ridge.

What we're looking for isn't at the top, anyway. Malrec wanted this job done and over with. It was past midday, so he lifted his arm in the air, calling a halt.

Malrec and Vargen settled close to a chattering stream, Ralken joining them soon enough. He settled upon a boulder and chewed on some dried meat, letting out a long, rumbling sigh as he did so.

Malrec took a sip from his water-skin, then passed it to Ralken.

"What?" Malrec said as the Scorpion-kinden took it.

"No point saying it," Ralken said.

"Just say it," Malrec muttered.

"I've got a bad feeling," Ralken said with a shrug. He did that a lot. "You asked."

Haven't we all, after Strakus, Malrec thought.

"You've always got a bad feeling," Vargen grunted.

"This one's worse," Ralken said. "And I'm cold. I don't like the cold. I am a warrior of Nem, born to the desert and sun."

"I'll add *cold* to the list of things you don't like, then," Malrec said. "Right next to *spiders.*"

Vargen barked a laugh. "You're the size of a horse, and you've killed more people than Tynan's Gears."

Scorpion-kinden.

Ralken shuddered. "They were no ordinary spiders. They grew, before my eyes."

They did. Malrec suppressed a shudder of his own.

"This is a strange land, true enough." Vargen agreed.

"All the more reason to get the job done and head back south," Malrec said. As he spoke, he stared into the stream they were sitting beside, the water clear and pure. A shoal of whitefish were gathered in the shelter of a rock. As Malrec watched them darting above the stone bed something long and sinuous caught his eye. A water-scorpion slithered out from behind a rock, a wake of ripples as it swam towards the unsuspecting fish, striking fast and catching one. Malrec blinked and frowned, staring harder at the rippled water.

Looked like…no, 'course not, must be a trick of the light. For a moment, it looked like that scorpion had two heads…

"Chief," Ralken said, nudging his arm. Malrec scowled, staring at the stream, trying to catch another glimpse of the water-scorpion.

"Chief," Vargen added his voice to Ralken's. Malrec looked up, following their gaze up the ravine. His eyes narrowed.

"Weapons," he growled, standing and drawing his short-sword. In heartbeats Vargen and Ralken were spread either side of him, amongst the boulders in a loose half-circle. Ralken gripped a throwing axe in each of his fists. Vargen had a knife in his left hand, Strakus' snap-bow in his right.

Drae came speeding down through the ravine, passing over the rocky terrain as if it were a wasp-built road.

"What?" Malrec called as she drew near. Her rapier was in her fist, and the jagged spines that edged her forearm were dark with blood.

"Trouble," Drae said, and then figures were behind her, crossing the ground almost as quickly as she had, though far less elegantly. Six, seven of them, lumbering, squat and low to the ground. They looked to be Beetle-kinden, a mix of male and female, wearing long artificer's leathers, though as they drew closer Malrec realised they were not like any Beetle-kinden he'd ever seen before. Hairless, with pale, bluish skin, and something about the way they moved, in ungainly, sporadic spurts.

What are they?

And then it was too late for thought, the first of them upon Malrec. He swept a crude thrust from a short-sword wide, side-stepping and back-swinging at the same time as the Beetle's momentum carried it past him, felt his own blade chop into the flesh and vertebrae of the Beetle's neck. He gave the Beetle-kinden a parting kick in the back for good measure, and turned to meet the next. The clash of steel and he glimpsed Drae dancing around two others, parrying and stabbing, arcs of blood tracing her sword's trajectory.

Another Beetle was surging at Malrec, this one a woman, some old wound mapped across her face by coarse stitches. She raised an axe in her fist, swung at him. He pivoted on a heel, nudged the descending axe-head with his blade, sending it slicing a hand-span wide of his shoulder, at the same time slamming his own blade down hard into the woman's skull, an explosion of bone and brain. Her legs gave way and she collapsed in a heap at his feet, heels drumming as he wrenched his blade free.

"Down!" a voice yelled, Vargen, and without thinking Malrec dropped to one knee, a life-time of trust and instinct taking over. He felt air whistle where his head had just been. The Beetle who's throat he'd cut was standing behind him, blood leaking from the gash across its neck, but nevertheless swinging his short sword with extreme vigour in Malrec's general direction.

He shouldn't be able to do that.

There was the hiss of a snap-bow and bolts appeared in a cluster around the Beetle's heart, piercing the thick leather of his coat, sinking deep. The Beetle staggered back a handful of paces and dropped to one knee.

Then he stood up.

What?

Another bolt, this one through its eye, only the fletching of the bolt still visible. It toppled backwards, a spasm through its legs and then it was still.

Malrec nodded his thanks to Vargen. Ralken was gore-spattered, bellowing a wordless battle-cry as he stood with a mass of decapitated torsos and separated body parts scattered in a loose circle about him. His double-bladed axe swung a bloody loop as it took a head from a man's body. Drae was having a more difficult time of it, though, her rapier buried deep in a man who seemed determined to continue his attack, despite the fact that an arm's length of steel was lodged in his belly. Drae stumbled backwards, blood sheeting into her eyes from a gash somewhere on her head, using the spines of her forearm to block a flurry of axe blows from her impaled attacker. One got through, chopping into the meat of her thigh. Malrec and Vargen shared a look and together they ran to Drae's aid.

A dozen blows from them and the Beetle-kinden was on its knees, one half-severed arm hanging limp, Drae kicking it off of her blade, stabbing and slicing at its face and neck. With a gurgle, it toppled sideways and lay still.

The three of them stood in a circle, all breathing heavily.

"They don't like to die," Drae observed, pale-faced and swaying.

"Didn't seem to mind for me," Ralken said as he strode over to them, grinning as he wiped his face, doing little more than smearing the blood of his enemies across his features.

"Glad someone's happy," Vargen said.

"I feel better, now," Ralken replied. "My bad feeling's gone."

Mine hasn't, thought Malrec.

They cleaned and bound their wounds, Vargen tying a tourniquet around the wound in Drae's thigh, stitching a flap of Drae's scalp back to her head. She sat on a rock in silence as he did so.

"Did you see where they came from?" Malrec asked her.

"There's a wall and gate, further up the ravine," Drae said. "Buildings within. Quite a few. Then *they* saw me."

"Hold still," Vargen mumbled, holding thread between his lips.

"They saw you?" Ralken said, raising an eyebrow.

Not like Drae, to be spotted by anyone.

"Yes," Drae hissed between clenched lips. Vargen had moved on to stitching her thigh, now.

"Were they guards from the gates?" Malrec asked.

"No. They came from behind me. I don't know where they came from. Somewhere in the ravine."

A band of brigands? Are there more like them roaming the cliffs?

When Vargen had finished, Malrec gave Drae a water skin and a pack.

"We'll be back soon," he said to her.

"I'm coming with you," Drae said, climbing to her feet.

"No," Malrec shook his head. "If there's more like them," he pointed at one of the dead. "I'll not see another of my crew slain, if I can help it."

"I'm good to go, chief," Drae said. "And I'll not be *protected*." She said that last word as ig it was a crime.

Malrec pushed her shoulder, hard. She staggered back a step and her leg gave out beneath her. Ralken caught her before she hit the ground and lowered her gently onto a boulder.

"Careful," Vargen said, scowling at Malrec, "you'll open my stitches."

"You'll be no help to us. A liability," Malrec said, his voice cold. "Wait for us here." This time Drae nodded, unable to meet his eye.

"There's no shame in taking a wound," Vargen said, putting a hand on her shoulder.

Drae didn't look as if she agreed.

"What's the plan, then, chief?" Ralken grunted.

They were standing behind a boulder, peering out around it at a stone-arched gateway, behind which the hint of a courtyard and buildings. The gates were open, but there was no sign of movement.

Malrec whispered quietly, Ralken and Vargen nodding.

The sound of Malrec's boots scraping and scuffing on stone echoed around the courtyard. Buildings were carved into the cliffs that reared around him, doors and windows shadowed holes into darkness. There was no sign of life, no movement.

Malrec put his hands to his mouth and shouted.

"Ariadne, I come with a message from Dariandrephos." His voice echoed around the courtyard. *"Drephos, Drephos, Drephos..."* He thought he heard a sound, high, to his right, his head snapping around, but there was only the sheer cliffs and shadows. The biggest doors were directly ahead, so Malrec drew in a deep breath and headed for them. They opened with a creak of hinges, and he stepped in, pausing for a moment to allow his eyes to adjust to the light.

It was a huge room, vaulted with a balcony above. Torches burned and crackled in wall sconces, sending shadows flickering.

So, not abandoned, then.

Long benches littered the room, iron rings and chains set into them, leather straps hanging. Elsewhere there were rows of cages and containers. Racks of tools lined the walls, saws, clamps, knives, other, strange-shaped implements. At the far end of the chamber there was a raised dais, and upon it, half in shadow, was a chair, and beside it a door. Malrec walked into the room, down a central aisle edged with the long benches. Now he was closer he could see dark stains upon the worn wood, reminding him of the tables butchers had used back in his village when he was a child.

When he was about half way through the chamber, he saw a corpse upon one of the benches. He stopped and studied it. A Beetle-kinden, skin coloured like the ones he had fought in the ravine. Its chest had been cut open, skin and muscle and flesh peeled away, held in place by clamps, and the rib-cage had been sawn open and spread wide. Not as in battle, but carefully, meticulously, revealing the heart and lungs within. One of the lungs was missing, cut away. Malrec felt a worm of fear uncoil in his belly.

What place is this?

His hand sought the hilt of his sword.

You have come so far. See it through now.

He walked on.

More benches, littered with bodies or body parts, sharp-edged tools scattered about them. Then cages, creatures within them, mostly dead, though a fox lifted its head to watch him as he walked past. As he approached the far end of the room, he saw one last cage, big as a man, and within it a green-leaved bush and a mountain goat. Cobwebs trailed the branches, fine and delicate. From one of them, suspended by a single thread, an egg-sac hung, pulsing and squirming with the life within it. The goat bleated, pushing itself into the corner furthest from the egg-sac. Even as Malrec stared a split appeared and miniscule spiders emerged, bodies translucent. Malrec took a step back, because he had seen these spiders before. They swarmed towards the goat, sweeping over it, beginning the same grisly spectacle that Malrec had witnessed upon Strakus. He slapped his palms against the iron bars of the cage, felt the heat rise in his palm, his art appearing unbidden.

"They have to feast when they are born, or they will die," a voice said, startling Malrec. He stumbled back a step, eyes searching. Then he saw her. A shadow, rising, detaching itself from the chair. A woman, tall, pale, skeletal thin. From the shadows and sharp angles of her face red eyes glowed at him.

Give her the letter and leave.

The terrified bleating of the goat rose in pitch, and Malrec remembered watching helplessly as Strakus died.

A flare of uncharacteristic anger overcame his fear, and he opened his palm and loosed his sting, killing the terrified goat in an instant, more flashes as he released sting after sting, a foul, acrid stench as the spiders burned.

The bush burst into flame, over the sizzling and crackling a sound rose. The woman. She was shaking with rage, a hissing scream emerging from her lips.

"Bring him to me," she roared.

Shapes moved above Malrec, shadows leaping over the vaulted balcony, four, five, more, man-shaped, a blur of wings and they sped towards him. They wore ornate, wood-lacquered armour and carried bows, spears, gleaming swords.

Dragonfly-kinden.

The first one to approach Malrec fell with a charred hole in his face, the second spiralling and crashing to the ground with a smoking wound in his throat, then the others were upon him. There was an eerie silence about them as they beat him with their spear shafts, sending him to one knee. He loosed his sting amongst them until his palm burned and his art ran dry, swung his short sword, felt it bite time and again, slicing through flesh and crunching into bone, and still they fought him in silence, battering him to the ground. He felt his wrist break and his sword fall from suddenly-useless fingers, and then he was grabbed and dragged semi-conscious towards the dais, thrown down upon it at the feet of the pale woman.

Twisting his head he looked up at her.

"Ariadne," he said through swollen, bloody lips.

"Yes," she answered, "I am Ariadne. Help him to his knees," she ordered with a gesture and arms grabbed Malrec, hoisting him upwards, onto his knees. He took a moment to study his victors, saw they were Dragonfly-kinden, though only three were left of the many that had attacked him. Something was not right about them, though…

He recoiled when he saw it, their mouths stitched shut, thin lines bound by thick cords.

"Men have very little of worth to say," Ariadne said. "You mentioned Dariandrephos. My brother."

Malrec blinked at that. Drephos had told him something of this woman, but had left out the detail that he was her kin.

"He, sent me…" Malrec paused to spit a glob of blood onto the floor. "He sent me to give you this," and he reached inside his leather vest. In a heartbeat swords and spears were levelled at him, hovering over his heart and throat. He moved slower, gripped the letter and pulled it out.

Ariadne regarded him a long moment, her red eyes boring into him. Then she took the parchment, breaking the wax seal, unrolling and reading.

"So," she said once she'd read it. "If I am to believe this, then my dear half-brother needs me. He asks me to go to him, to aid him." She stared at Malrec. "Is he in trouble? He must be, to be so polite. Is he?"

"I… don't know," Malrec said. "The world is at war, and rumour says he has…talents, and secrets, that the wasps want." He shrugged. "If Drephos doesn't give them what they want, I doubt they'll be happy with the thought of what he could do for their enemies. *If I can't have it, no one can.* That's what the wasps are like."

"You're Wasp-kinden," Ariadne pointed out.

"Deserter," Malrec said. "Not one of them, now, never will be again."

"But, what if you're lying? And if it is the truth, for our dear-departed mother's sake, I should go. Truth or lie, lie or truth?" Ariadne crouched, low enough to look into Malrec's eyes. He didn't like what he saw, the red-glow, a hint of madness in her stare.

Drephos is her half-brother. His mother was a Moth-kinden, father a wasp. So who was Ariadne's father? What kinden? But as soon as he thought about it he knew.

Mosquito. She's half Mosquito-kinden. That explains all. He felt his world fall away, knew that he was a dead man. Hoped he was, because the alternative was worse.

"I can do things to you, make you scream, make you beg, make you silent for ever," she said to him, matter-of-factly. "I need to know if you are telling the truth. I am happy here, with my experiments, my research."

Malrec remembered Drephos leaning forwards and whispering in his ear.

"Adne, say that to her, if she doubts my letter, if she doubts you. It will prove much to her."

"Adne," Malrec said.

Ariadne recoiled at that, swaying back as if struck. Her face softened, just for a moment, as the word seemed to stir some memory deep within.

"So," she said, a smile twitching her lips. "The truth, then. Only Drephos ever called me by that name. My brother needs me." She clapped her hands and laughed. "My great brother, the engineer, needs *me*. You know why? Because I make things, too. But where he experimented with metals and gears and coils, I always experimented with flesh, and blood, and life." She smiled, a cold, bloodcurdling thing.

"My task is done, now," Malrec said. "Release me. I have honoured your brother's request."

"Release you?" Ariadne said, frowning. "I could, I suppose. But, I have so few visitors. Only the goats, and the spiders for friends…" She smiled at him again, and he liked it even less this time. His eyes twitched to the door behind her.

"Waiting to be rescued?" Ariadne asked. "Come," she called out, and the door opened. In strode more Dragonfly-kinden, with their ancient armour and engraved weapons, four of them, and then two figures he recognised, Vargen's limping gait, and Ralken's bulk. They were bruised and bloody, wrists bound. Behind them another four Dragonfly warriors, and more shapes flitted at the edge of torchlight above.

Vargen and Ralken were shoved to their knees either side of Malrec.

"Well, look what my servants have brought to me. A scorpion, and another wasp. Such gifts to play with. My brother is kind, indeed."

What?

What else did Drephos write in his letter?

"I have long wished to discover where your art is housed, somewhere deep within that frail cage of flesh and blood," Ariadne said, stepping close to prod Malrec in the chest. "I wonder, could I find your sting, and extract it, somehow?"

Ice ran down Malrec's spine.

"What do you mean, gifts?" he said.

"My brother knows me well, knows my pleasures and desires. You three are a gift, a taste of what I could have if I joined him." She frowned, "Though his letter said there were more of you."

"It's been a difficult road," Malrec said, thinking of Drae back in the ravine, hoping that she would somehow escape from this place.

"Three will do," Ariadne said, snapping her fingers and uttering orders. Hands clamped around Malrec, Vargen and Ralken, the three of them dragged in different directions. Malrec was carried to one of the long tables and thrown onto his back, leather straps buckled tight around his wrists and ankles.

Drephos, if I get out of here, I swear I will kill you with my bare hands.

Close by, he heard Vargen scream.

The Mantis Way

Peter Newman

The bulk of the Wasp army had left the Felyal, taking their heavy artillery and their fire throwers with them. Despite this, much of the great forest still burned, and even where the fire had gone, guttered by its own greed, the smell remained, so strong that when Adamae closed her eyes, she could still feel the heat on her cheeks and see the ghost flames dancing on her eyelids.

Days ago such a world was beyond imagining. The Wasps had come, as others had come before, and the Mantis had gathered to fight, Adamae among them.

She was not the tallest of her kind, nor the quickest, nor the strongest. Her hours of training had made her a solid, not exceptional fighter, a cause of disappointment to her parents rather than one of embarrassment. Though the grief tears were still fresh on her cheeks, Adamae was glad they had not lived to see what had become of their second daughter.

She had never exactly fitted in, though not for want of trying. It was hard to say why. She wanted to, oh how she wanted to! And yet her achievements always had a workmanlike quality to them, no amount of effort matching the sure grace of her contemporaries.

But, average or not, she was a Mantis, with the same amount of pride as the rest of her kinden. When the call of the elders had gone out, she had answered it as a warrior.

Like many of the younger ones, she had not seen battle before, and even Uncle Rademon, most far travelled of the family, had never seen one on such a scale. Every Mantis hold had come to face the Wasp threat, gathering silent as the night within the Felyal's depths.

Old enemies who had fought for years put aside their grudges, petty feuds forgotten in order to meet a greater threat. For another kinden, such a violent history might have tainted things, leaving cracks for the enemy to exploit, but not the Mantis. They knew each other, had stared into each others' eyes over crossed swords and seen the fierce spirit within. Each had learned to respect the others' skill, there was even an excitement, a joy at being able to stand shoulder to shoulder and turn the anger outside.

Adamae had finally understood why her people fought among themselves so often. It was not to destroy, but to strengthen, each hold becoming a whetstone for its neighbour to brush against, honing, sharpening.

She often struggled to comprehend what seemed instinctual, even obvious to everyone else. But on that day, when her people gathered in strength, arrayed in their ancestral armour, each with a history as unique as the one that wore it, with claws, swords, bows and bodies honed for battle, for this battle, she understood. For this was the Mantis way. They were born for this.

As the light of day began to fail, the Mantis force had made its way towards the Felyal's edge, a whisper of steel and claw amid the leaves.

Her people had moved together, not regimented but organic, a shoal of spine-armed, blade-wielding fish, each with an instinctual awareness of the other but each warrior distinct, able to react to change at a moment's notice.

Gradually, Adamae had fallen towards the back. She could not hope to match those riding the great mantids for speed, nor could she quite match her fellows on foot. She saw in the dark as well as them, she told herself that she wanted the glory as much as them but, increasingly, that wonderful sense of being part of something bigger began to fade, a dream that she had to labour to keep sight of.

Her brothers and sisters had already vanished into the trees ahead, even Uncle Rademon, who usually waited for her, had gone. A part of her was glad, for it meant he recognised her as an adult and a warrior, while another part wished he had stayed close.

By the time she reached the edge of the forest, the battle had already begun, not that the Wasps knew it yet. The scouts they had out on watch saw only darkness around them, the Mantis archers picking them off with casual ease as they raced by.

Adamae saw the Wasp camp and was amazed. Where she remembered open fields, they had constructed a fortress big enough to encircle their entire army.

While her own footsteps faltered, the Mantis forces accelerated until they were at the base of the Wasp's wall, and then surged upwards, leaping, flying, legs and art-wings making mockery of the fortifications.

She readied her own bow, going through the steps in her mind, considering which part of the wall would be best to approach, worrying if she would be able to scale it at all.

Ahead of her, the Mantis continued to flow up and over the wall, pouring into the Wasp camp, a rain of blades and arrows.

And then something strange happened. It was as if the sun had been smuggled into the camp and was sleeping there, hidden, and the Wasps had drawn back the clouds; for suddenly the sky above the wall was lit, blinding white, an immediate and brutal dawn.

Mantis silhouettes hung above the battlements, black specks, elegant even in confusion. And then the Wasps returned fire, and the air was thick with bolts. In the past, Adamae had seen a group of archers loose together, and thought how it looked a little like rain. What she saw that night was a deluge, a wave of bolts, so thick it nearly blocked out the giant light below.

Black specks began to fall, training and grace and skill rendered meaningless. There was no space to dodge and the projectiles were too fast and too numerous to parry. As they had for generations, the Mantis trusted to their rage and speed, but this time, it was found wanting.

And yet Adamae could not help but find it beautiful. There was a cohesiveness about the Wasps that was different to that of her own people. Horrific as it was, it stirred something in her.

If the Wasps thought this marked the end of the battle, they were wrong. The Mantis fell back from the wall to fluidly regroup and surge again, accepting losses, taking wounds, risking all to get close to the Wasp archers.

She could not see past the wall but she could hear the screams of the dying. It was not just Mantis blood soaking into the earth, of that she was sure.

Again, and again, the Mantis were thrown back. Again and again the survivors threw themselves into the fray, always fewer than before.

To her complete and utter shame, Adamae dropped her bow and the arrow she had nocked to it.

They were going to lose.

She'd known it as surely as she had ever known anything, the certainty freezing her where she stood.

Such knowledge had not reached her kinden however, who continued to hurl their bodies at the Wasp forces, as if the relentless spitting of the snapbow and the crossbow and the Wasp stings could be overcome by sheer bloody mindedness.

She watched as the Mantis fell. The Wasps had regained the top of the wall now, firing down into the faces of her people as the last dregs of them, many already threaded with arrows, made a final futile attempt.

She watched as these brave remnants were cut down, and how a handful managed to gain the battlements again, laying about them with astonishing fury. She watched as these few were steadily overwhelmed, the Wasp generals paying the cost clinically. A bold Mantis might claim to be worth at least three of a lesser kinden, but what matter if there are four times as many?

The worst however, was yet to come.

There came a moment, long after Adamae had seen the truth of it, where the Mantis warriors looked about them and saw it too. There was a shift in their stance, a slight slump of the shoulders. Despair was passed from eye to eye. They had come here ready to die, for many Mantis seek honour in death, but there was no honour to be found, just slaughter in a night dressed as day, at the hands of a foe they could barely see past the glare.

It was not just the blades of the Mantis that failed that night, it was their hearts too. And when they fled into the sanctuary of the Felyal, broken forever, Adamae became one of them, her bow left behind in the dirt.

She had not gone back to her hold. Shame had kept her at bay for the rest of the night, then fear when the Wasps had started their advance the next morning, their coming heralded by fire and smoke.

What could be done against an enemy such as this, thought Adamae. Nothing. If she were a true Mantis warrior, she would seek an honourable death, preferably one that shed a lot of Wasp blood. But she did not feel like a true Mantis, she felt like a lost child, a failure, too stupid to live, too craven to die.

For days, fear and fire drove her from one hiding place to another, stumbling, struggling to see past tears, self-loathing. Not even daring to give voice to her grief, lest the enemy notice her.

In the end, it was hunger not valour that brought her back. Not to her own hold, she could not bear the thought of what, or who, she might find there, but to a neighbouring settlement.

Like the trees of the Felyal, the houses had been reduced to charred, shrunken versions of their former selves, and Wasp boot prints tracked over the ashes in all directions.

Bodies, unrecognisable but without doubt those of her people, were half buried where they'd fallen, cremated at the location of death. In each she saw the faces of her family, staring at her with accusing sockets.

With no food in her belly, Adamae could not be sick, but she could retch painfully as her body tried to claw out the bottom of her stomach for something to eject.

Afterwards, she forced herself to go closer. The Wasps had been thorough in their looting, and even more so in their burning but perhaps something was left, something only a Mantis eye would be able to find.

A child's corpse caught her attention, a crossbow bolt sticking from her back like a flag-less pole. Once the shock had passed, she was struck that it was the only child she'd seen. Looking at the scene with fresh eyes, it was striking how many of the tracks were deep and easy to follow, and there were several tell-tale drag marks going in the same direction. It could mean only one thing: slavers.

She was not sure why she followed them. She was, after all, only one, and hardly the best of her kind. Where a Weaponsmaster might hope to surprise a group of Wasps at night and defeat them, she had no hope at all. She didn't even have her bow anymore.

They weren't hard to find. The Wasp camp sitting boldly in a clearing, its fire bright, merry even, with a number of Mantis children chained to each other at its edge, blank eyed. There was robust banter from the Wasp soldiers, aided in no small amount by a hip flask being passed surreptitiously from one to another.

It took her a while to spot the officer in charge, a pale-haired man, so blond as to appear grey before his time. He stood on the opposite end of the camp, uninterested in what was going on by the fire. She wondered why he was not in his tent, and what it was he seemed to be looking for.

After a while he came back to the campfire, his eyes sweeping the darkness not far from where Adamae crouched, making her withdraw further. But Wasp eyes fared badly against the night, especially across the flames, and soon his attention returned to those close by, a look of disgust crossing his face.

"Still no sign of Hien, Lieutenant?"

One of the Wasps stood up and saluted. "Nothing, Captain. You want me to go look for him?"

"No, we stay together. I'm surprised we haven't had more trouble, to be honest."

"I'm not, sir. There can't be many left, not after what General Tynan did to them."

"Don't make the mistake of thinking that the Mantis are like us, Lieutenant. Odds and reason don't matter to them. They'd gladly sell their lives to a lost cause if it took a few of us with them." He looked out into the forest again, clearly unhappy about something. "The sooner we're away from here, the better. I want you to lead a search for Hien in the morning, keep it quick. If he's not close by then we move on. Until then, I want at least half the men ready at all times," he leaned in slightly, "and I want them sober."

The lieutenant saluted and returned to the campfire, while the captain returned to his tent.

With a little grumbling, the Wasp soldiers organised themselves into watches, and the bottle of drink was put away. Adamae was struck by how average they appeared. How had this brutish kinden managed to crush her own so completely? It seemed impossible, laughable even.

As she watched, the lieutenant took out a weapon she'd never seen before. Something a little like the crossbows outsiders favoured but more intricate. He handled it carefully, taking his time, and Adamae could see his lips moving as he checked each moving part in turn.

Some Mantis said that a weapon could contain the spirit of others, either pressed into it by hands of the forger or absorbed by those that wielded it, but this was different. There seemed to be no blurring between Wasp and weapon, no real connection at all. Instead, the bow seemed to her like a creature all of its own.

The Wasp lieutenant was asking one of the soldiers for something, and from the conversation she plucked a word: 'Snapbow.' Adamae nodded to herself, it sounded appropriate, for now the lieutenant had loaded the bow and put it down, it seemed poised, a small hunter ready to spring.

She found that she wanted it; the need to understand the weapon that had broken her people overwhelming.

The lieutenant was settling down to sleep, leaving only one soldier on watch. The guard had been one of the ones drinking earlier, and he seemed more interested in the way the flames danced than anything outside the ring of its light. His back was to her. The Lieutenant was asleep. There would never be a better time.

Adamae crept to the edge of the firelight, moving with aching slowness, willing the soldier not to look round, willing the lieutenant to remain undisturbed.

Her hand reached out towards the snapbow just as the lieutenant turned over, mumbling in his sleep.

She froze, preparing to dive back into the darkness, but the soldier stayed where he was, and the lieutenant did not wake. The Wasp had been using his bag as a pillow, and in turning, had left it free for her to take. Thoughts flew through Adamae's mind. The bag would contain rations and other things she would need to survive. It might also contain the key to the chains that bound the Mantis children. The thought of them sent her gaze in that direction.

One of them was looking back, a flicker of something other than despair in his eyes.

That settled it. Adamae would take the bag and the snapbow. She would find a way to free the children. She would take revenge on these Wasps, killing them one by one, until she was bathed in their blood.

It was the Mantis way.

She picked up the snapbow, her finger moving naturally to the trigger, and slipped the strap of the lieutenant's bag over one shoulder. But as she started to edge backwards, she felt resistance. A corner of the bag was still caught between the lieutenant's ear and the dirt.

She glanced back up at the soldier. He was busy rubbing his hands together over the flames and muttering something to himself. She felt sure her luck would not hold much longer.

Like a mother slipping her hands from beneath a sleeping baby, Adamae began to ease the bag free. The fabric was slightly thicker at the edge where it had been sewn together, and she was forced to tug hard to get it free.

Instantly, the lieutenant was awake. He rolled onto his back, reaching for the snapbow that had been by his side but was now in Adamae's grip. She dropped the bag so she could point it at him as he raised his hands.

If Adamae had known about Wasp culture she would have known

that when one Wasp surrenders to another, they do so with raised fists but as it was, she saw only a defenceless man and wondered if she had it in her to kill him?

Adamae had never taken a life before and had always imagined that when the day came it would be on the battlefield, or in a duel, not like this.

Up close, she could see the lieutenant was not entirely unlike her. His skin was as fair, though his hair fairer. His features were blunt in comparison to her own, but the fear on his face was familiar, and much as she hated him, she could not help but empathise.

She hesitated.

He did not.

While she stared at his face, the man's palms crackled to life, and his Wasp's sting seared her side, sending her staggering backwards.

The lieutenant roared for aid and the camp sprang into action.

Adamae squeezed the trigger of the snapbow but was unprepared for its eager response. She had expected it to behave like her own bow, with a relationship between the effort to draw and the power of the strike, but the lightest touch of her finger had discharged the shot early, sending it spinning harmlessly into the night.

And then she was running, her wounded side screaming at her, the eyes of the Mantis child following her, blank again.

Stings crackled nearby, warming the air but lacking the strength to reach her. A crossbow bolt thunked into a blackened trunk to her left, and she heard the sound of pursuit.

As the pain won her over, Adamae's grace failed, and the young Mantis stumbled, knocking into trees, feeling brittle wood snap against her shin and shoulder.

She pushed on, driven by fear, sure that the Wasps would bring her down at any moment.

But they didn't, and when she fell down, unable to get up again, the Wasps did not see her. And when she passed into exhausted sleep, she did so alone.

The groan of Adamae's stomach woke her. She was curled up in a ball in the ash, the first glow of dawn's light reaching her through the naked branches above her head.

Several of the trees had partly fallen, leaning low over her, their looming forms almost like people.

She sat up carefully, mindful of the burn on her side. Relief followed a quick inspection. It was not as bad as she'd feared. There was no sign of infection, and though the skin was scarred and tender, she realised she had been incredibly lucky.

The snapbow was next to her. She picked it up without thinking and stood, taking in her surroundings.

One of the trees had snapped, the top half drooping forward in a sharp bow, while the broken wood of the stump stabbed directly up towards the sky. A Wasp soldier was impaled on the stump. It looked as if he'd tripped in the dark and fallen backwards onto it. Shards of wood poked from his chest and belly, while his head had fallen back to rest on the sloping trunk.

The man's face was locked in an expression of surprise, his eyebrows raised in almost comic indignation.

Adamae screeched and backed away. She wanted nothing more than to run from the sight and never look back, but she could see the Wasp still had his pack and she needed it.

The Wasp's limbs were stiff and unyielding, forcing her to wrestle with the corpse in order to free the bag. She tried not to think about how cold he felt, as if there were ice in his veins rather than thickening blood.

Putting a bit of distance between her and the body, Adamae examined the spoils. The first thing she found was food, dry rations, and all other thoughts vanished as she began to eat. Some piece of common sense surfaced from her hunger, reminding her to eat slowly and to chew. He had a canteen as well, and she slaked her thirst as well as her hunger.

There were other useful things too that she pocketed: a small knife, some coins, a rough inked map that looked as if it had been copied from something else in a hurry.

But most importantly, she found snapbow bolts.

She sat down with the strange weapon and the ammunition and tried to see how one worked with the other. For a time, she forgot her grief and her despair, becoming entirely absorbed in the puzzle. Once she stopped trying to get her head around what the strange canister might be for, it was surprisingly simple to operate. Each part of the snapbow had been carefully worked, and there was a logic to the way the parts fitted together.

It was almost as if the weapon were speaking to her, guiding her hands as she loaded a bolt and primed the weapon for firing.

Having learned how sensitive the trigger was, she lifted the snapbow with care, taking aim at the dead Wasp. When she had sighted between his eyes, she squeezed the trigger and felt a slight kick from the snapbow as it loosed.

The bolt struck the Wasp square in the forehead, not quite where she was aiming but not too far off either.

Adamae nodded to herself, feeling suddenly calm, the necessary adjustments to her positioning already suggesting themselves.

She knelt down in the ash and started to reload the snapbow.

The Wasps were huddled close around the fire that night, the wind colder and more spiteful than usual, stirring clouds of ash that stung the eyes.

Adamae was able to walk right up to their camp, the darkness and the wind seeming to come with her.

"Captain's right," muttered one of the soldiers. "Sooner we're out of this cursed forest the better."

"Just one more night," said the lieutenant. "With a good march we'll be clear by tomorrow afternoon. Remember, Mantis slaves fetch a good price when they're got young enough." He pointed to the line of children, bigger than the last time Adamae had seen them. "We get this lot back to Capitas, we'll make our fortune."

"What about Hien?"

"What about him?"

"What if what happened to him happens to us?"

The lieutenant snorted. "Looked to me like he shot himself in the face with his own snapbow. You're not planning on doing that, are you?"

"No, sir. It's just —"

"Just what?"

"Nothing, sir."

"Exactly, it's nothing. Hien's stupidity means more money for us."

Adamae worked her way to the captain's tent. It was easy to identify, being bigger than the others, a shuttered lamp lighting it from the inside. Through the fabric she could see the captain's silhouette sitting hunched over some papers.

The wind howled loud in her ears as she raised the snapbow.

The lightest touch of her finger was all it took, the bolt like a hunting animal straining at the leash. In a blink it had punched through the side of the tent and through the captain's neck.

No one but Adamae noticed, the soldiers straining to hear each other over the roar of the fire. Using the knife, she cut her way inside, opened up the captain's lamp and tipped it over the papers, slipping out again as the flames took hold.

Then she began to circle away from the tent, reloading as she went, her hands moving of their own accord, fluid, the smooth engineering of the device making every movement natural.

One of the Wasps had gone to the edge of the camp to relieve himself. She shot him and two more before the others even realised there was a problem, but by the time the camp was rousing to put out the captain's tent, she was already on the opposite side, putting bolts into the backs of unsuspecting skulls.

The Wasps had dealt with enemies that could see in the dark before. They lit lamps and flew into the night air. But the winds and the ash-clouded skies threw shadows everywhere, and Adamae simply fell back from the little rings of light, beyond their ability to see her, but well within her range.

It was almost too easy, circling them at leisure, shooting Wasps at alternate ends of the camp, keeping them guessing, and all the while the snapbow greedily accepted new bolts, ready for the next kill.

The Wasps called to one another, identifying targets that were no more than shadows. To listen to them, it would seem that a hundred Mantis were stalking the camp, one for every tree on the clearing's edge.

She saw the Wasp lieutenant turn and run, his feet kicking up little clouds of ash as his art-wings flared to life at his back.

With their captain dead, and their only other officer showing his true colours, the remaining Wasps scattered. Adamae raised her eyebrows in surprise. There were still more than half of the Wasps left. Why were they quitting so easily? Why did they not rally?

Anger stirred in her. She wanted them to stay and fight so she could kill them all. She wanted to go and hunt them down one by one.

"Come back!" she shouted. "Come back and die!"

None of the Wasps seemed to hear her, each one shrinking rapidly as they raced over the tree tops.

Adamae narrowed her eyes and scanned the air until she spotted the lieutenant. With his lantern sparkling, he looked like a distant firefly, zig zagging in the sky, as if he knew her intent.

She raised the snapbow and fired, watching as the tiny bolt raced after its bobbing target. For the first time that night, the wind worked against her and the bolt went wide.

Her Mantis blood soared with frustration and she took three strides after her quarry before remembering the little figures chained together, shivering in the night.

She put the snapbow away and began searching the camp, finding the keys in what remained of the captain's tent. There were nearly fifty Mantis children chained together, most with only a handful of years to their name. The Wasps had killed the weak and the old, taking only those strong enough to endure travel and still fetch a good price.

They watched her with distrust as she unlocked their manacles and it hurt. For she knew that though they were one kinden, she was not like them, and had never been like them.

She was a different kind of Mantis.

Daggers and swords were placed into the children's willing hands, and supplies distributed. Adamae did not ask them to go with her and they did not ask her to come.

But they saluted her nonetheless, solemn faced, as she set off in pursuit of her prey.

Adamae found the lieutenant midmorning the next day. The rain fell hard, filling in the holes made by his boots in the mud.

The skeleton of the Felyal was behind her now, and she walked in the open. There was nowhere for her to hide, no way for her to conceal her approach. Just the way Adamae wanted it.

A Wasp could fly swifter than most but the use of art-wings was tiring. As she'd suspected, the lieutenant had been forced to land and continue on foot, hoping that he'd put enough distance between them to throw her off.

When he realised that he wasn't going to be able to escape, he'd turned round and waited for her, hands raised, palms open.

At some point he'd abandoned his helmet and the rain plastered his hair to his head, dulling it. Perhaps it was her imagination but Adamae fancied that his hands shook a little as she drew nearer.

To his credit, he didn't cry or grovel. He waited, saving his strength for their fight, watchful for any opportunity she might give.

Adamae stopped before she got within range of his sting and fired her first shot. The snapbow did not seem like an extension of her wrist, rather it felt like a loyal servant, ready to obey her commands. And she had just given a very specific one.

A second later, the lieutenant screamed as the bolt went through the palm of his right hand. His left palm crackled and a golden light flared between them, dissipating in the rain long before it reached her.

She fired a second time, hitting his left hand, snuffing out the light before he could prepare another blast.

The lieutenant crossed his arms over his chest and hunched forward with the pain. "What are you waiting for?" he shouted. "Why don't you kill me?"

Her third shot drove into his foot, the tip lodging in the thick mud underneath.

Adamae reloaded the snapbow and advanced closer.

The lieutenant was shivering now, though it was unclear whether this was because of shock or fear or cold. His eyes widened as she got closer. "You're... you're no more than a child."

"I am going to kill Wasps," she said. "And you are going to help me."

"What?"

"You are going to tell me where they are and how they think, and then I am going to kill them."

He laughed, though it sounded more hysterical than derisive. "What makes you think I'd betray my own?"

She tilted her head to look at him. "Because more than anything, you want to live."

He had no reply to that.

"This is an incredible weapon," she said. "You call it a snapbow, yes?" He didn't answer but she carried on as if he had. "It was this that killed my people. Now it will kill yours. I will show you what it is capable of."

The lieutenant shook his head. "We have thousands of those and thousands of us to wield them. You're just one. It doesn't matter how good you are with it, the Empire will hunt you down and kill you eventually. But spare me, and I could get you in. The Empire always has a place for people like you. They'd put that skill of yours to good use as an Auxillian. You could have a life! A rich, fulfilling life!"

"No, it will be as you say. I will die young, but I will be steeped in Wasp blood. And before I am gone, the Empire will learn to fear my

117

people again."

"But... that's madness!"

"No," she corrected him. "It is the Mantis way."

The Poor Little Earwig Girl

Tom Lloyd

"I'm looking for a thief."

"You must be lost, then," Marigh replied without looking back.

"I'm looking at you."

She paused. "That much I worked out."

A glance over her shoulder revealed a burly man with dirty blond hair and a neat beard. Nothing on his battered jerkin identified him but with a face like that, nothing needed to.

"You won't find a thief staring at my arse now, Mister Wasp."

A small smile appeared on his face. "Sure about that?"

"You ain't finding nothing there." She scowled and went back to the wood she was carving.

"I'm not so certain."

She looked at the wood, wanting to slam it down on the tabletop in irritation. Marigh didn't move, however. Her grandmother's words echoed in her mind "*Always quiet, always unseen. Forget that and others will turn on you.*"

"I am."

"Man I know said I'd find what I was looking for here."

She looked back at him. Typical Wasp-kinden; big, brash and full of himself, but handsome enough, with dark eyes and a narrow nose that had a tiny scar near the tip. Just by the way he stood she could tell he was no lumbering brute, but a fighter who'd have the measure of any local brawler. His kind had hardly won themselves many friends in recent years, even in places unscathed by war as Ishiel was, yet this one had the easy manner of a man with few cares and fewer enemies.

Teach me that trick and I'll do the job for you.

"If you want a thief," she said, "I suggest you head to Amayl's Caskhouse. Order a drink and put your hands in your pockets. Most likely you'll be holding hands with the nearest thief."

The Wasp's smile widened. He looked around her workshop, brushing his fingers through the pale blue forget-me-nots trailing from the tall pots that flanked the doorway. "Ah, but I don't just want a thief."

"Still doesn't mean it's anything to do with me."

Marigh couldn't help but look at the man's hands. Neatly kept nails and scrubbed palms couldn't hide the marks of his past. The little finger on his left was missing and that wasn't anything near the only scar to mark his rough skin. A man used to physical work and blade work too, no doubt, but she knew the real danger of those hands. That searing gold flash, quick as an arrow, and the ruin it could leave in its wake. Her hands tightened. For a woman with surprises of her own Art to hand, the presence of a Wasp's sting in the room was not a comfortable one.

The Wasp cocked his head at her. "What kinden are you?"

"Beetle. Got a problem with that?"

"If it were true, I wouldn't. But you're like no Beetle I've ever met."

"That's the best line you've got to spin?"

To her surprise, he laughed – not so coarse as she would have expected, either. There was a depth and richness to his voice that put her in mind of a singer's training, or perhaps an actor. Neither of those seemed likely of a Wasp and she looked again at the man, struggling to see past the trappings of the Empire.

"I think perhaps my friend was correct in his recommendation," he said.

"Who's this friend?" she asked quietly. A lifetime as an outsider made her wary of what others were saying. A recommendation from anyone round here was to be treated with suspicion. "Some gossip spreading rumours that I'm a thief?"

"Don't worry, your secret's safe with me."

The smirk on his face never wavered and Marigh took a breath, aware she was being wound up and hating herself for rising to it. Her grandmother had raised her better than that.

Pride never did this family any good, the old woman's voice echoed in Marigh's memory, *dead or fugitive is all it ever made of us – don't let it take you too.*

Marigh made her hands relax until the tingle in her palms subsided. Now was not the time to show her temper – certainly not to a Wasp soldier who could fire his sting as quick as a snap-bow and from across the room.

"Who?"

The Wasp nodded as though she'd passed a test. "Man named Ubest."

"Never heard of him."

"Probably not one of your gossips, then."

She frowned. Ishiel was a fair sized town with half of its streets perched on the sunny slope of a hill and a skirt of farms and vineyards running for miles past the walls. It was too big to know everyone, but still she was disconcerted that this Ubest person knew her name even.

"Sounds like he was mistaken," she said. "I don't know the man and can't see how he'd have heard of me."

The Wasp gestured expansively. "Ah well, Ubest is a good man for that sort of thing. He and I go back a few years now, so I trust his judgement – and his discretion."

"Maybe you shouldn't." She turned her back on him, doing her best to ignore the prickling feeling on her neck. "Now if you don't mind, I've got work to do."

The man snorted. "As you wish. What are you making?"

"What does it look like?"

He took a step closer and she felt his presence disturbingly close as he leaned to look over her shoulder. "A stick." The faint odour of cinnamon on his breath accompanied the words.

"It's the neck of a fiddle."

"Ah. So you're making a fiddle then?"

Marigh bit her tongue to stop herself snapping at the man. It was easier than that normally was, given he was twice her size and looked like a veteran.

Are there any other sort of Wasps in these parts? She reflected. *Rekef, soldiers or ex-soldiers. None of them are here to be nice and do an honest day's work.*

"I'm making a fiddle," she confirmed.

"There's good money in that?"

"Good enough."

He grunted. "I'm Olric."

"Sounds about right."

The Wasp ignored her comment, which she was glad of. Pointing out a man's name as typical of his professed homeland wasn't exactly a clever come-back, she just hadn't been able to think of anything better.

"You're Marigh, right?"

That tripped her. He really had come here looking for her, on the suggestion of someone she'd never met. "I am, but I'm still no thief."

"Fair enough. Do you have a buyer for the fiddle?"

"You want to start playing the fiddle?" Marigh asked irritably. "You don't look the sort."

"Might be I don't look much like what I am," he replied, his tone lowering a significant shade. "How about this? I pay you what the fiddle's worth and you come eat lunch with me instead of making the thing. No commitment, just hear me out."

She took the change in his voice as a small warning. "I don't know what you've been told, but I'm not a thief. Ask anyone."

"Good." He stepped back, finally affording her some room again. "The last thing I need is someone who's known to be a thief. They might get noticed, or caught, if that was the case. Some young, ah, *Beetle*-kinden girl who's lived here all her life and makes an honest living carving things – folk would look straight through you and that's an attractive quality to a man like me."

"Which would be?"

"I'm sorry?"

"What sort of man is like you?" she said, unable to stand it any longer and turning back to face him. She didn't say what she was thinking but the word hung in the air all the same. *Rekef.*

This time his smile didn't reach his eyes. "You Beetles, you see a Wasp and you think we're all spies and assassins, ready and willing to slaughter the whole town in a heartbeat."

"Some might say you are. All the ones who come round this way, anyway."

"Well, be fair, the Empire's not attacked anyone near here, has it? I mightn't know about further abroad, but given Collegium's full of words and hatred for us, I'm not surprised rumour is all you have here. As it is, I'm just a businessman looking to get a little help in trade."

Olric stepped to one side and indicated the door. "Come, let me make my proposition over lunch. There's an eatery I always visit when I'm here, join me."

She almost laughed at that, but then the image of her eating in public with a man like this appeared in her mind. Just that one glimpse was enough to send a chill down her spine.

"Out in public?" Marigh gasped, feeling faint, "with you? In front of everyone?"

The calculating looks of the old women in the neighbourhood danced in her mind; the anger in the eyes of girls who'd tormented her since childhood, the outrage of the men who'd ignored her almost as long. Her stomach clamped at the thought. She felt the heat of their silent judgement on her skin and an ingrained desire for a dark corner welled up inside her.

"Too good for the company of a Wasp?" Olric laughed. "Don't worry, it's across town." His tone lowered again. "A better part of town, you won't be seen by folk you know."

He stood where he was, one arm raised to usher her out. Marigh straightened and faced him down, every instinct screaming to lower her head and not look so defiant. That he was so much larger and carried himself like a fighter only strengthened the feeling and eventually she submitted.

Her shoulders sagged and the tingle in her wrists subsided – the fight driven out of her by her own fears. Wordlessly she shuffled outside into the alley. The noon shadows of neighbouring buildings filled it while sunshine cut an uneven path across the walls of the higher storeys.

"This way," he said, thankfully pointing away from the main street. The alleys were narrow and deserted but for a sandy-colour beetle the size of a child that nosed between cobbles.

"Where are we going?"

"Artifice Square," Olric said.

Marigh pictured the district she'd rarely visited. This southern face of the town took the brunt of the wind, rain and sun – enjoying the worst of each season – so the better-off had houses on the east-side, sheltered from the extremes.

At least they won't recognise me, east-side, Marigh said to herself as she set off, trotting ahead so she wouldn't be seen as some companion of a Wasp-kinden.

A belligerent kinden like the Wasps didn't care they were unpopular. They surveyed every room like it was a country to be conquered, should they choose to. Marigh and her people didn't have that luxury. She might be no more popular than a Wasp, she didn't need their baggage on top of her own.

She looked down at her clothing, realising she was still in her stained apron with just a shirt and breeches. Her feet were bare and now she paid attention, also dirty and callused. More boyish than anything else and hardly fitting to be seen on the better streets.

They won't care what I am round Artifice Square, she realised with a sinking feeling. *They'll just see someone too poor for her surroundings. Will that be better, worse or just a new shade of shit?*

"If I were Emperor," Olric declared expansively, making Marigh flinch, "I'd conquer this town and all those near it, fast as I could."

She peered around at the warren-like restaurant he had chosen, sparsely occupied and of those none were Beetles so far as she could see. Theirs was a cool, dark corner across which the scents of grilling meat drifted however. Most of the patrons were seated at tables on the vine-shaded terrace overlooking the busy cobbled square.

"That's not the best way to make friends round here," she said. "This is my home, remember?"

He made a dismissive sound and gestured at the food in front of him. "Don't be so touchy, it's a compliment."

"That you want to conquer us?"

He grinned. "For food like this? Damn right I would. This cured aphid haunch alone is worth it."

She blinked at him. "You'd bring your armies here for the food?"

"If I were emperor, I'd want the best and here, even the poor eat almost as well as the rich back home. I admit it might look a little simpler than what gets served on the tables of the powerful, but the quality..." he shook his head and popped a small tomato with vertical ridges into his mouth. "Ah yes, why play with the food when, in its simplest form, it's fit for emperors?"

"It's just a tomato," Marigh said.

"Indeed – but you come to Capitas and try a tomato there. For one who's grown up here, it'd be as ashes in your mouth."

"Typical bloody Wasp," she muttered before she could catch herself. Olric raised an eyebrow and she reddened.

"How so?"

Marigh took a long breath. "You, ah, that's your way of complimenting my home. Most folk'd say they could stay for years; that they'd take a cartload back home and make a fortune. Something like that, anyway. You lot, your first thought is conquest. You like something, you take it by force, and the fact you want it is meant to be a compliment."

Olric shrugged, smiling at her words. "We're all slaves to our heritage," he admitted, "one way or another. You're born a Wasp, grow up a Wasp, and yes I guess conquering is in your blood. It's just the same for you, isn't it? Whatever kinden you are." His voice became more pointed, hand paused over a chunk of crumbling white cheese in a terracotta dish. "Beetle, you said?"

Marigh nodded. "It's those who've ended up slaves to your *heritage* I feel sorry for," she added sourly, as much as anything to get him off that subject.

"For a Beetle you've got something of a temper on you."

She resisted the urge to squirm. It was true – and she wasn't the only one in her family to be that way. Uncomfortable in the light of attention, there remained a spark within them all that refused to quietly crawl into the shadows when roused.

The Wasp proffered a bowl of olives stuffed with garlic. "I'm sorry," he said in a voice that almost sounded genuine, "I didn't mean to upset you. I didn't bring you here to pick a fight."

"Why did you, then?" Marigh said, swallowing her pride and taking an olive to follow it down.

"To offer you a job –" he raised a hand as though to correct himself, "to persuade you to take a job."

"I'm not a thief."

"Perfect."

She frowned at him. "What?"

"I don't want a thief, not really – they tend to be stupid and opportunistic. You can't trust them and in a small town like this, people know who the thieves are. What I want is someone who could be a good thief if they were so inclined, but has the sense not to be – or at least to have never been caught."

She shook her head and took another olive. "So what is it you do want?"

"Someone who can't afford to be too picky about breaking the law if the right offer comes her way. Someone who is on the small side and agile, who might have some natural gifts towards housebreaking and has brains enough to follow instructions to the letter."

Silence fell over the pair of them, Marigh looking at the utterly self-assured Wasp with suspicion while her various money concerns jostled for attention at the back of her mind. Her grandmother was getting old and frail. Marigh had been meaning to save more for fuel and doctors come winter, but somehow they were barely paying the rent with what she earned. Fears of the war turning in this direction weren't helping anyone.

It was just the two of them now, her only other relations lived out of town and they'd not spoken in years. Marigh didn't even really know what had started the argument, only that it had happened around the time her father died. The one time she'd asked about Uncle Padrin had been the one time she's seen her grandmother angry enough to swear.

"So someone told you I'm poor, there's a lot of it about."

"Clever, agile and poor, rather less so."

With great ceremony Olric rolled a paper-thin slice of sweet-cured aphid and raised it in both hands to his mouth. There was a reverential look on his face as he bit into the salty-sweet meat and despite the strange conversation Marigh reached for the plate herself. Ishiel sweetcure was a luxury she couldn't afford – aphid haunches cured in honeydew, salt and the wild thyme that grew only in these parts. They bought it for feast days only and even then she had to scrimp and save.

She crammed a piece into her mouth and tried not to moan at the flavour, but Olric was making enough appreciative noises for both of them. For a few minutes the pair attacked the plates of food in silence. Olric delighted over every plate and bowl as though greeting old friends before he devoured them, Marigh just wanted to eat enough to give her grandmother two portions of supper.

Eventually they slowed and Olric poured himself a cup of wine, offering the jug to Marigh who shook her head. She didn't want anything muddying her thoughts when dealing with this man and wine at midday had never suited her.

"So what is it you want stolen?" she asked eventually, unable to contain her curiosity.

"Nothing."

"Nothing?"

"Not one thing."

"I don't understand."

Olric cocked his head at her. "Does this mean you're in?"

A familiar flutter of worry appeared in her stomach but Marigh ignored it, speaking carefully as though they were being listened in on by the local magistrate.

"You're saying you don't want anything stolen, but you do want a thief's skills. It could be I need the money if there's a job that doesn't involve stealing. I'm guessing it's easier to explain yourself to curious watchmen if you're not carrying stolen goods – not saying I'm in, but I'm willing to hear more."

"Now you're just being coy," Olric said with the smile of a man who enjoyed the chase all too much. "So you're interested, that's a first step I suppose."

"How do I know you're not just after some fool to pin whatever this is on?"

"I'll pay half up front, does that help?"

"A bit," Marigh admitted, "but a heavy purse only makes it easier for them to hang you."

He sighed. "It's a job, I'm offering money. There's risk involved, I'll not lie there, but at some point you need to take a chance. No enterprise like this ever worked if the parties refused to trust each other."

"What's the risk for you?"

"Half my money for a start,' he laughed, "but I've no wish to have my name offered up to any curious watchmen either." He clapped his hands together and stood. "So here's my offer. Come to my house tonight and you'll get half the money – assuming you can break in without my guard catching you. Call it a little test. I need to know I'm investing in the right person, after all.

"Once you have the money I'll tell you the job. You can walk away with it as an aid to forgetting you ever met me, or you can do the job with a promissory note in your pocket. I'll see you to the job and watch you in – if you're not caught you can cash the note yourself and never see me again or return it to me to swap."

"Sounds like you've got it all worked out."

"I like to plan things," he replied casually, "and I like to find people I can trust to do a good job. This is business. In business, you stick around and you protect employees who get the job done. The Imperial Army might chew through a town like this one without caring what happens to those in its way, but I'm here to make money. That means doing things a bit different."

He slid a scrap of paper across the table. "Here's where I'm staying. I'll see you tonight."

Marigh stood in the shadow of a silver-leafed aspen and checked the paper again. The address was certainly correct so she carefully tore it up and let the pieces fall to the ground. The leaves overhead rustled a warning, shivering in a wind that came down from the north – Empire lands. She looked around again, out of habit as much as anything. It was late in the evening and there was no one outside.

She had spent an hour scouting out the house and its surrounding streets. It was on the outskirts of town, a large detached property with a mud-brick wall running around an expansive garden. There were three more aspen inside the wall, looming high and casting their weak moon-shadow across the garden. The wall was too tall for her to look over, the gate just as big. Finally accepting there was no one watching, Marigh crept forward to the gate and paused. She realised she had no way of knowing if this was Olric's house at all or whether he was setting her up for something else entirely, but there was no getting around that.

The gate was seven feet high and made of thick oak planks. There was no way to casually look through it, but there was space at the hinge where it hung on three fat metal brackets. She crouched down and held her breath as she peered through the gap. She could see little of what was behind, just a white-washed wall and the edge of a window frame, but she had heard footsteps when circling the wall earlier so she kept still and waited – all the while trying to ignore the prickling feeling on her neck.

Before long she heard the footsteps again and presently a figure crossed her view. It was only a glimpse but he was out in the open – a man in a studded jerkin carrying a long club. Most importantly, he was pale skinned with sandy hair tied back in a topknot – Wasp-kinden.

Maybe this isn't some elaborate ruse, then, Marigh thought with a flush of relief. *Now to get inside.*

Paranoia made her look around again as she pulled back, but there were no town watchmen bearing down on her and the street remained empty. This was a newer part of town, full of prosperous merchants and landowners. West of here was the dyke that served as a town boundary and then just miles and miles of vineyards, orchards and grazing land for the aphid herds that made the region rich.

She waited a few seconds more then pulled herself up to peek over the wall. Her heart jumped into her mouth as she caught a glimpse of movement, then realised it was the guard rounding the corner of the building and disappearing from view. Marigh eased herself down and continued on around the wall in the same direction.

He wouldn't be patrolling all evening and there were similar houses to this all over town. He would head to the rear servant's door and go inside there, venturing out every half hour or something. The household would mostly be turned in by now – *any normal household would be,* she corrected herself – but there were lights shining behind more than half the shutters here.

At the east face she paused, checked her surroundings and put her toe in a small crack in the wall – just large enough to assist her up to reach the top of the wall and pull herself gingerly up. The garden was empty, starlight showing a long vine-draped pergola occupied much of the ground to her immediate left. That was the best cover on offer, the rest of the garden no more than child-height shrubs and turf-bordered herb beds, while a pair of sunken ponds flanked the main path.

No point in waiting around, then.

She wriggled over the smooth top of the wall with innate ease and dropped quietly down on the other side. When no shouts of alarm or anger rang out across the garden, Marigh padded into the fractured shadows of the pergola and moved from one support to the next in brisk bursts. Before long she was at the house and surveying the obstacle. A three-storey central block from which later additions protruded on three sides, shallow tiled roofs with a thick parapet around the edge of each. All the ground floor windows were shuttered and she didn't bother to try them. If this was a test, Olric wanted something a little more deft than slipping a catch.

With two steps' run up, Marigh hopped onto a window ledge and hurled herself towards a gutter spout on the eastern extension. She hung by one hand for a moment then managed to get a grip with the other and begin the climb. It wasn't an easy route she'd picked, but she was light and nimble. Before long she was crouching on the parapet and looking out over the darkened town.

When the stolid tramp of footsteps came from the garden below she felt a flutter of panic in her stomach, but managed not to catch a roof tile as she lay flat on the inside edge of the parapet. Before long the Wasp came back into view, but she realised he wasn't hunting an intruder, just doing another lap. She kept very still, willing him not to look up and notice the grey shape against the line of the roof.

Crawl into the cracks, Marigh, wriggle through the dark.

The spiteful voices of her childhood echoed loud in Marigh's memory. She'd had few friends. Beetle-kinden made up the majority of the locals here and they could somehow tell she wasn't quite one of them. The more they'd picked on her and shouted at her, the more she'd wanted to do just that; hide herself away in the dark, squeeze herself into some hidden space.

She blinked and the voices vanished, present day reasserting itself as the Wasp below trudged out of view again. She turned and looked up. More shutters, but while the grand south-facing ones had glazed doors leading onto narrow balconies, this side had much smaller windows flanking the chimney stacks. She gave the guard half a minute to complete his lap then began to scale the main building.

It proved no great challenge and once she had reached an upper window she slipped her hand up to the clasp of the shutters. Using her Art she could reach just far enough to slip inside the clasp and jerk it open with a sharp twist of the wrist. That done, she eased it open and reached up to wriggle her head through the narrow frame.

Despite the gloom Marigh saw immediately the small guest room was empty. The furnishings were bare and neat so she crawled all the way through the window, head first and upside down with her feet set against the sides of the window.. It was an undignified, almost lizard-like movement that rekindled her sense of shame, but she ignored it and focused on pulling the window shut behind in case the guard noticed.

Easing the door open a crack, she peered out into the dim corridor beyond, adorned with long canvasses of clashing colours and a dark, polished wooden floor. Unable to hear anything she slipped out, fighting the tingle in her palms that wanted to unveil her Art once more in case there was a guard inside too. Directly ahead was a wall, but past that a balustrade opened out over the central hallway. Marigh slipped forward and saw an open doorway spilling light. Inside were oil lamps on carved wooden stands beside the ornate roll end of a sofa upholstered in pale green. She could smell cigar smoke and there was a silver haze to the room so, with nerves jangling, she moved as silently as she could around to the threshold.

"Don't just stand there," called a voice from beyond the open door. "Join me for a drink."

Marigh stepped reluctantly inside, anxious as she left the gloom of the corridor. Olric lounged on a second sofa at right angles to the first, an incongruously delicate, long-stemmed glass in one hand and a short cigar in the other.

"Wine? Something stronger?"

"Where's the money?"

He pointed. "On the table."

A long chequerboard table sat before the unlit fire, its surface almost entirely light and dark wooden squares each one an inch across. There was a small flat purse lying in the middle beside a swan-neck decanter of some amber spirit. She picked up the purse and looked inside, gasping at what she saw. There had to be fifty silver pieces packed neatly inside, slotted into folds of cloth so they would make no noise when carried.

"And that's only half, remember?"

She closed the purse, feeling suddenly afraid. "I remember. Just how dangerous is this job? I won't murder anyone – if that's what you want, best you say nothing at all. Just take your purse back and I'll walk away."

Again that easy smile of a handsome man in his prime. For all that he'd asked about her kinden, Olric seemed not to care what the answer was. The townsfolk mostly looked at her with faint suspicion, even those she knew were somehow discomforted by her presence. Though Olric had guessed there was something different about her, neither that nor his ignorance about what that was appeared to matter.

Or maybe some Rekef are just practiced at that, Marigh thought darkly.

"The purse is yours no matter what," Olric said after inspecting her for a moment. "I appreciate your consideration, but there'll be no murder. A certain dubious legality is only to be expected in business, but murder's the province of criminals and soldiers so I leave it to them."

"Guess I'll take that drink then," Marigh replied, slipping the purse cord over her head and tucking it into her belt. "Wine if you've got it."

Olric stood up smartly and poured her a glass from a sideboard behind the door. He handed it over with a small bow of playful chivalry then draped himself back over his seat and indicated that she do similar.

"You climbed your way in?"

She nodded. "I'd have a hole burned through me otherwise, no? So what's this job?"

"A girl of little foreplay," Olric sighed. "The gods are so cruel to me."

Marigh said nothing. She had no wish to stay in that house any longer than she needed to. While Olric had given no indication of expecting anything other than burglary, she didn't mean to play coy to appease some indolent sense of drama.

"Very well," Olric said after a pause, "the job. Meet me at dusk tomorrow, the Aristoi cemetery. Wear what you are now. The work isn't so arduous but will require time and a certain grace. You'll be out all night I expect."

"Why me?" she asked all of a sudden. "Why not find a Fly-kinden?"

He cocked his head at her. "Fly-kinden and their extended families aren't good at keeping a secret and I don't want gossip about me flitting about town. They also have a less than hardy constitution and aren't much for patience. I'm assured *you* are well suited and now I see you here, I think Ubest was right. Given that, I'll put aside my curiosity and just be content that you can get it done. And keep your mouth shut afterwards.'

There was no mistaking the faint note of menace in his voice – not so much a threat as a reminder. He, and likely his friend downstairs, were hard men who lived by a set of rules different to her own. He might call himself a businessman but she wouldn't be fooled as to what business that was. Criminal, Rekef spy, solider, it didn't matter; those worlds overlapped often enough and even Marigh knew what happened if the rules got broken. If they did, it would be briskly dealt with then they'd move on to the next bit of business just as soon as they'd washed the blood from their hands.

Marigh ducked her head in acknowledgment and set her glass down, a sour taste in her mouth. Olric saw the look on her face and saw she understood. He gave a nod and stood. "I'll see you out. No point climbing back out now is there?"

The next evening Marigh perched on the pedestal of a large statue just inside the gates to the Aristoi cemetery and watched the world beyond. There were few Spider-kinden in the town, but an intermittent flow of adventurers and exiles passed this way – enough for some to settle down over the years. The cemetery was, in truth, for all Spider-kinden who died hereabouts not just Aristoi, a chance to rest among their own kind. While it wasn't large, there were a number of impressive statues and memorials dotted around it.

The evening shadows were long by the time Marigh chose her spot. Golden shafts streaked the gravel paths running between plots. Strands of white jasmine climbing the perimeter wall waved in the breeze and the voices of children echoed from behind the cemetery. It was a quiet and peaceful moment, but though she tucked herself into the stony shadow of a robed Spider-kinden statue, Marigh could not shake the anxiety crawling through her body. Her palms itched as her pincers demanded to be unsheathed, as though she could cut her fears free, and she was forced to rub and scratch her hands together to try and quell the feeling.

"Ready?"

The voice made her jump, her Art half-unveiling until she recognised Olric's voice. Marigh bit her lip and dropped her hands, cheeks burning with shame and fear as she hoped he hadn't spotted them. Even now people took fright of bony points sliding free of her wrists, as though she was some raging Mantis warrior.

Olric stood haloed by the fading sun, the battered lines of his face now smooth and gilt-edged. With golden triangles embroidered down his tunic and a fat, ornately striped belt around his waist, the Wasp looked every inch like an imperial envoy or nobleman to Marigh's unschooled eye. It didn't hurt that his handsome face wore a gentle smile the likes of which she rarely saw. In one hand was a nondescript canvas bag, cinched shut with a long shoulder strap hanging loose.

"I, ah, yes – ready."

He inclined his head and pointed away to her left, within the bounds of the cemetery. "Over that wall is a yard owned by Ulbrec Curer. You know the name I assume?"

"Of course, most likely that sweetcure you were stuffing yourself with came from his farms."

Marigh turned in the direction he was pointing. She could see nothing over the cemetery wall but knew there were long warehouses reaching right into the body of the hill itself. Every week there would be a small procession of carts from the farms beyond the town, laden with the legs of freshly slaughtered aphids the size of children.

"But there won't be anything there to steal, that's not where he lives. That's just the salting and curing warehouses."

Olric's smile widened. "True, but there's value there all the same." He proffered the bag. "In here you'll find ten bundles of sticks wrapped in cloth and some resin-treated squares of linen, damn sticky things they are too. Beyond and beneath the warehouses there are the caves inside the hill where the haunches are hung for the final curing. There are ventilation shafts connecting them all, narrow shafts too small for most people to enter and covered by grills to keep out animals or insects."

Marigh frowned for a moment then her mouth fell open. "You want to taint the stock? Drive him out of business?"

"It won't be a fatal blow, but enough to give his fortunes a knock and allow for some competition," Olric explained. "Ignore the salting warehouses, they're too well ventilated, it's just the stores where the haunches are aged. Ulbrec can afford to take the hit without anyone starving, but he'll not sell any Ishiel sweetcure this year or next."

And it's coincidence he's the guiding hand on the town council? Marigh kept the question to herself. *Didn't someone say he's got a portrait of Stenwold Maker in his hallway? But I'm sure that's nothing to a businessman like you.*

"How many guards?"

"The workers will have finished for the day. Just two guards at night, a guard beetle with them. I've got a distraction planned, once you hear that, get over the wall and into the nearest ventilation shaft. You'll need to close up all the ventilation shafts with the pieces of linen to stop the smoke escaping, then set the bundles and light them all. Retreat into a shaft and close it up behind you, the smoke's nasty stuff but a Beetle won't get more than a headache from it. Give the smoke three or four hours to taint the meat, then clear up as best you can and clear the shafts again."

"Four hours hiding in a ventilation shaft? How do I even count that?"

"I'll have a man here five hours from now, he'll ring a bell twice – piss off the neighbours mebbe, but he'll be long gone before they come to complain. If you don't hear that, wait until the sky starts to lighten. Do the clear-up and you'll be out before anyone returns. With luck no one will even notice anything's wrong in the morning – I'll double your fee if no one notices before the town's officials grade the sweetcure next week."

Unexpectedly, he took her by the shoulders and looked her hard in the eye. "Can you do it?"

Marigh hesitated. Her dalliances with crime had been minor thus far, her housebreaking skills only tested when fleeing her peers. The prospect of the money was enticing enough, but more compelling still was the way Olric looked at her – not with desire or anything like that, just a measure of respect. He had his suspicions she wasn't your average Beetle-kinden, but he didn't seem to care. It went against all she'd heard about Wasps and all she'd put up with from the regular Beetles and other kinden of Ishiel.

"I can do it."

"Four hours in a ventilation shaft, it won't be fun."

The young woman suppressed a bitter laugh. *Not fun, but something I was born to do. Hide in the cracks, Marigh, wriggle down the shaft. That's where your kind belong, the dark and narrow places.*

"I'll manage."

That easy smile blossomed once more on Olric's face, gentle for all the man's strength. "I know you will."

He brushed a finger down her cheek and turned to go, swift enough that he might not have even noticed the blush he'd provoked. Marigh looked away, hiding her embarrassment in the shadows until the Wasp was out of sight. She took the bag to the wall she needed to scale, setting it down to investigate once she was out of sight of the gate. Everything was as he described, along with a fire-lighting kit and some sort of alchemical lamp, so she cinched the bag shut again and slung it over her head.

Her fingers soon began to jitter as the sun's last rays vanished and the sky became dark. The jasmine flowers lowered their heads with the dusk and the night chill had started to descend before raised voices echoed out across the town. Marigh paused a while longer, trying to pick out words from the sounds, but all she could fathom was a jangle of men's voices shouting each other down.

Now or never.

She took a breath and pulled herself up to look over the wall. All was clear. Angry voices echoed around the buildings off to her right, but she did nothing until she spotted her destination – a flared wooden box set halfway up the wall of the nearest warehouse. Round the top of the building were long banks of open shutters, covered with netting to keep insects away. The wooden box faced away from her, toward the prevailing wind so it could bring air down into the caves under the warehouse. She slithered over the wall and went to the box, freeing the netting down one side so she could push past it and look within.

The shaft was narrow indeed, a natural fissure in the rock that had been chipped away until it was wide enough to serve. They must have got Fly-kinden or children to do the work, no one else would fit down to wield a tool, and there would certainly be no space for her to turn once she was in the shaft.

Marigh knew her night vision was excellent, but still she could make out nothing of the shaft below. Arranging the netting so it would slip back down once her feet were through, she took a deep breath and wormed her way inside. Despite her heritage there was a small moment of panic before she got her bearings. Suddenly the walls felt too close, too constraining and tomb-like. She almost backed out right there, while she still had the chance of working her way back up and escaping, but as panic ran through her, Marigh pictured that confident smile Olric had worn.

He's confident. He's seen these shafts, he must have. He knows I can fit or he wouldn't have sent me. My getting stuck and dying here doesn't serve his purpose, it might even lead Curer's men back to him.

Marigh closed her eyes. It made no difference to what she could see but helped calm her. *Time all this was more than a burden. Time all the shit I've put up with got balanced out.*

Slowly she worked her way down the steep slope of the shaft, the surface rough enough to ensure she didn't slide. The bag she pushed ahead of her as her hands quested forward, discovering as she went two alcoves that had been cut into the rock. There she perched, checking she could turn around comfortably and taking her time about the descent rather than get tired.

Eventually she reached the bottom, feeling the spring of netting beneath her. Already there emanated a warm, rich scent from below – the curing haunches filling the air with a heady perfume so thick she could almost take a bite. The net was tied to a nail driven into the stone at each corner, but she couldn't afford to let go with both hands above an unknown drop. Instead, she slid a pincer from one hand and sawed at the lower knots, the edge barely sharp but eventually it did the trick and she felt the net hang open.

Using the bag as a guide she tested what was below the mouth of the shaft, unable to see anything still, and to her relief it bumped against something not far away. She knew the caves would be full of solid wooden frames that the haunches hung from and let the bag rest on top as she worked her way out. Soon she was crouching, blind in the darkness, on a narrow wooden plank just a yard or so from the ceiling of the cave.

Marigh climbed down and found the tiny alchemical lamp just the size of her palm. One twist and a dull light began to emanate, enough to make Marigh jump at the sudden looming shapes of haunches that now surrounded her.

She gave a nervous laugh at herself and held the lamp up. Its light was the palest blue and barely enough to give any sense of outline, but it was all Marigh needed and she set it down to begin unpacking the bag. Lining up the stick bundles that smelled of some bitter, pungent oil, she touched her finger to the sticky resin linens that sat inside a waxed pouch then set the rest of the fire-lighting kit to one side. Last, she found the promissory note in a sealed envelope. In all her anxiety she'd forgotten about it completely, but now she had it she gave it a cursory inspection, tucked it in a pocket and went to scout the caves.

It was cool and silent as she walked through them, five in total and all full of the pungent dry scent of Ishiel sweetcure with barely a breath of air to disturb them. Solidly-build frames stood a yard apart throughout, mostly laden with haunches though there remained space for a few hundred more she guessed. She kept well away from the tall doors leading off the largest chamber, not knowing where the guards would be beyond that, but once she had scouted the whole network Marigh felt a semblance of calm descend. She had the place to herself and so long as she was quick and quiet, there'd be no trouble.

Looks like Olric's friend was right, she realised with something of a smile. *I really am suited to the job. Might be grandmother's last years will be a bit more comfortable after all.*

She found two vents in each of the caves, the two beneath the warehouses high up on the uneven ceiling but the ones inside the hill would be harder to reach. When it came to pressing the resinous cloths onto the netting, she had to climb the frames and lean precariously, but the one time she almost lost her balance her quick reactions saved her.

It took a little while, but soon she had the vents covered and the stick bundles set on the floor in every cave. She didn't know how much smoke would seep through the door, but it was perfectly possible there were several between her and the guards. She resolved to simply place the bundles as far from the door as she could and put the worry from her mind. She tossed the bag on top of the first wooden frame then headed to the furthest cave and set about lighting a cloth from the kit.

The first of the bundles caught easily, emitting a thin spire of dirty smoke as it started to burn. A bitter chemical-laden scent, sharp as bile, began to fill the air. In moments she could taste it right at the back of her throat, a thick, heavy taste that seemed to coat her mouth and leave her skin greasy and sticky. She needed little imagination to work out what it would do to the delicate, sweet flavour of the aphid haunches all around her. Just a moment of standing there made her yearn for a bath and if she didn't move quickly her clothes would be fit only for burning.

As fast as she could she retraced her steps, lighting the rest in her wake and ending up at the first vent as smoke began to build and drift towards her. Marigh scrambled up and hung the bag around her neck, trying not to breathe too deeply as she went. Climbing inside she ascended to the alcove and quickly set about using the remaining sticky cloths to seal the shaft behind her.

In the feeble light of the lamp it proved tricky to ensure the edges were fully sealed, but eventually Marigh was satisfied that she was not going to choke. She settled into as comfortable position as possible – aware all she could do now was wait quietly and patiently, listening out for sounds of alarm.

And here you are, Marigh said to herself, *tucked up in a dark little hole of your own. Only this time you went willingly, you weren't shoved there by Obolan Hoon or Geress.*

She pursed her lips, feeling a slight urge to both laugh and cry. It hadn't happened very often, just twice in fact, but she remembered all too keenly the humiliation – the laughing voices and shouts of a crowd of children – when she'd been shoved and punched into some gap too small for most Beetle infants. The first time she'd wedged and become hopelessly stuck as she tried to escape. The laughter had only increased then and she'd spent more than an hour there until someone bothered to fetch help.

Her hand tightened. The second time she'd a few years older, still small for her age but old enough that her Art had come on. It hadn't saved her, Marigh had still ended up forced into a crevice that she'd had to crawl and slither out of, but she'd left one with a nasty pincer-wound in the process. They had thrown rocks at her until she escaped for that, then as punishment the magistrate had forced her hands bound for three months.

Punishment for defending myself. She wiped a finger delicately under her eye to sweep away the bead of sweat there. *The others got nothing, even the ones who threw rocks at my head.*

She shifted her position and let her feet dangle limply on the stone shaft slope. *And here I am again, how many more times I wonder?* She pictured Olric, his assurance and un-Wasp-like calm.

Maybe there'll be more jobs, maybe this is me from now on. I'll walk the Lowlands, living the high life as a master thief. Out there few will know my kinden or ever be able to work it out. I'll gather a crew of my own, men and woman like Olric who don't give a damn about your heritage – men and women like me who're blamed for what they are.

She sighed and sat back. Day dreaming was a wonderful thing, but she had her grandmother and nothing would separate her from her last remaining family.

Perhaps when she's gone, no – definitely then. There's nothing holding me here, not without her. There are more people like Olric out there, people who care more about what you can do than what you are.

She looked down at her hands and slid the pincers free of her forearms. Maybe six inches long and dull edged, each was simply a bony spur only a little darker than her skin, the point slightly turned inward. She knew men with the Art had longer, more curved pincers, but they were better-know for the tulwars they were taught to use almost from birth.

It was impossible to gauge how slowly the minutes and hours dragged past. Marigh tried to sleep, propped up and wedged so as not to fall, but every time her thoughts began to drift some instinct panicked and jerked her awake. After a long time her nerves got the better of her and she climbed almost to the mouth of the shaft. It would be a tricky climb back down, but she was more confident with the faint glimmer from the lamp. Once she was close to the top she stopped and waited, letting her breathing settle into a rhythm and her body find an equilibrium on the rough surface. She stayed that way for a long while, listening for sounds of outside, but when one came she almost let go of her perch in her surprise.

The steady tramp of feet echoed down over her, fading as the night watchman continued away. Marigh clung desperately on in an uncomfortable, shifted pose until she could hear no more and was sure any movement she made wouldn't be carried up. She worked her way back down and passed a long while on the alcove ledge – comforted by the glow of the lamp and contriving increasingly bold schemes that would be her future.

A notorious jewel thief, a spy – a feared assassin. The fantasies built and evolved as the minutes drifted by. She won and lost fortunes in those minutes, took Olric as her lover and cast him out in the next heartbeat –

was forced to kill him in some rooftop showdown as he threatened to expose her past. She became the power behind Collegium's Assembly, the trusted advisor of a feeble and aging Wasp Empress, and...

And she was always sitting in the shadows. One way or another she would squeeze into a dark crevice and haunt the unlit places. Marigh felt an ache in her gut as she realised her blood would always call to that, that her first instinct was to shy from the light of attention.

But it's what I am, she reminded herself, *and I'm too old to cry about that any longer. I am this, for all the good and the bad that comes with it.*

To take her mind off things she crawled back up again, listening out for the guard on his rounds to be reassured that all remained unnoticed. This time, after he'd passed, she moved further up – close enough that she was sure, if the sky was beginning to lighten, some measure of that would seep down into her little shaft.

There was nothing, however, so she worked her way down again, settled in and began to spend all the money she had earned – on fresh clothes and tools for herself, for treats for her grandmother. Her ambitions were more modest this time round. She knew the value of what she bought and did not dream too hard, did not forget the reserve for doctors she had promised herself. It passed the time as well as anything and for a long while she just stared at the alchemical lamp, wondering what forces inside it made it work and how long it would last.

If she left things too long and dawn crept up on her, would the lamp flicker and die? Would she be forced to clear up in utter darkness – risking arrest or injury as she fell from a tall frame? Those fears themselves occupied some time and she left it as long as she could before climbing back up again. She had heard no bell at any point, or rather she had heard it a dozen times in her imagination, so again she waited a long while for the guard to pass then worked her way up to see if dawn was approaching.

For a while Marigh was not sure and she crept right up to the shaft mouth, confident now in the navigation of her little sloped world, until she could see a sliver of sky beyond the wooden hood. Dawn had certainly not come, but she reasoned that the sky was a shade lighter than the dark edge of wood around it and that was enough for her. Back she climbed, forcing herself not to rush as she descended and gathered her things. She tucked the precious lamp inside the bag, held her breath and peeled back the sheets that blocked the lower part of the shaft.

There was a feeble gust of the disgusting smoke, but nothing so strong as she'd been expecting. After twisting her face up against the taste Marigh put it from her mind and went to clear the others. By the second room her head was swimming and she was forced covered her nose and mouth with a torn piece of sleeve to try and filter the worst from the air.

Whether it was that or the hardiness that all Beetles seemed to enjoy, she couldn't tell, but she struggled on through the caves and pulled down each cover – hoping against hope the guards would not smell the smoke as it escaped and come investigate. Soon she had a bundle of sticky linens and boots caked with soot after scattering the ashes of each little fire as best she could. She climbed back up into the shaft, turning at the lower ledge to use a strip of the remaining linens to try and glue the net back into place.

How well it worked she was unsure – less so how long it would last – but it was as good as she could manage so she headed back up. Encumbered by the bag, she waited again for the watchman – feeling a flush of relief when he passed by – and ascended far enough to see a definite brightening of the sky. She left the remains of one linen sheet to let the cut net settle on and stick to, then headed out across the gloom of the empty yard with her heart hammering in her chest.

She climbed the wall without incident and dropped down into the dark cemetery – half expecting to see Olric waiting for her, half ready for a blade in the dark. There was neither. She was alone and after a moment to check her surroundings, she exited the cemetery and trotted off through the stillness and stuttered birdsong of early dawn.

Back home however, she saw as soon as she turned into the little courtyard that something was out of place. The door was slightly ajar and her heart leaped into her throat, fearing the worst at last. Unable to do anything about it she got ready to unsheathe a pincer and crept inside. There, flanked on one side by a lamp and on the other by a tall bottle of wine, sat Olric, head cocked to one side as he watched her silently enter.

"Good morning, Marigh," he said, a faint smile on his lips. "Fun night?"

She coughed to cover a laugh but it turned into something more real. For a moment she could only restrain a full wracking cough as the taste of the smoke filled her mouth again.

"Might I suggest tepid water and lemon juice to scrub the flavour away? You might want to lose those tainted clothes too."

This time she was composed enough to raise an eyebrow and that prompted Olric to laugh – quietly still, so as not to wake her grandmother next door. Clearly he was a little drunk, but at the same time Marigh appreciated turning the tables a shade.

"I'll be scrubbed and changed by dawn, then an early trip to the baths I reckon, sweat the stink off."

"All went as planned?"

"Close enough. I wouldn't say it was fun, but it's done."

Olric pushed himself upright. "Will they notice?"

"Who knows?" Marigh said with a shrug. "I was as tidy as I could manage, looked enough to me but who can say in the dark?"

"Then I'll call it a job well done." He nodded to the clay bottle. "A drink to celebrate."

She was about to refuse then caught herself. *Just a moment in the light, that can't hurt now, can it?* "Go on then, a bath can wait a few minutes more."

He poured her a cup and handed it to her, raising his own in toast. "Here's to business by other means."

Marigh gave a snort at the affectation. "Here's to getting paid and not getting caught," she countered.

"Lacks a certain poetry, don't you think?"

"I can't eat poetry, can't drink it neither. What I can do is take my money and go back to my quiet little life, a bit more comfortable than it was yesterday."

Olric grunted. "Very sensible. Best not to draw attention to yourself."

"What about you?"

"Me?" That seemed to catch the man out and genuine surprise crossed his face. "Nothing changes for me, not yet. It's a long game I play, but the rewards will trickle in and one day they'll become a flood. Until then, I might even have a little more work for you if you're interested?"

She nodded. "Sounds better than what else you could be offering right now."

"A knife? A sting?" He cocked his head. "I'm not that sort of Wasp. I've spent enough time in foreign lands to lose most of that foolishness." He paused. "I know when I see worth with my own eyes."

Her heart swelled a little at the conviction with which he said that.

"Let's hope you can pay for all that worth then," she forced out in a slightly choked voice.

The comment seemed to diffuse the heaviness that had appeared in the air and he smiled. "It's more than likely you've made me a rich man tonight so have no fear there."

She nodded, suddenly feeling unaccountably shy as though this was the moment of quiet before her first kiss.

"Just tell me one thing," he said softly. "Indulge me? You don't have to, I'll not hold it against you, but I'm a well travelled man and I'm always keen to learn."

Marigh paused, seeing in his eyes what he meant – seeing too that it was still just curiosity about her kinden, nothing more. No Wasp superiority or Beetle prejudice, just a man interested enough to want to know. She took a breath, one that seemed to drag on so long she almost couldn't speak, but as she released it a few of her fears went with it.

Marigh told him – the first time ever she'd offered the information and it felt a wonderful release. Just for a moment.

But then she saw it, that flicker in his eyes – that twitch of the cheek she'd seen before. Not scorn or any other hateful emotion she'd faced most days of her life, but one even more hurtful. One that cut her to the bone, that drove the wind from her lungs and the strength from her limbs.

Just a flicker. Nothing more. Just a hint, but in a less-composed man one that might have become an involuntary bark of laughter. Dry-eyed but hands shaking, she turned away and as she did so her cup fell from her hand. It hit the floor and shattered, and with it her fractured heart was breaking.

Forwards

Joff Leader

"Is he still drawing, Hepsos?"

"Yes Domina. We did try taking his charcoal away. It... got messy, so we gave it back. And we give him sheets of paper now, to spare the walls any more abuse."

"Would any of it... work?"

"Some of the designs are coherent enough that they could probably be built, but that's not quite the same thing. I mean, there's the one, for example, which is supposed to heat the ocean – the whole ocean, mind – to a comfortable temperature for bathing. Me and the boys, we went over it, took us days, and we couldn't work out what nine tenths of it were even supposed to do, and the bits we could work out had nothing to do with heat or water. And of course, when we finally found the power source, it was a single hand crank again, same instructions..."

> Forwards
> Up
> Back
> and Down

FORWARDS:

When a Karinael set his mind to a thing, it got done. Seiris' family had not established one of the Spiderlands' broadest trading empires by accepting the popular wisdom regarding obstacles. So it was, then, that when Seiris woke one morning with an unbeatable plan to remove his cousin Rhialli's greatest advantage over him (her genius Bee kinden artificer, Hepsos), it was a foregone conclusion that it would come to pass exactly as he intended.

The glory of the plan was not in the killing of the wretched tinkerer, but in the method by which all suspicion for the murder would slide from

Seiris' head onto, well, any that he chose out of a vast range of possibilities. And this despite the fact that he would have the visceral pleasure of, reasonably publicly, landing the killing blow himself.

Skipping breakfast, he swept down the long, sunlit staircase from his rooms to the servants' huts in a flurry of gilded green silks and silky brown locks. Without warning or formality, he flung open the hatch to the apartment-workshop of Ovina, Martinis, and Gerrinus, prompting an eerily synchronised yelp of surprise from the little Ant Kinden collective he employed as engineering advisors.

"New project", he announced to the three startled, blue-white faces, atop bodies frozen at various stages of breakfast and ablution.

"Yes, Dominus?" Prompted Ovina, after a second or so of silence.

"Yes, Ovie. You're going to make me Apt!"

UP:

Gerrinus stood in the fencing circle, swathed in padded silk that bulked him up like a well-fed Beetle-kinden, clutching a practice sword and shuffling uncomfortably. He watched the Dominus swing his new sword experimentally, then turn to Ovina with a question in his arched eyebrow.

From her spot outside the circle, Ovina answered the unvoiced query.

"There are no records that we can find of an... of a person of magically inclined lineage becoming Apt, Dominus. However, the House is aware of two examples whose activities affected the last war, who were the other way around. A Wasp diplomat to the greypates joined in their rituals, although he appears to have been born with, shall we say, older blood. More excitingly, reports suggest that Empress Seda learned magic and forgot gears and levers and such as the conflict progressed."

Martinis took up the tale here.

"So we can look at her and see that aptitude is perhaps not as stark a state is it often appears, but possibly a gradient one can inch up or down with study, luck and," here he puffed out his chest, just a little, "excellent advice."

Seiris looked again at the pommel, well, really the whole hilt, of his unusual new practice blade. A squashed sphere of polished wood connected directly to the shockingly basic crossguard, and thence straight to the blade.

"The hilt is shaped just like a Collegium doorknob, Dominus."

Stammered Gerrinus, very conscious of the form the next hour or so of his life was going to take. "Once you've thoroughly retrained your hand and wrist to do that clever little twisting parry and riposte thing you do, but with that shape in your hand, we'll move on to a real door."

Seiris nodded.

"Well then, lay on!"

Seiris grinned.

Gerrinus closed his eyes, gritted his teeth, and raised his sword arm.

BACK:

They were on the ship bound for Collegium by the time the three increasingly concerned Ant Kinden engineers felt that their master was ready to attempt the crossbow.

"On the one hand," Seiris murmured as he hefted the unloaded weapon to his shoulder in the section of cargo hold that Gerrinus had outfitted as a practice range, "it's about bloody time. The Symposium Hepsos is speaking at is less than four days away, and we've been at this for weeks now. On the other hand, I don't feel any different. Any... Apter? How sure are we that this is working?"

Martinis grimaced and only barely managed to avoid sucking air noisily over his teeth.

"Well, Dominus. See, the thing is, we're a lot less sure than we were that we can actually radically alter the fundamental nature of your being in such a way as to grant you your actual Aptitude, as such."

Ovina stepped in smoothly as the three of them observed a dangerous tide of anger rising in Series' eyes.

"This is, of course, to your ultimate advantage, at least in the context of the plan."

"Oh?" Seiris' voice was rising in pitch and volume, though he still stood motionless with the crossbow held as if ready to loose. "Do explain how your failure to meet the objectives I set you is to my advantage?"

"Well, Dominus, it's as simple as this: were you to be revealed at some point in the future as an actual Apt person who could very well have shot the crossbow, the deception is revealed and suspicion for the assassination falls squarely back upon you. The thing is, right now, you have learned by rote how to open doors with knobs and handles instead of simple latches, and in the time we have you can learn by rote to load and shoot the bow, but you'll never be clocked as different by the rest of

Spiderlands society."

There was a pause. Two deep breaths, and Seiris brought his anger back under control.

"Fine." He said, flatly. "Just teach me how to kill with this thing."

DOWN:

And of course it had gone like... those clever Collegium contrivances with the little interlocking spikey wheels in that are ever so precise and effortless. Like those.

Obviously securing legitimate entry to the College for the Symposium once they had docked in the Beetle Kinden capital had required simply cash changing hands and no thought or effort at all. Martinis, Ovina, and Gerrinus had separately smuggled in the parts of the weapon and assembled it by candlelight in a servant's supply closet. They left it under a bundle of cleaning rags in a corridor of teaching rooms which had been kept clear on the day to maintain a buffer of quiet space between the ongoing business of education, and the large public lecture hall where the Apt genii of the world were presenting their grand theories and achievements.

Once that was done, so was their part in the venture and they went their separate ways into the gathering audience.

Seiris swept through the backrooms and corridors of the college with an ease that genuinely surprised him. Unlike during his practice runs on the ship, the doors were just opening as he turned the handles, not taking three or four attempts each time (although they had, of course, allowed for that).

He scooped up the bundle of rags that was exactly where he had anticipated it would be, shook them off the crossbow, slung it over his shoulder by the strap and hopped out of the window to scale the wall to the roof.

Above the centre of the grand lecture hall was a copper dome, and in the brickwork around the base of the dome, two dozen little glass windows. Working quickly and silently Seiris prised the correct window free, affording him a clear view of the stage from a position of perfect concealment. He reckoned he had an hour to wait at least. Hepsos was certainly not the final, keynote speaker, but nor was he on the crackpot fringe like those who were expected to give their presentations while the audience were still milling around, securing their drinks, and finding their seats.

He sat half listening to the enthusiastic chatter of the opening few presenters, as images illustrating their points were flung up onto the wall behind them by means of painted glass and bright-burning lamps, until at last his hated cousin's favoured pet sauntered out onto the boards.

Seiris lifted the crossbow and wound the gear as had been drilled into him every waking hour on the ship, all three of his servants telling him the same

"To shoot is easy, hold it as you have been, look all the way down the length of the bolt at the person you want to kill, and gently close your right hand." And he had mastered that, oh how he had mastered that. "The complicated bit is loading. Before you put the bolt in the groove, you have to wind the handle. Now, it goes in a circle, which is easy enough, circles are one of the few concepts the Apt and the Old Blood truly share, and it will give a nice obvious click when it's ready, but to remember the correct way to wind while you have the crossbow shouldered, just remember this sequence:"

Forwards
Up
Back
Down
Forwards
Up
Back
Down
Forwards
Up...

It mattered not that the bolt went wide, because in its path he saw the movement of the air and understood exactly what sharpness and speed actually were.

He was not overly concerned by the reaction of the crowd, as he saw them move almost as a single mass, he also perceived the secret of why dirigibles seemed to defy the pull of the ground below.

There was nothing to fear as the crossbow splintered under the strain of some inexplicable winding error, as his eyes reflexively closed he saw great confluences of lenses, lightning, and lodestones reshaping the world at the command of the wise.

He felt no pain as the burly Beetle guards roughly manhandled him down from the roof, and no fear or worry as the Beetle magistrate consigned him to the care of Rhialli, as his nearest kinswoman available. None of that was important, not in the face of the great expanse of gears and levers and pistons, flames and fumes and endless possibility that now stretched out before him, waiting for him to take that first step FORWARDS.

Recipes for Good Living

Justina Robson

It wasn't the fact that there was a Spider in Hamfist's office that caught her attention so much as the tone of voice. Obviously with a Spider you expected a certain quiet lilt suggestive of complicity and corruption, that went without saying, but this one had an edge of urgency to it that made Jerit swerve slightly in her course down the corridor and take a much slower stride or two, glancing in while pretending to be casually passing – well, the door was ajar. One might suppose they were planning to be overheard.

She saw almost nothing. Hamfist was a bulk behind his massive desk, hunched over a sea of papers and their attendant islands of mugs and discarded plates. A veil of smoke from his pipe hung beneath the low ceiling, giving the room a look of imminent precipitation. A slender, velvet cloaked figure with pale brown hair wound in fine gold chain was simultaneously crouching over the desk to get closer and bracing its arms on the desk for safety's sake. Its voice was female, dulcet but agitated as well in a most unprofessional manner. It was saying,

"... and marches upon the city of Kanaphes as I speak. I need someone capable of understanding this to act as a translator and analyst of the situation. Somebody, Hamfist, is moving towards this place in the dark and they are coming for the text."

... and she was out of range.

Damn it all! Hamfist was in on some scheme. Of all the people to be dealing with something illicit or ill advised, how could it be him – least adventurous Beetle of all the scholars in the Academy? But as the words sank in, repeating themselves in her mind as she took step after step away like a fool leaving an ember to burst into flames behind her, she felt not heat but cold creep across her flesh and make her take an unplanned turn into the lavatories.

She went inside and bolted the door, fingers lingering for a moment on the familiar curve of the latch, its solid iron and oak so sturdy. There was something very unsturdy about Jerit Goodmeet, Beetle scholar, right now that needed the strength of that door Who was marching on Kanaphes? Marching on meant armies, meant invasions. That kind of power could only mean one person – Seda, the Empress of the Wasps. One could not reasonably come to this place in Collegium and bandy these terms about freely unless one hoped for... but her imagination balked at what a Spider might hope for. In the room next door she heard the facilities flush. Flush out something, yes. They could come looking, seeding notions that would create a fuss and a scurry in which careless, frightened people would reveal things that were better hidden.

It's your guilt, talking, she chided herself silently, still holding the latch, her forehead pressed to the ancient wood that had been here even before Collegium: this door had been repurposed from a fine and fancy Moth mansion when her people were only servants and slaves. It had survived the revolt and found a new home in the Academy, guarding the modesty of female scholars about their ablutions. And now it was preserving her from giving away something to watchful eyes.

She thought of her family books for the first time in a long time and a pang of longing to rush out and make an excuse to go home struck her deeply in the gut. But that was exactly what she must not do. Was it even possible that the Spider knew anything or was it her own fears and worries doing all this by themselves? Like the door, the books were generations old, handed down lovingly from mother to daughter. They contained recipes and home tips on most pages, but with hidden secrets woven carefully here and there; the gift of a Moth mistress long since dust, who had bid her Beetleservants keep esoteric knowledge of value and return it, when the Moths and the family were restored to their rightful places.

There was no chance of that now. The Moths had retreated to their oldest cities, fading, the world's magic only enough for parlour tricks where once it had razed nations. And the forest. One did not forget Drakaryon easily, or ever. But since its destruction and in the absence of a return of the Moth-kinden the books had become of interest to Jerit only as academic artifacts – it wasn't the information they held but the way that information had been preserved which charmed and romanced her and set her to studying them late into the nights. She loved puzzles and there was no better puzzle than the family books.

Her ancestors had developed a code for hiding language within numbers; a little engine of faultless timing that would ensure that nobody in ignorance of it could read the things, even if they were prepared to wade through Grandma Aln's endless pot pie reworkings and Aunt Genua's ahead-of-their-time theories on child rearing. To further complicate matters a good many of the volumes were in fine needlepoint and the paper versions much illustrated and coloured over by enthusiastic but innocent Beetle children. Some parts would not survive the black crayon that Jerit herself had deployed. No amount of careful ironing between tissue sheets could leach out the determined fortitude of the colour. A monster crab had come from the depths and obliterated several significant footnotes and that was all there was to it. It wasn't the crab that had caught at Jerit's heart and rushed up to try and strangle her though, it was fear of what the books said.

If Seda was going to Kanaphes... No, no. Who cared? What could anyone among the Wasps possibly know about the books or what they might contain? Get a grip, Jerit, she told herself, your mother would be ashamed. A Beetle is the least fanciful and most practical of all the kinden, and, in that, superior. But she didn't feel superior. She felt sick. The Moth family that had kept the Goodmeets as house servants hadn't been killed in the uprising of the Beetles, merely 'returned' to more suitable places. It was unlikely a sorcerer would forget where they had left important things and the Moths were still reputed to live lengthily. Seda could only be going to Kanaphes for magical reasons of power-gain and Kanaphes was a home of the Moths and the only home of their much older, stranger Masters.

"Stuff and Nonsense!" she heard her mother say, resoundingly, in her head, where the woman had been forced to take up residence since she'd died fourteen years previously. "Those are only the tales, child, the tales and stories of old to scare little ones into bed and to stop them going where they shouldn't. Read Genua. She'll tell you."

Jerit had read Genua when the time came for her own children and knew it to be true. Those Old Master stories were great for that, although she'd put her own spin on them because she didn't want them to be complicit in even the most innocent way with the truths in the tales. As a scholar and not a mother she'd decoded them for herself when the time came, to prove that she was a capable keeper of the knowledge. This effort and its success had taken away all the romance from the project in one immediate swoop. Whereas before the guardianship of the information had been terribly charming and daring, a secret thrill, now it was a burdensome worry that gnawed at her in the stretches of the early morning, when creeping age decided it was a good idea to wake at 3am and do all the horrible, terrifying contemplating of the future that she had completely ignored for the last fifty or so years.

Of course it wasn't true that there had once been a Kinden of the Worm who had stolen and remade children in their own image within cauldrons of magic deep in the earth. Poppycock. Ridiculous.

And yet, as part of the Inapt, of course neither Jerit nor any of her most clever and learned foremothers had been able to read or understand the bulk of the spells and cantrips that the Moth had chosen to leave with them. She could not and would never know what they said. She could only read the historical bits. Where the stories went off into convoluted metaphors that were the traditional Moth way of communicating their idiosyncratic alchemies she could not translate that into actions. It was a code within a code, but one she could never read. Which was another reason that the stuff hadn't been on her mind so much, not, compared to say, the heating problem now that her boiler had broken down and the engineer to fix it was always busy elsewhere – there was always a call on his time to do this and that and winter was a coming on, as Auntie Aud would have said. "Bide thee only after the house is secured against famine, pest and the cold." Bloody Aunts. How right they were, but their advice on workmen ended in the firm insistence that workmen be visited and, if necessary, dragged to the task by the ear, in a manner which Jerit would never get away with now that so many inventions and developments required their time. Probably in the old days workmen had long ears from all the dragging. Now they were as small as her own. She had lain awake only that morning wondering if a family sized fruit pie and a jeroboam of ale might sweeten the deal. Ears out, stomachs in, so to speak.

The mind did jabber, when it was on the run, Jerit thought, and firmly and quietly shut it down. It could have its go later on. For now she had spent a suspicious amount of time in here and that wouldn't do.

She washed up, folded and hung the towel, checked herself in the mirror – a sturdy, greying woman in scholar's robes, a bit dishevelled by hair raking in the course of a morning of tough mental labour. Yes, that would do. Slightly mad, but you were expected to be by now. Lipstick would have gone some way to saving things but why bother? She opened the door and gasped, startled to the point of heart failure by the Spider-kinden woman waiting outside, tapping her toe on the flags and twitching a bit as she moved from foot to foot.

"Hurry up!" With a twist and a flip of her hair the tall creature whisked past and into the privy, the door closing behind her with a forceful slam and click.

Jerit stood a moment, a scent of jasmine eddying around her that said some people took pride in their presentation and it was actually rather nice. She put a hand to her face to see if guilt was actually oozing out of it like a snap sweat. Seemed not.

She went to the dining hall and got herself something to eat, made herself sit and eat it where she always sat, remembering a treatise on spying she'd read recently, from the pen of a Spider general, no less, which advised anyone with business afoot to assiduously make sure to rid themselves of every kind of habit or pattern. For the sake of something to distract herself she sifted among the handful of flyers left on the boards by various interest groups, societies and student bodies. One, a brilliant orange, caught her eye.

"Tonight and for two nights only the immaculate, infinite, amazing Circus of the Fireflies hosts a variety of plays, musicals and culinary delights. The Fairgrounds of the Long River, from dusk till dawn!"

Jerit hadn't been to or heard of the Circus since she was a child, well, a teenager. She'd never thought to see it again but now that the war was done it seemed they felt it safe to return. Her heart leaped a little in remembered happiness and hope. The Circus, come again to Collegium! But relegated now to the Long River fields, outside the city walls. Probably they were not trusted enough now to be let inside, bringing whoever could pass as an actor along with them. Any assassin could juggle, and any spy be on hand to pass out flyers...

A child with burning flame red hair went rushing past between the trestles. Ribbons ran from her wrists and her bonnet. Squealing, she was chased by a boy in yellow and blue, sparkling dust in his wake that lit the air as the groups of lunching professors and students bustled in a sudden grumble and complaint. A moment later they were left silenced and speechless by the glittering powder and the sound of distant laughter that must, but could not be, magic in the children's wake. More flyers rained down, and free tickets to this and that, and they were gone.

155

Jerit watched a falling ticket and stretched out her foot, putting her shoe on it and dragging it to her, hiding her smile as she bent to pick it up. Spies indeed. You should be ashamed of yourself Jerit Goodmeet. It's the fair. Songs and good times. And handsome young men in colourful suits, leaping like acrobats and breathing fire like dragons and showing off curiosities and monsters. They had had a gigantic scorpion that followed a woman around like a pet though it was as big as a barn. Its carapace was painted like a sunset sky and it had obligingly lifted the roast carcasses from the fire pits with its pincers, a tiny chef hat balanced between its shining eyes.

Some things were just worth seeing. She folded the ticket and slipped it in her shoulderbag. It would be a perfect way to get out of the house, a good reason definitely not to be in. As she let the ticket go her fingers brushed a brief accordion of folded pages. They were soft with handling now, the letters. She'd had them so long. She pushed them down, although they were already at the bottom, and looked up to find herself face to face with her friend, Bren, the archivist, who had just landed by her plate.

Bren was Fly-kinden and chose to sit on the table rather than on a bench and have to peer over the top like a child. She liked floral dresses and leather boots that laced up and straw hats. She wore yellow like it was going out of fashion and looked concerned as she peered out from all her happy fripperies. "Are you all right, Jerry?"

"No, not really," Jerit said. "But the fair's in town. You'll come with me, won't you?"

"Wouldn't miss it!" Bren said, excited. She sipped her tea, the steam rising and making her curled hair slowly straighten out beneath the hat brim. "And then you can tell me what's bothering you."

"I will," Jerit said, pushing the last bit of bread around her plate and then away from her. She felt ill, nothing digesting. "Just wish I didn't have to go through the afternoon."

"You work too hard," Bren said. "Nobody will notice if you go early."

"Well, they might," Jerit replied and smiled. "So I think I'll try to finish up that presentation on the early history of the Dragonflies."

"You always did have an eye for them," Bren said. "Handsome men, dashing women, and the intrigue and the dynasty!"

"It's not a romance novel, Bren," Jerit said with a haughty air. "It's history."

"Of course it is," Bren winked. "Should I invite Celador?"

"Sure, why not? It's not a party if he's not coming." Jerit got up and made a few deliberate, getting-out-of-here movements with her bag.

"See you at dusk then, by the river."

"See you there."

But back in her office, no signs of any Spiders around, Jerit didn't touch the Dragonfly paper. Instead she hauled the steps out and poked around in the dusty upper shelves of her personal library until she had dug out the sparse volume on Ancient History of the Inapt by P. Purslane. She carried it to the creaky leather sofa by her leaded window and opened it in the low light of the afternoon sun. P. Purslane had been a Beetle of note in his day and had written exclusively and rather feverishly on the very dimmest of distant pasts for which there was any trace data. He was not above rifling bins, taking anecdotal references from drunks at out of town inns and reminiscing with old soldiers and thieves alike, for which Jerit liked him enormously. There was little P. Purslane wouldn't do to get his hands on a tablet or rune and nobody he wouldn't pester for stories but, even so, after a lifetime of travel and work under life-threatening conditions, all he had to show for it by the end was this skinny little book. Perversely, considering the contents and how they had been come by, he had given it an incredibly boring title. Jerit liked to imagine that this was a deliberate test to put off all but those who really, really wanted to know about history.

Of course he was massively discredited now, a figure of gentle mockery in the corridors of academe. The man wrote about the Worm, for goodness' sake, with the conviction and authority of someone dealing in firm facts rather than a feverish interpretation of some alleged cave paintings and the ramblings of drugged shamen.

It was to these pages that Jerit turned, ignoring an impulse to dart a glance out the window and into the corners of the room to make sure she was not overlooked. She had every intention of convincing herself that there was connection between the Moths mentioned here and the Moths which had been unhappily related to her own family but instead, as page after page turned by themselves, she found herself embroiled in a convoluted mystery world which referred to magics of unimaginable power as if they were accepted, everyday things. The world was smaller, wilder, a far more unfair place than Collegium, steeped in the primordial brutishness of master and slave with her people cast in the latter role, largely unseen.

This was a book she'd last read as a teenager, about the time she'd gone to the Circus and fallen hopelessly, stupidly in love with a carnie of all people. Although in retrospect perhaps not such a bad choice. Absence on his part and a surfeit of imagination on hers had rendered him impossibly perfect and impermeable to change. Also impermeable to criticism, failure or any other influence. He was the best boyfriend ever, especially once the fair had left town. Jerit had kept him on, in mind only, for those occasions that she felt the need of such company. He'd preoccupied the attachment slot of her life all through her education and her slow progress to one of the few seats in History that the Beetles had bothered with in the Academy. He'd been sympathetic and helpful with her determination to pursue stories through thick, thin and academic disapproval. He'd slid gracefully aside once she met her husband, the much more embodied Atwud Castright. Now, smelling the old paper and turning the loved pages, Jerit felt his presence again, faint as a ghost.

She wondered if he would be there, setting up the tents, juggling the fire batons. It was stupid to think so and ridiculous not to assume that he was greyer, wider and far less interesting than she'd thought. She had a way of adding to a person in her mind and knew it. But the notion made some dry old kindling in her heart catch light. Fine, she'd go and see. She'd...

There was a sharp rap at the door and without waiting for a reply the door itself opened and there stood the Spider woman, green cloak swirling, hair afire with subtle gold.

"I.." began Jerit, not sure what she was going to say but that didn't matter because the Spider woman had enough to say for two and began it without a pause as she leaned theatrically upon the door she had closed behind her.

"Not a word, Doctor Goodmeet! I already know who you are. I am Myenrath Dawn. I understand from Doctor Hamfist that you are the one to turn to if one has questions about antiquities."

Jerit folded her hands protectively over P. Purslane as a lot of thoughts went through her head. "I don't know anything about antiquities, you must have got the wrong end of the stick. I'm a historian." She made no move to get up. Once the sanctity of the office was breached, trying to position a defence at the desk seemed a bit of a pathetically late showing. She studied Dawn's person acutely. The velvet and gold had a certain tattiness in a good light, reminiscent of an actor's garb.

"I regret the intrusion and the extreme manner of my behaviour," the Spider said, although there was a tinge of pleasure in it. "It is most unseemly but time is running out. There is someone ahead of me in coming to Collegium who has instructions to spare no effort in discovering the whereabouts of antiquities that are rumoured to be here. It is vital that said items do not fall into the wrong hands."

Jerit looked at her earnest face and smelled a rat. "You're no Spider."

With a surprising speed and completeness the poise of Myenrath Dawn collapsed on the instant and instead of the elegant aristoi Jerit saw clearly now the physique of someone who was a halfbreed with one half obviously being Wasp. It must have taken some skill and much dieting to get this gawky woman to be so adept at pretending but once she dropped the act the contrast was astounding.

"Shit," the mystery woman said and dropped into the student chair which faced Jerit's desk. "You're the first one to notice." She eased her neck and flopped into a lassitude so profound that she looked like a ragdoll draped on the wood. Resting her head on the back of the seat she allowed it to flop in Jerit's direction. "Anyway. The point remains the same. Have you had any approaches before me?"

"No," Jerit said, cautious. "Should I have?"

"No. Good. But Hamfist was confident you were the person in all Collegium who would know about ancient objects, rituals, stories, whatever. He said 'She's the only one who bothers with all that blasted useless hearsay'."

"That does sound like him, but, Miss Whoever You Are Really, the point remains that the only artifacts of antiquity you will find in Collegium are at the Museum under glass or in the locked archives and most of that is fairly boring arrowheads and broken vases and the like."

"Not after that. After things with power in them. Inapt things. Writings maybe. Did they have books in those days?"

"Scrolls, a few. Tablets. The majority of things were committed to memory if they were truly useful, people weren't in the habit of leaving stuff around where anyone could get it. An Inapt's power was their person and the Apt rarely had need of writing to transmit their arts." Jerit used the time she spent talking to study the half Wasp more acutely. There was something so flashy about her, a mercurial quality, an energy and also a brutish straightforwardness that no spy would use. "Who are you asking for? Who is ahead of you?"

"Wasps, innit?" The guest looked around in the manner of someone hoping for something worth stealing or at least picking up and in that moment of assessment Jerit made her analysis.

"You're a thief."

"D'oh. Actually, Doctor, I am a bounty hunter and I am late, late, late!" With a swift jerk of her body Dawn was upright, boots slammed to the floor, shoulders jerked back. "I can offer my services in return for information."

"What services?" Jerit said, bewildered by the speed with which events were pivoting about.

Dawn looked insulted, "Finding. A historian must need some things found out and stuff, right?"

"I'm not into stealing antiquities. My interest in history is entirely from a legitimate standpoint of investigation..."

Dawn tilted her head and broke in, "Seda's going into Kanaphes. Everyone knows she's doolally Inapt now and listening to the secret chatter of the ancient ones or whatever. I'm telling you. She's sent her scouts here on the words of some Moth trying to ingratiate itself into her financial and whatnot good graces. They claim that they left important material in the city generations ago which would be of definite interest to her ladyship. Is that enough payment for you yet?"

Jerit stared at her with her jaw hinged half open, incredulous. "Do you never watch your words or your volume?"

"Subterfuge is not my strong suit," Dawn said. "But I figured if there was such a thing then you might have heard of it because you like old stories. So I'm just asking. No harm in asking. I've asked ten Beetles if I've asked one and they all think I'm full of rubbish. I couldn't get them to believe me so I figured that I'd be a Spider aristo from one of the lesser families who was worming her way up the slippery web... what?"

"You said worming. You can't worm up a web."

Dawn rolled her eyes. She held up her hand and the soft intimation of a Sting glowed briefly in her palm. "I could zap every last one of you pedants. Look, I had a cover that made sense. Spiders are worried about Seda but good, and I don't need people knowing who I am. What am I even talking to you for? Do you have any idea what Kanaphes is about?"

"Yes, I do. I think that there must be some residual magic or knowledge thereabouts and Seda is merely going to find out what that is."

"There's Inapt chatter of a bigger picture."

"Do you have any sources for your statements or are you simply fishing, dear?" Jerit tried a motherly tone, matronising, to see if it had any effect.

"I hear things."

"At wayside Inns, perhaps? In taverns, brothels, barracks, places where people love to make a tall tale the tallest in the land?"

"Look, lady – doctor – I hear things often enough that they make for a tickover, a notch upwards on the way towards something real behind all the chitchat. I know that's not how you proper people work but I've found... never mind. I followed the guy here but I lost him soon as we reached the city. Wasp spy. Sure of it. Psactim told me and he's a Mantis merc. Knows all the big faces, names, who does what. Worked for most everyone. He said it's Seda's man. But if I can beat him to it and bring in whatever it is then..."

"Then you'll be dead," Jerit said, feeling herself looking at the strange spirit child of the unusually investigative P. Purslane and knowing that she was stitching herself up into something much bigger and more dangerous than she was prepared to deal with. "Are you listening to yourself?"

"The Spiders sure would pay well for it."

"Suppose it's all a lie? The man is here for something else. After all, nobody has shown up asking for ancient histories but you."

"Mantis, lady! Mantis. Them guys don't mess about. It's real. Look. I'll be at the fair later tonight. Meet me when they do the bug roasts and everyone's drunk. At the cherry ale stand. If you know anything, if you've got anything." She adjusted her emerald velvet cape and for an instant the last of the afternoon sunlight shone off the hilt and scabbard of a very impressive dagger which changed Jerit's mind once again about the woman. It was no toy. With a soft sigh the Spider-kinden resumed her place, entirely in character, all elegance, grace and poise. A haughty disdain lengthened and gave authority to her face. There was a subtlety that gave the lie to her earlier statement of ineptitude.

Moth, perhaps, Jerit thought with a shudder. Or something like Moth. "Right. Roast time. Cherry ale stand. Oh wait. What's in it for me again?"

"You tell me," the Spider arched one beautiful brow and gazed down her narrow nose with a flash of guile that said she knew, she knew it all and was only waiting for bumbling Jerit to give herself away in some gawkish blunder once trouble came calling. Dawn could wait and wait.

The thrall of that gaze was such that Jerit was still sitting there dumbstruck and alone when the sun went down and she found herself in the cool darkness of early evening, clutching Purslane, her finger jammed into the pages on Kanaphes where he recounted the glory days of the Moth-kinden and their secret masters talking, talking from the darkness far beneath the earth. There was something like that in one of the recipe books too but Gramma Bolst had rested a freshly baked pie on it and burned out some of the story with a ring of carbonized berry filling.

It wasn't the stories on her mind now though. It was the code. Her books contained the secrets of the old masters and could usher them back in the wrong hands of the right Wasp Queen. This thought would not be still. It would not.

She glanced at the clock, feeling a chill, and got up, time to go home making her move with purpose and speed, not fear, no, not that. She closed and locked her door, hesitated, looked at Hamfist's door but it was closed and given the hour he was likely already heading towards the Professor's Lounge for early drinks and talks with colleagues. Jerit felt a longing to go that way which had never before seized her, thinking of the warm light, the comforting, tedious chat. Instead she folded her cloak closed and went out into the frisky wind, making her way on her usual path, saying goodnight to the porters, always planning to take the circuitous route while her feet trod swiftly and surely on the direct way to her home. She felt a sense of unreality and found Sizer Darten at her side, hurrying with her, his face anxious.

Sizer was a ghost. She saw him only when she was afraid that death was near, or if it was after midnight. He was real. At least, she was pretty sure he was.

"What's up, Sizer?" She sounded so gaily light of humour, it was a dead giveaway.

"Worried about you," Sizer said, striding with a much slower lope, his gangling figure cutting the wind like a knife, untouched by its bluster and threat. His wrinkles had wrinkles, she noted, face working itself in and out of concern, in and out of speculation. "Does anyone know where you are?"

"What's your point?" She realised the answer was no. It wasn't surely possible that she was the one member of the family that time had come to call on. She knew that. Nobody needed to know where she was or should be. She was a Beetle in her home city and the war was over. It was over. Her hand jammed in her bag gripped the letters, pushing them down, her other hand held her cloak close around her face. Sizer's librarian's acuity was a kind of searchlight going through her soul, watching for anything out of place.

"My point, dear lady, is that you are thinking one thing and doing another. Might I suggest that you at least make a contact with someone before you go..." But he was too late. Jerit was on the street, a few houses away, and she could see a darker line around her door that said it was unlocked, ajar, not enough to look open but not closed as she'd left it.

"Don't go in alone!" Sizer protested, sensibly enough.

"I'm not alone. I've got you," she said and pushed the worn wood aside. There was no sign of force. The lock was undone.

Jerit knew that she had an advantage in the dimness of the twilit interior. She told herself that as she dithered and wondered if she could call a neighbour, if she should. But Ver Ketch had children on the left and Upsisan on the right was away. She went inside, leaving the door wide, followed by a silently anguished Sizer, wondering why she'd never bothered to make a will yet and feeling irritated by that at the same time that she was glad her own children were safely grown and gone.

Her moment of pleasure was brought up short as her eyes adjusted to the darkness. A cold, slippery feeling oozed over her, making her wish she could escape though that was foolish because clearly it was too late. Everything was ransacked. From the coat rack to the closet the hall was littered. The drawers of the sideboard hung murdered at odd angles, ravaged, their contents spilling over the sides, scattered on the floor. She had to step over things. Her foot skidded suddenly with a scrape as she trod on loose keys and dragged them across the worn stone. She froze, heart in her throat, but no sounds from deeper in the house came to warn her of a waiting slayer. From beyond the door footsteps and the trundle of a cart came noisily to tell her that nobody knew or cared.

"Crikey," said Sizer, the silly word in a small tone, so like him to try to deflect with humour. She was grateful but she couldn't speak.

After minutes she moved again, determined to see. It was her fault this had happened and she must witness what had been done to her home – which felt like it had been done indirectly to her – making her clutch her cloak close to herself as though she had to hold everything in.

Each room was the same. There was nothing that had not been examined in detail and thrown aside as worthless. Every piece of upholstery was sliced open, wadding bulging out from its wounds. Floorboards had been levered aside where their mismatch made it seem there could be a hiding place. A hole was bashed in the living room ceiling where the plaster had been cracked for decades around a loosening panel.

Sizer went with her, crane-stepping over the guts of her life. He was silent of course, being entirely insubstantial, and she tried to be so, in case the spirit of the dead place rose in anger. She must get it to rise only when things were straight. *If* they were straight again. Because it pulled at her with the force of a lodestone she left the kitchen for last. Stubborn Beetle refusal to be pulled it was, and a need not to discover her complete failure in protecting the legacy.

She planned to be thorough, to be calm, but instead she moved straight to the worktop under the low window. The legs and feet of those hurrying home moved past in a constant flicker and their alternating light and shadow fell on the untouched row of blown glass grain jars and the neat backs of the six books that they held up against the wall. The slim books and their brightly coloured, obviously home-made cloth covers were untouched.

When she saw them she felt herself grow taller and a breath went into her lungs that lifted her up into that extra height. Wasps. Send a man and he thinks nothing like this is worth anything, she thought, proudly, and reached out to recover them.

"I thought so," said a smug male voice from the shadows behind the pantry door.

"No!" Jerit said, though it came out as a squeak. She cringed, the books clutched to her chest. She was trying to back away. His silhouette filled the doorframe only a few feet away, growing every second. Then she felt something bump against her ankle as she stepped. It put her off balance so that she had to grab for the counter to stop herself going over. The books went tumbling away from her as she felt a desperate terror. Against the black outline of the intruder's raised hand a bright spark was forming. She had nothing in reach to use as a shield or weapon, nothing to put between them.

A sudden whine and a stinging sensation in the tip of her ear made her cringe, though as she fell clumsily against the sideboard she thought it had come from behind, not in front, there had been no flash. Then from her seat among the cabbages and the remains of the breadbin she saw the silhouetted Wasp fold up and became a heap. Her ear burned like a fire as she looked around wildly and saw the tall, statuesque shape of a hooded Spider woman standing just outside the kitchen in the hall, her arm raised, tiny crossbow in hand.

"Hah!" said a familiar voice, with much too much vigour for any Spider. "Take that, you smug bastard."

"Dawn?" Jerit turned around on her hands and knees. Staying close to the flags seemed the best bet at that moment. Safe. She found a book under one palm.

"Tis I!" the hand with the crossbow made a kind of flourish but both it and the voice were shakier than they had been a moment ago. She came forward into the grisly twilight of the kitchen and stepped around Jerit to take a poke at the body. It did not react. "He's dead," she said, almost to convince herself, Jerit thought, and figured that killing wasn't something Dawn did often, at least not so far.

Moving slowly, as if to not spook a monster, Jerit began to gather the books up and slip them into her satchel. She glimpsed Sizer, silent, hovering in the far corner, unnoticeable. *Really?* she thought at him. *No quips to make?* But he didn't speak. As she began to get up, using the counter for aid, Dawn made a quick rifle of the spy's person. Her cloak must have been lined with a million pockets for he was stripped in seconds and she upright, apparently none the wealthier. Jerit wasn't fooled. At least two daggers and other sundries had gone. A ring too, she thought, though she wasn't sure about that last one.

"We have to call the guard," Jerit said, horrified to find that she was panting and heaving, sweaty and unable to get her head to stop spinning, never mind the damned ear.

"Not yet," Dawn corrected her. "Are you all right?"

Jerit took a step back as she advanced, the satchel like a hot lead sack against her leg. She tried to look formidably put together but she didn't fancy her chances against Dawn. "Just stand still, you, you thief!"

Such gibberish! Shameful, but it was out before she had a chance to engage her brain.

"It's all right," Dawn said, as though soothing a bullock in the cart traces to prevent a bolt. "Why don't I just get you a glass of water?"

And put something in it, Jerit thought, "No. No."

But she was already in the fourth cupboard. "A brandy then. D'you have some? I need one."

"Last on the right," Jerit said, clutching the counter and the bag simultaneously, wondering how she was going to go on from here. She waited and gave out instruction as Dawn located mugs and liquor and poured them generous shots. After a few swallows Jerit went to light a lamp and then wished she hadn't. In the soft gleam of the mirrored flame everything looked so much worse than she had imagined. And there was a dead man pooling blood in the pantry door. His leg was askew almost comically. Instinctively she wanted to right it because it must hurt terribly and that it would never hurt terribly seemed a much worse thing again. She felt out of her depth and longed to be somewhere else.

"Rum punch, innit?" Sizer said from his corner and she said wearily, "Oh, shut up, you idiot."

"Who are you talking to?" Dawn said, glass in midair halfway to her mouth, eyes surprised.

Jerit turned to her, trying to think of an explanation. "Nobody."

Dawn gave her a long look.

"I've lived alone a long time. I talk to myself," Jerit snapped, swigging the last of her drink before thinking that was not a good idea and then slamming the mug down with a bang. "And what are you going to do about it? Have you come to get him and then take my books?"

Dawn took a drink and pointed at Jerit with one gloved finger, "You make a really terrible guardian. Led us right to it."

"That's because I'm an historian," Jerit said. "But even so we haven't got all day. Come on, what're you waiting for?"

"I'm not sure," Dawn said, less Wasp and Spider than ever. What in the world could she really be? "But I've been thinking that if those books have something in them that Seda wants and the Spiders want or anyone wants very badly then maybe they shouldn't have it."

Jerit rolled her eyes. The feeling in her legs had returned now. "You're a crap bounty hunter, then," she said.

"That has been noted before," Dawn nodded thoughtfully and put her drink down half finished. She looked at the dead Wasp and a sudden laugh came out of her, all strangely buoyant and light. "I'm a good shot, though. But before I make my mind up I thought it best if you read them to me."

Yes, Jerit thought, *foolish to consider the other option, that I not give them to you no matter what and you have to shoot me too. I suppose I might. I might not. I can't. Oh, damn. But reading them at least provides time and with that opportunity, for something to happen which might turn things for the better. I don't know what you are. Maybe I can figure it out.*

"Very well," Jerit said aloud. "Find us some chairs and let's take them to the table."

As the wind died down and the night drew dark Jerit showed Dawn the stories, the coded spells, the symbols. She spoke about the ancient beliefs that someone reading this could easily be fooled into thinking true. Somewhere in there they drank another glass each and Jerit's love for the tales came up and led her into animated conversation with the younger woman, late into the night, until she came to her senses and realised she had said too much to go back, too much to go forward. She was an old fool, lost in her memories, stories and dreams. And all the while the dead man lay obediently in the door, waiting for someone to summon the guard. Inexplicably late it would be now.

"Oh dear," Jerit said, to herself, and to Sizer and Dawn. "We're done for."

"Nope," Dawn said. She was like someone who had been out late, a glamorous woman at the end of an evening of fine dining, inhabited by the spirit of a naughty urchin. "Toss the glasses..." She illustrated her meaning by throwing hers to the flags where it broke. She pushed the decanter after it as she got up. Grandma Ynes' decanter, with the bubbles caught in the glass that made it look like water. "We're going to the fair."

Jerit looked at the broken jug which she had prized all her life. Shards everywhere and the suddenly nauseating stink of strong alcohol. Yes. Why not? The fair. It was a perfectly reasonable move to complete an insane afternoon. She had loved her home so much but now only the bag and its contents were of importance. Bafflement at this rooted her to the spot. It had meant everything, this place. Now it didn't exist.

"Dr Goodmeet," Dawn said crisply. "Come on."

Before dawn-the-real-thing comes and claims you for its real, consequential self, Jerit thought. "I'm ready," she got to her feet, found them stable, and followed the Spider's regal sashay out of the door, pausing to close it behind her and then to lock it. She didn't want anyone, especially any children, finding their way in and coming to harm.

The night of Collegium was a thing of deep darknesses punctuated by the soft lights cast out of its windows and from the major streets where lamps burned and guards patrolled in the relaxed way of people who didn't have a lot to do. They were hardly the only figures moving about although they drew a bit of attention thanks to Dawn's height and bearing contrasted with Jerit's obvious Beetleness and greater age. But many had gone to the fair and there was a lot of to-ing and fro-ing between the fields outside the gates and the city within. They showed their tickets and passed the ropes largely unnoticed and were soon lost in the throng. Jerit shadowed Dawn, partly out of numbness and shock, partly because Dawn had momentum and seemed to know where she was going. She cut a swathe directly to a set of caravans in a ring around an area of small bonfires awhere tables were set. With a wave of her hand she bought them a sickly sweet and powerful cocktail in a chipped container the size of a small bucket. Those who had already partaken were slumped and carousing everywhere. Jerit sipped and winced and followed Dawn's billowing cape meekly, trying to see her schoolgirl visions in the tattered drapes and vivid tents. She felt as she had the first time she'd come to the fair: awed, frightened, small and out of place. It was not a time for that. She made herself come to a halt.

"Where are we going?"

"Come, there's a play you must see!" was the unexpected answer.

A play, at a time like this? But then Jerit felt that time was shorter than she knew. In fact it had all but come to a halt. So why not a play? She let Dawn drag her into a show tent and sit on raised planks a few feet from a tiny stage where actors and actresses were already well into their performance. She recognised it as a version of A Mage Out of Time where a powerful Moth magus plotted to discover the powers of the older worlds. His adventures were rendered comical and foolish for the entertainment of the crowds as he was led to ridiculous conjurations at the whims of a clever woman. Soon, as they were late to the story, he would run out of money and then out of magic, all siphoned to his mistress' grasp. Jerit wondered, starting to feel sick, what the point was. She let her cup of liquid spill at her feet without Dawn noticing and then started to look for exits when the actress playing the mistress gasped –

"Here, in this ring, this trinket, my darling. Infuse your desires upon its form for it contains the most powerful magic of all, the circle of infinite return, whereupon even the dead may walk again. Behold, the Clutch of the World Worm!" And she brandished a very large and flashy copper curio.

Dawn stuck an elbow in Jerit's side just in case it was going to be lost on her. "See?"

Jerit held the satchel closely on her lap as if it were a baby she was nursing. She didn't see what Dawn was getting at exactly but she'd begun to feel a terrible tiredness and a cold. Perhaps it was the hour and the shock. She suddenly didn't know what to do. As the mage poured his power into the empty copper ring onstage she felt as though all her power was draining away.

"Why did you bring me here?" she hissed, clutching the satchel, thinking at the same time that this bag was all she had left of everything, and then castigating herself because that was rubbish. It felt true though. And there was a dead Wasp spy in her pantry and she wouldn't be explaining that away without some very quick thinking. She would have left right then and there but the trouble was that everywhere she looked she could see Sizer. There he was, in the seats, behind the stage set, in the darkness of the wings, behind the bun vendor standing in the aisle, his lined, caring face with its large eyes insisting that she stick put. She trusted him, even if she didn't trust anyone else. She stuck put.

"It's all here in this play, right out in the open because nobody believes it. That's what made me pick up with it in the first place. The circus was down near Kanaphes and a cadre of Wasp men came, from the army, and were watching the play and asking a lot of questions. They only wanted the stories, every little detail, but only this play, not the rest," Dawn was saying as if puzzled that Jerit didn't see it. "That's why I think – there's something in what you have there, Doctor Goodmeet. And if you've had it all this time then you should decide what to do with it and not them. You have it for a reason."

My family history, all my past, my love, my books, thought Jerit. My job. Is it all over? What even is this secret we've held and not known? A reason. Yes, there's a reason. A Moth mage hid it with us because they knew none of their kin would look here. And they never did. And all my family kept themselves in danger all the time because of – I don't even know, a sense of being special and chosen, of being singled out by the Masters as worthy. Idiocy, but really such a good, good story. Did Aunt Fea and Gran Aud ever really think someone would come and be willing to kill them for it? How could they believe that and keep it? But how could they not keep it, because that Moth could still be alive somewhere with its many stolen years and as long as it knew then there was always this chance for someone to come calling and ask for their magic back. Which is why the code existed. We had it, but we didn't have it. We were no danger to it. And the only weakness in the whole plan was that Jerit knew the code. Now Wasps knew that there was more to the Kanaphes story, and that there was somebody with a written treasure, likely some clever Beetle who would enjoy the revival of the old stories and come to see it at the Circus and be sitting like a mutton-head in the audience with a spy because a ghost told them to.

Seda was coming.

The leather of the bag creaked in Jerit's fingers as she watched the end of the play with a compulsive force of attention she'd never used before, searching anywhere for a shred of hope.

The mage fainted as his power was siphoned off into the Clutch. The scheming woman who had crafted it, and lied about its provenance purely to deceive him into giving himself away, picked up the World Worm and clasped it about her wrist. "For all men are fools," she turned to the audience to declaim. "For power they will hand over their life as easily as asking. And fools they are to be deceived when the deceiver is the master true. Now when he wakes he's time to rue. The jest of the infinite was ever thus. To live but once, and briefly, and not come again. But I shall, with his life, last out the longer day. I take twice what I should owe – and never pay."

There was a moment of silence and then thunderous applause from all sides.

And was this the play the Wasps had seen? They must be thinking of the life, the magic, the transfer of one to another. And was that in the Code? Was this the trick hidden in the recipes? Ironic really. If one were writing an essay one could point up that food is life, so it was an apt place to conceal the eating of souls. Even if it wasn't, that was likely what Seda believed or was willing to take a risk on. Even if it turned out only to be the magic that could raise bread and brew beer. Eternal resurrection was worth the risk of a few dead Beetles.

Applause and cheering drowned Jerit. She watched the mage get up and take off his hat and mask. Beside her, Dawn was clapping and whistling, bouncing off the seat. She caught the eye of the male actor onstage and they nodded to each other with a grin. Jerit's heart stood still, startled out of time by the shock of those features. Was it, could it be HIM? She must be having a turn but it looked like him, that carnie from years gone by, the same jaw the same nose the same glint of eye and curl of lip. That hair, just so.

In the same moment that she saw the resemblance and reeled with it she realised with a flash that Dawn was in fact an actress, and a rather good one. She wasn't a bounty hunter even if it was her chosen profession, she belonged here with the carnies. She was partly their kind. The players on the stage were a head shorter and of a different build entirely. Delicate, pretty, ethereal. She remembered that. And the stories they brought from all over the place on their never ending tour: the whole world rendered as stories from ancient to recent. They were a troupe and Dawn was one of them.

From a dark corner poor old Sizer nodded at her. *Yes. That's it.*

"Dawn," Jerit said, suddenly confident again now that she wasn't in the company of a master thief or a vicious criminal. Sizer was close on her other side again as she asked, "How come you know them? Who are you?" For the mystery of her unexpected friend was biting her, even more than the desire to ask the actor for his name. She nudged Sizer so he didn't get any ideas about making remarks but she was spared the bother of more awkward questions as the crowd filed out because the actors came over to greet Dawn.

"Mimi!" they said, embracing her and laughing as she overpraised their drama. "Who's your friend?"

"This is Dr Goodmeet. An historian," Dawn said, as if introducing royalty. Of the trouble they were in she gave no sign at all.

Mimi? That was her real name? It sounded a lot like mimic and that was no accident, was it? Jerit had heard of mimics but she'd never thought they were real. Was that why it was impossible to tell what Dawn... Mimi – really was?

"Ah and did she put your mind at rest?" the woman asked, pulling off her elaborate wig to show much shorter, more practical hair beneath. Her manner suggested that she felt Dawn had been bothering her for some time with fanciful notions that she hadn't been able to quell herself and now she was hoping that someone else had done the job for her.

Jerit clasped hands with her and found a firm, practical handshake there. No fancies, whatever the art demanded. "At rest about what?"

"Some nonsense about spies and daring do," the woman said, giving Mimi a friendly chuck under the chin with her finger. "She can't stop herself when she gets a notion in her head no matter how far-fetched it is. She wrote a play about Drakaryon you know but we can't put it on. It'd stir up too much anxiety. Ancient history, isn't it, Dr? Nothing to worry about."

"Yes," Jerit said. "Quite."

Mimi smiled at her.

Then the man who had played the moth mage took Jerit's hand and she paused to look into his face, couldn't prevent herself saying, "Are you a relative of Redfan Rye, by any chance?"

"I am. Great grandfather of mine, he is. Well, was," the actor said, wiping at greasepaint on his face casually as it revealed that he was far older than he looked. Her age if not more. "Saw him last time around, did you?"

"I... yes," Jerit said faintly. She wanted to ask how it was possible, wanted him to turn and say it was him, the real thing, and he remembered her and... But they were busy and dragged away by their fellows and stagehands and that never happened nor showed a sign of happening.

They said their goodbyes and Jerit followed Dawn who was really called Mimi out into the chilly shock of night air. "I don't understand," she said to Mimi, hurrying to keep up with her long stride as they wove a way through to the glow of the roasting pits. The smell of savoury beef and spices flitted winsomely on the air making Jerit's stomach hurt.

"They're Mayfly-kinden," Mimi said, offhandedly, her words lost to anyone but Jerit in the flow of traffic. "And they've always been the circus that travels the world. It takes ten years to get all the way around, and if they're lucky they'll see it all once. They don't tell people. They always say they're lost Dragonfly royalty who fell on hard times because otherwise everyone feels sorry for them."

Jerit thought hard. "Then it's true. He really was that man's grandfather?"

"Great great," Mimi said. "They never live more than twelve years, but they're old by then. Ancient. They don't all last that long."

"But I've never heard of Mayfly-kinden."

"They never tell people. They don't want to be pitied."

"So, but... Are you one of them?" Jerit was aghast, her mind already travelling the world with the circus, seeing everything, doing everything, knowing that she must pack every day with wonders and joys because the days were so short, meeting people from other kin that would outlive her four times, five times, a hundred times over. How stupidly pedestrian, how wantonly selfish they would seem with their preoccupations, their sadnesses, their troubles, all the benefits of feeling they had so much time yet to come that they could waste it on these things. No wonder she had fallen for the power of such a fierce joy.

"Yes, after a fashion. Not so short but not so long. That's why I do this, play all these roles, so I can live all the lives. That's why I brought you here. Because Seda might have a lot of things but I don't want her to have more time. The Wasps have everything and look what they do with it." There was a bitterness in this that Jerit felt as keenly as a serrated blade stuck in her heart. It wasn't that Mimi envied the longevity of Seda or the rest. She merely hated them for what they had allowed time to make of them. She'd seen them all and the futures they'd make and she was greatly disappointed.

Jerit understood. She knew very well what a sense of time, personal and historical, could do to someone's mind. Beneath her fingers the folded letters pressed. She drew them out as they arrived under the lamplights of the bug roast at the edge of the crowd waiting to see their monstrous food unveiled and served by a monster. She opened her letters one more time.

They bore the letterhead of the War Office. Each one read identically: "We regret to inform you of the death of... who died during performance of their duties during the war." Only the names were different, and the softness of the folds depending on how many times she had touched and read them. Sizer Darten. Kobalen Kossifry. Tillin Oarblade. Gensin Goodmeet. All alive to her, in her head. All dead and gone everywhere else. And now only Sizer remained here and there. The others had faded away over time. She didn't even know why he was the last. Maybe it was because he had been the funniest. In any case, all of them had lived much longer than Mimi would, or could. And of course there was Redvan Rye too now to add to the ghosts, forever young.

Jerit felt Mimi looking over her shoulder. She handed her the letters. "These are my friends. I have a son, out west. I have a daughter, studying away." She added the last defiantly to assure herself that she wasn't alone, not left behind but staying on.

Mimi took them and read. She folded them back up. "I'm sorry."

"Don't be," Jerit said. "Now I know why you never mention what you are. I don't want pity. I only wanted to let you know."

They moved along, the walkway ropes guiding them in an orderly queue as the ancient scorpion, somewhat doddering but well trained, dug out the ground ovens and began to heap huge chunks of bug meat onto platters that were taken away to be neatly trimmed and portioned. It was quite the primordial sight, in a strangely hallucinatory way. The scorpion's paint was bright and festive, its movements alarmingly swift and choppy: a clown officiating at an execution. Snip snip, thought Jerit. Here today and gone tomorrow. It was the oldest member of the circus by a long way. She remembered it from last time around. It still had the same chip out of its tail spike.

Mimi nodded, her eyes bright. "What will you do with the books?"

All my history, Jerit thought, my family, my friends, "I'm going to burn them, find me a fire."

In the end they used one of the braziers at the edge of the encampment. Jerit watched each page blacken, eaten by an orange line that didn't catch light, only crept steadily in arcs, until every bit was ash. Mimi sat by her side the while, tense and watchful. When it was done she said "Thank you," in a brittle voice.

"Thank you," Jerit replied, feeling numb. "I'd be dead without you. Do you suppose I can borrow that crossbow?"

"What for?" Mimi reached into her cloak to take it out. It had folded down neatly into something like a scroll case.

"Because I'll need to explain how I killed that Wasp," Jerit said, taking it and putting it into the place of the letters. She tossed them as one into the fire with a sense of completion. That was everything taken care of and high time too. "How long will you be staying here?"

"Just one night," Mimi said.

"Then I won't see you again."

"No."

"Well," Jerit straightened up her cloak and bag. "It was good to meet you, Mimi."

"And you, Dr Goodmeet," the woman's face turned to a smile at the name. "One last drink?"

"Don't mind if I do," Jerit said and together they went back into the fairground, arm in arm.

The God of Profound Things

Adrian Tchaikovsky

Nemoctes had thought to find them private guests of the Edmir.

Admittedly, until recently that had not been such a great honour –
for Land-kinden or anyone else – but now the boy Aradocles had taken
the Edmiracy from his uncle. Not so unreasonable, then, to expect a
couple of landswomen to be given the best of care while they waited for
the man they had summoned from the depths. And yet here they were,
in a common chamber surrounded by the crafters and workers and idlers
of Hermatyre, as though the very thought of Land-kinden wasn't still the
stuff of fearful story for plenty.

Of the two, one was plainly in charge, and just as plainly quite
heedless of the looks she and her companion – servant? – were getting.
She was compact and tough-looking, with blue-white skin and blue-black
hair, and Nemoctes had seen her like before. He had to thoroughly turn
over his memories before the names came to him, though: this was an
Ant-kinden (whatever an 'ant' was) and she came from a far-away city
called Chen or Tzen or something. That made a little sense of her fearless
attitude. He had a good idea that there were other colonies over where
she lived, and land and sea lived in a more open relationship than ever
they had in Hermatyre's waters.

The other one was more familiar from recent excursions. Shorter,
darker of skin, stouter of build, she looked to be one of the Collegium
colony. That was the coastal place that had been the centre of so much
of the recent comings and goings – the one that the new Edmir was
keeping up a careful dialogue with. If she had been the one in charge,
then Nemoctes would have gone up to them without much worry, but
she was very plainly junior, and very plainly ill at ease with her
surroundings.

I could just leave, of course. Somewhere around here would be a
Deepclaw named Yosl, who had put out the call that a couple of Land-

kinden wanted no less a man than Nemoctes to be their guide. Less flattering, of course, when you thought that his was probably the only Pelagist name they knew.

Nemoctes was not used to being called on, save by his own people in times of need. To be a Pelagist was to travel far and free. But that travelling was apparently exactly what the landswomen wanted.

He studied them. The Collegiate was sitting down, writing on a scroll of paper so thin it looked as though it should just fall apart. The Ant woman, who had been standing and spying on their neighbours with an unabashed stare, now stepped into a sequence of elegant moves, unselfconscious and automatic. They were just some sort of exercises, but the sight of them weighed the scales in favour of him stepping forwards. He had never seen anything quite like it. He could practically see the glitter of a sword in her empty hands as she killed enemies of the imagination in a sequence of perfect steps. She was a hard-faced woman, expressionless as an Arketoi, but she was very beautiful indeed when she moved like that.

She glanced up before he had closed even half the distance between them, finishing her exercise with a single graceful step that also served to kick her associate. The Collegiate looked up nervily, flinching back from him. Like most of the Sea-kinden around them, Nemoctes was wearing little more than a kilt, with a sling bag over one shoulder for what he should need to carry. The landswomen were both dressed up as though for the icy depths, neck to toe. He had an idea that so much exposed flesh all around her was leaving the stout little woman in a frenzy of land-locked propriety. If the Ant cared, none of it showed on her face.

"You look like a Nemoctes," the paler woman stated flatly. The odd, direct words put him off balance, a little. He learned later that she had been given the image of him from the mind of a kinswoman, and that these Ant-kinden shared their thoughts just like the Arketoi they faintly resembled.

"Consider my coming here a measure of my curiosity, not my willingness to serve," he told her, clutching for the initiative.

"I don't want servants. I want a partner," she told him. "Carabin, find us somewhere we can talk in private. Chuck someone out of their cave if you have to. Master Nemoctes and I have business to discuss."

Carabin was the Collegiate, who pushed herself to her feet unhappily, plainly without the first idea of how to go about doing so. She was young,

Nemoctes judged – maybe two decades, unless her kinden aged very differently to his. Her face and body said she was fighting a creeping fear of just about everything around her.

Nemoctes took pity. "Where is Yosl, who called me?" Had he been back within his living ship, and Yosl in hers, they could have spoken easily enough through their Art. Here, in the chalky tangle that was Hermatyre, he would never find the Deepclaw woman.

And yet here she was, just as though she had caught him thinking her name. She was dark, more grey than the Collegiate's brown, and her scalp was bristly with barnacle-like stubs. She was old, was Yosl, and prone to making mischief and bringing down the good name of her kinden, but Nemoctes liked her.

"I knew I could hook you here," she told him, her smile wrinkled and mobile over toothless gums.

"Apparently we have much to discuss, or so the landswoman tells me," Nemoctes observed.

There was something disturbing in Yosl's gleaming eyes: plainly she found something amusing in this business. At his request she found a chamber in Hermatyre that could contain their private speech, and the four of them crammed into it.

The Ant Land-kinden named herself Orethia. Her proposal was brief and to the point and fully justified Yosl's expression. *Not amusing: insane.*

And yet... and yet... once set, it was like a lure in his mind. He told them it was foolishness; he told them it could not be done, that it would be the death of all involved, and yet... and yet...

He was half-expecting what came next, because probably the Land-kinden had been loose-lipped before they had met Yosl, and of all the Pelagists in the ocean, Yosl sought company and couldn't keep her mouth shut. So it was that he received an invitation to meet with the Edmir of Hermatyre.

Old memories, new circumstances, again. Back in the days past, such invitations had come by way of armed guards, or perhaps even the Thousand Spines warriors. The new boy owed Nemoctes his throne, at least in part. More surprisingly, he was of a temperament that meant such a debt meant something. It meant, for example, that a wanderer like Nemoctes could ignore such an invitation. For that reason, if no other, he came when Aradocles called.

"They're mad, of course," was his diagnosis.

"Are they, though?" the young Edmir asked him. They were in the boy's private quarters, attended only by the Kerebroi woman who had served the old Edmir as major-domo, but had for a long while been working with his enemies. Her reward, it seemed, was to keep her place as the swift currents of change rushed through the city.

"They say they want to find a Seagod," Nemoctes pointed out.

"Not the most lunatic quest in our histories."

"This Ant-woman, she says it will know her. She wants to touch it. She thinks it will care what she is."

"And your opinion?"

Nemoctes shut his eyes. "The Seagods might care about us – *all* of us, as a whole. They rise up to us when great matters wash over us, as though they are curious. They have inspired. They have destroyed. Our stories are in very many minds about what a Seagod's attention means. But will they care about one Land-kinden woman? No. How could they?"

"Perhaps she is a great matter," the major-domo suggested softly. Nemoctes shot her a look that said, *You're not helping.* They knew each other of old.

"I would think as you," Aradocles admitted, "but I have other advisors who want to see her try."

"What advisors…?" but Nemoctes had seen the flick of the Edmir's eyes, cast in a direction that took in the unseen vastness of the sea beyond the coral wall. "*Him?*"

"Whatever this woman is, word of her has reached Arkeuthys."

Nemoctes had no fond memories of the cunning old beast that ruled the octopi of Hermatyre like a second Edmir. It had been Claeon's enforcer back in the bad days. Now its words crept into Aradocles's head. Better, surely, that the creature had died in the coup, but history was seldom cut so cleanly into segments.

"So you're telling me you think this should happen?" he demanded.

"If any know where the Seagods may be found, the Pelagists do," Aradocles observed. "We here know only our own little space of sea. Even our neighbours exist mostly through the tales of your fellows. The whole breadth of the oceans is yours, from the sunlight to the darkness."

"That's very poetic." Nemoctes scowled. "And are you sure you *want* the Seagods to take notice of this woman? What might they do next?"

Aradocles shared a look with his major-domo that told Nemoctes they had all this planned out in advance. "Are you telling me you're not curious at all?" he pressed.

"You want to keep them sweet because they're Land-kinden," the Pelagist guessed. "That's why all this."

"It seems wise. The other woman is from Collegium after all, one of Stenwold Maker's people."

Nemoctes was far from sure that meant much, and he wondered just how far the Ant woman had been inflating her and her companion's importance to get even this far. The people of Hermatyre were used to thinking about communities. Nemoctes thought more naturally of isolated and maverick wanderers. He knew which category he would place Orethia and Carabin into.

"You didn't answer the Edmir's question," the major-domo observed. "You who have seen so much of the world, only to discover how much more there is to see: don't you want to know what will happen when Land-kinden meets Seagod?"

And he did; of course he did. All of this had just been dancing about that plain fact. He was protesting for form's sake, for when things went wrong later. In his heart of hearts he had already made his decision.

The Seagods, though. The sea was full of a bewildering variety of denizens, great and small. There were enough wonders and terrors out there that a Pelagist might spend a lifetime hunting them and achieve nothing more than a greater understanding of his own ignorance. But the Seagods were special. They held a place in the legends of the Sea-kinden, all the way back to when the sea had been a new and hostile place for them. The Seagods had spoken to them, so the stories claimed. They had taught them the Art all the sea people now knew, regardless of kinden. They had brought those ancient fugitives of the land to the beasts that would name them and shape them. Was there some hero you wanted to sing of? Then she had met a Seagod once, to mark her out. Was there a great event of times past, a catastrophe or a salvation? Then a Seagod was there, coursing through the dark waters in the background. Merely to see one was an omen of great and terrible times. So: they were special, in the minds of the Sea-kinden. Nemoctes was not a credulous man, or so he assessed himself. He knew there were beasts that were beasts, and there were beasts like Arkeuthys that could grow as wise and wicked as men. So what were the Seagods? Minds, myths or monsters?

Nobody sought them out. No – he corrected himself – nobody sought them out and lived. Surely there had been mad-eyed mystics over the years who had tried to impose themselves on the gods of the deep, to anoint themselves with the glow of greatness by that contact. None had come back with that approval written in their face, certainly. Few even tried to make such a claim in jest or earnest lie. None took the Seagods lightly. None, it seemed, except this Land-kinden woman.

"I knew you'd come round," Orethia told him. Her smile was hard, like a little crescent knife, there and then gone.

"You don't know me," Nemoctes stated. In the face of her self-possession he was less than sure of it.

"I hear things."

What was he to make of that? Surely no land-kinden would have been skulking unobserved through Hermatyre, gathering rumours.

"How did you get here, Landswoman? And how will you hunt the god? Swim and hold your breath?"

She was undaunted. "Carabin brought me in a Collegiate submersible, and we will take it with us, when we go. But for board and lodging I must call on you. There's no air in our craft for any great voyaging across the seabed."

"What makes you think I can find a berth for the two of you?"

"I hear things," she said again, and the smile came and went again. "I expect we'll be cosy."

There was an invitation there, none too subtly phrased. Awkwardly made, though. Nemoctes had wooed and been wooed in his time, by men and women both. Orethia could move on land with a swimmer's languid grace, but she was all raw edges talking to him: too brash when confidence was off-putting; too reticent when one true word would open doors. It was as though the pieces of her that faced outwards were ill made and ill fitting.

He looked to the other Landswoman, Carabin, who appeared acutely embarrassed. Embarrassed about her companion; embarrassed about everyone's bared skin; embarrassed just to be someone called Carabin, here and now, or perhaps anywhere.

A pair of broken shells indeed.

"Show me your craft," he directed.

He had seen a Land-kinden vessel before: an oval of metal with beating legs that swum like no creature he had ever encountered. He had expected another such, and probably the principles were the same, but the aesthetics brought him to a dead stop.

The docking pools were busy, a dozen slender siphon-powered craft floating there while some sort of mechanical crab-looking device was half-disassembled in and out of the water. A dozen Smallclaw mechanics were crawling all over it like scavengers. Nobody was going near the Landswomen's vessel, though, and Nemoctes didn't blame them in the slightest.

They had made it to have a blunt, rounded prow, and a jointed body that swelled for the first few segments and then tapered towards a flat paddle tail. He saw a knot of legs and paddles hanging in the water below it, like the appendages of a thing long dead. It would come to life at their command, he knew, in that disturbing way these machines did. More, he knew how it would swim. He knew the shape it would make in the water.

"You made it like a Seagod," he observed hoarsely.

Carabin surprised him by elaborating. "It was a challenge because I only had Orethia's pictures and descriptions to work on, and it's a departure from the Tseitan hull, but when I got into it, there wasn't all that much to worry about, and the shape is obviously seaworthy-" She broke off abruptly and Nemoctes guessed that Orethia had given her a Look.

"You think you will fool the Seagods?" he got out.

"We think they will see, and understand that we come to meet them," the Ant woman explained. "I assume your own craft can carry ours without much difficulty?"

"I'll say this, there's one way your toy there fails in its resemblance," Nemoctes told her. "It would fit neatly in the claw of a real god."

Carabin shuddered, her face twitching all over with the thought, and he wondered, *Why are you even here?*

"Summon your beast," Orethia told him.

He gave her a level look. "And if I have questions?"

"Let them enliven the journey. After all, we'll be in each other's company long enough, surely. It must be a long way to where the Seagods dwell."

He opened his mouth once, twice. Of course he should insist on answers. Of course he could not trust them. When they were in the open

181

ocean, though, they would live or die by his good graces. They could hardly seize control of the great creature he travelled within. There would be a time for answers, certainly.

And it was a while since he had travelled in company, just heading out into the glorious vastness of the world. Pelagists were loners, but they were human. The old call of their own kind brought them back to places like Hermatyre or the Hot Stations.

And there was something attractive about Orethia, for all her edges and oddnesses. Perhaps she was not the mystery that she tried to create, but she was a mystery for all that.

When he showed them the innards of his companion, his vessel, her reaction was cool, almost disinterested. She looked on his pearl-walled rooms, his treasures and trophies of a Pelagist's long life, and her face gained nothing in the way of expression. It was just a place, to her; just a means to an end. Carabin was quite different in her response. The Collegiate woman let out an exclamation of surprise and delight, eyes wide as though trying to see every detail at once.

"This is wonderful!" she got out. "It's just like civilization!"

Nemoctes gave the subsequent awkward pause time to sink in, seeing the precise moment when she realized what she had said, her face darkening further. "I didn't mean that!" she squeaked hurriedly. "I just meant this…" face twisting as she fought for words, "could be home. It's a little like home."

"You Beetles always did love your clutter," Orethia admonished absently. "This is where you live out your life, Master Nemoctes? Within the air-chambers of a fish."

"If you must bait me, at least do so with scholarly precision," he said mildly. "As you see, these chambers fit me well, but with three we shall be almost as snug as when my beast was living here. No doubt we shall fall to arguing swiftly enough, but perhaps you would rather begin on a more agreeable note?"

And her expression, turned to him, admitted precious little comprehension of what he even meant. He decided then that Orethia knew little of what agreeable meant – that those parts of her mind were the most ill-fitting, or perhaps had been left hollow and empty as she had moved on to greater things. There were plenty of similar temperament among the Pelagists, but then the Pelagists had the luxury of being a long way from other human beings for as much of the time as they liked.

He had his nautilus gather up their little mechanical god in the forest of its arms, hanging limp there as though it were prey. He felt the mind of his beast twitch and frown at the metal taste of it. Reaching out his Art, he smoothed over the feeling, lending his wider human understanding so that the creature's simple mind could reconcile the task with its instincts.

"So where are we…?" Carabin let her voice trail off, perhaps realizing that none of his landmarks or directions would mean anything to her. "How far?"

"Far." Nemoctes shrugged, feeling the nautilus's contentment as it swung about and began swimming for open water, away from the busy nest that was Hermatyre. In truth he was still not fully decided as to what he would do with the Landswomen. Curiosity, yes, but at the same time they were surely fools, and Orethia at least seemed mad. Perhaps he would simply take them on a tour of the ocean floor and bring them back, godless, lamenting that the creatures could not be found. After all, he was but a poor Pelagist. He could not compel the great beasts of the deep.

Or perhaps he would do as they wanted. Or perhaps the Seagods would find him.

He was still mulling the thought over when the decision was taken from his hands.

Carabin had been pottering about admiring his curios and stealing nervous little glances at him, as though any moment he might assault the pair of them. The Ant woman, though, had been standing perfectly still for some time, off in a world of her own. Nemoctes had thought nothing of it, until his beast, his companion of many years, bucked and shuddered around them,

Instantly he was reaching out to her, thinking: *predators? Men-fish?* but in her mind he found an unfamiliar turmoil, a twisting of her simple thoughts. *Are you sick? Are you hurt?* And for a long moment he waited, hearing no reply.

And then Orethia said, "She is well." She was staring at him, pale blue eyes in a paler face, and now there was an expression gripping her features. It was none he had ever seen before on a human being, though.

"What have you done?" he demanded. He had his pick in his hands instantly, threatening her with the hooked bronze point of it. Carabin flinched back with a hand to her mouth.

"Know this about me, Master Nemoctes," Orethia told him. "First is that I am not like any others you have met, on land or sea." There was room in that alien expression to fit her little crescent smile. "I am a freak, Sea-kinden. Where your Art - where others' Art - touches only the minds of kindred beasts, my mind can pry into the minds of them all: ants, spiders, mantids, crabs, squid. I even had a fine conversation with your kraken general back in your colony."

Arkeuthys. "You won him over."

"I fascinated him." The cutting smile again. "I fascinate you, do I not?"

"This is your plan? You think you can pry into the mind of a Seagod? You think you can have a *fine conversation* with one?"

She was practically shaking with the force of her certainty. It was matched only by his own that she was utterly mad. *Curse Aradocles and curse Arkeuthys and curse all Land-kinden.* But too late for that now.

And there was a little traitor part of his mind that asked, *But what if she can?*

"Your mount remembers where the Seagods were, those few times you met them together," Orethia observed. "She's afraid, of course, but she will go there, for me." And her eyes lost focus momentarily. "But she likes you, Nemoctes. She likes you very much." The smile, that damnable smile. "So if I killed you now, she would not do what I wished, not without fighting me every moment. So you're right, in the end. Let us be *agreeable.*"

He was standing there, armed and ready to strike, and yet he remembered the fluid ease of her combat exercises, the imagined glint of blades that her dance had conjured up. And she believed she could kill him, as she patently believed a great many things. Perhaps, in one like this, belief would be enough to make it true.

Then he started back, because she had reached out and touched his beard, a brief tweak that was full of a childish mischief she was otherwise entirely lacking. "You're a fair specimen, for a sea monster," she told him dryly, and then turned her back on him quiet pointedly, daring him to try something.

What he did was sit down on the matting against the curved wall, feeling as though a current had hold of him, and was dragging him helplessly into unknown waters. The worst of it was that his curiosity still had a pin in him, pricking away. Yes, he wanted to know what would happen when this mad, remarkable woman met a Seagod. Yes, the thought terrified him in equal measure.

"She must be a great woman of her colony," he said hollowly. "What is her plan? Will she try to make the Sea Gods slaves to her people?"

Carabin was regarding him curiously. "She and her people parted company a long time ago, Master Nemoctes. You won't know, but Ants don't much like people who are different. Whatever she's doing, she's doing it for herself."

"You don't even know?" Nemoctes demanded.

Carabin grimaced. "I'm sorry, but does she strike you as someone who confides?" Her voice was very quiet – not to escape Orethia's notice, he guessed, but because she was far from home and getting further.

"So why you, why here?" he asked her. "You don't seem to me like someone who dreams those dreams."

"I designed the submersible," Carabin said, as though admitting murder. "She came – she had gold." A guilty flinch. "Sea-kinden gold, she said. I'm sorry."

"For what?"

"She must have stolen it from your people. I see that now." Her eyes ranged over the opulence of his quarters.

"*Gold?*" For a moment this seemed madder even than Orethia's plan. "What was the gold for?"

"To pay for the..." A clenching shudder went through Carabin. "I needed money. I... Do you even have debts, down here? I had debts. I couldn't pay to finish at the College. I had – *have* – such ideas, but my family, we owed so much, it was like..." Her huge eyes goggled at him. "It was like being thrown into the sea with weights tied to every limb. But I suppose that doesn't really scare you, does it? You just sit in your magical travelling squid and go wherever you want and don't need to worry or to care or anything."

"My magical..." Nemoctes felt he was missing a great deal of what she meant. "So you are here because...?"

"The money. And because she's not a good pilot, and I am." Again that shudder, fear and frustration knotting her up. "I'm good at so many things, Master Nemoctes, but up on land, if you've got no money, then they never let you show it. And." She bit the sentence off, but he saw it plain enough in her eyes. *And now it's led me here and I'm afraid I'm going to die.*

Orethia left him to guide their travel after that. Sometimes, when he used his Art, he could feel her there too, crowding the mind of his beast just as she crowded his living quarters, impossible to ignore. There would be no fooling her, no fobbing her off with excuses. They were bound for the deep reaches of the ocean, and first and foremost for the Shellgrave. If there was word to be had of the Seagods and their wanderings, that was where it might be found.

Nemoctes had shared his chambers with others before, but never two at a time and never with such a woman as Orethia. As she herself claimed, she was like no other. Every glance or movement said that she was mistress there, and that Nemoctes remained only on sufferance. Her presence was inescapable through all the little nested rooms, even when she was sleeping. Or perhaps that was his mind, betraying him. She haunted his thoughts as much as she rode the mind of his beast.

Carabin, for her part, had taken one small part of one chamber and done her best to drape it off. Nor would she take off a single piece of clothing, even when the body heat of three people made the nautilus shell close and humid. Orethia herself had stripped down to just a shift, and the icy pallor of her slender limbs began to plague his dreams until at last he went to her. She received him with her distant humour, and he tried his strength against those limbs, a physical union as fierce and antagonistic as killing.

He caught Carabin peering at him from past her drapery, after that first coupling. He was tending to the bruises Orethia had put on his hide while showing him just who was stronger – more Landswoman Art he had not been expecting – and for a sudden moment he saw the world as most Land-kinden did. He felt naked and ashamed of himself, as though what he had done had stripped away some shell or armour that normally stood between him and the world.

He wanted to ask the Collegiate girl if she had a partner back in her arid home. He wanted to tell her to stop staring at him with that fear in her face, as though he would cut her throat the moment she let her guard down. He wanted to say that he would not go back to Orethia's bed, but that would have been a lie, and even then he knew it.

Shellgrave had been a place of heat and life, once. In the long-ago past, the vents there had spewed out a rich mingling of toxins that nonetheless had fed a vast menagerie. Snails and crabs and tubeworms of great size had congregated here in their thousands, long before ever there were human eyes to see.

And then the vents had gone cold, and those creatures that could move on had done so, and those that could not had cast their last larvae onto the ocean currents and then died. Ages later, the Pelagists had discovered the graveyard of empty shells and carapaces, and they had made some small corner of it their own.

Beyond Shellgrave, the ocean floor fell still further, into vast black and desert reaches, down to depths where the crushing weight of water would be too much even for the nautilus to bear, beyond even Nemoctes' Art to survive. And yet there were Pelagists who travelled those lightless marches, and they came up from time to time to places like Shellgrave, and told their tales.

There were never many at Shellgrave – the place could hardly have supported a thriving community. Enough, though that, when Nemoctes and the two landswomen stepped into the close air within a great whelk shell, a good dozen Pelagists, exiles and lunatics were there to greet them.

What the denizens of Shellgrave made of them, Nemoctes had no idea. Shellgrave was not a place to ask questions about anybody's past. The men and women there could be treasure hunters or explorers or fugitive murderers, for all he knew.

A handful knew him, though. The Pelagists lived a scattered existence, but their Far Speech lent them an illusory sense of community. Even the furthest-flung Pelagist might find a need for a colony's goodwill someday, and they knew Nemoctes was the name to conjure with, when venturing into the shallows around Hermatyre or the Hot Stations, or half a dozen other settlements.

Even so, he had come in his shell armour, because being careful cost nothing, and there were always those who cared nothing for any rules.

There were Polypoi there, a trio of them with skin the colour of bruises and deadly poison at their fingers' ends. There was a hulking Greatclaw woman in mail of overlapping black shells, in hushed conversation with a creased old woman of Nemoctes' kinden. There were two emaciated men whose folded limbs would have made them twelve feet tall if they could stand straight without the water bearing them up. Instead they crouched, or crept on all fours with careful, stilted motions, the deepest of the Onychoi who never came to the shallows at all. All these they saw, and more, but Nemoctes sought out a gang of ruffians who had welcomed him with a growling cheer. They were seated about a boulder someone had dragged in, playing Semk with black and white pebbles. He crouched down companionably beside them and watched, feeling all eyes in the room stray to the landswomen. Carabin was practically huddling at his side, a woman so uncomfortable he wondered if there was anywhere in the world, wet or dry, that she truly fitted. Orethia stood like a statue accreated from white stone and regarded the lot of them with haughty condescension.

The band he had attached himself to were Deepclaw: squat and robust men and women with basalt-dark hides. He knew them for travellers, scavengers, dour and secretive folk. They saw a great deal, though, and of all the things they might be hunting in the ocean, he was willing to bet his own quest would not conflict with theirs.

As they played their game, he began to work on them, drawing out snips and scraps of information about where they had travelled, what they had seen. And of course they were close-mouthed: far too much so to let anything the size of a Seagod out, yet he began to piece together a map of their exploits. He began to spot omissions, detours, a look that came into their eyes at certain points. They had what he needed to know, and he would winkle it out of them, piece by piece.

But Orethia was not content to be patient, nor could she see the delicate fishing he was about. She strode to the centre of the room and told them all in clear tones, "I'm hunting gods."

Nemoctes heard Carabin swear wretchedly, and he stood and let a hand drift near to his pick handle. Orethia was standing very straight, and taut tension was clutching at her. She looked like a woman ready for a fight; a woman who believed she was immortal. Everyone was staring at her: he saw plenty of blades and mauls and weapons of Art ready to hand. Any moment, any moment now...

"Come now, who's seen one?" the Land-kinden demanded. "Which of you will share in my greatness by being the one to show me the way." Her madness was plain in her face like a pale fire, or perhaps it was just that the blankness of feature of the Ants had reached some new perfection in her, some terrifying negation of the human.

She scared them. They were hard men and women, self-reliant, governed by their own codes and whims, but Orethia scared them. Her self-belief was vaster than the sea; so was her inability to engage with others on any terms but her own.

One of the spindly Onychoi crept forwards, his bowed limbs almost transparent. "I saw one once," came his whispering voice. "It was far from here, where the coldness seeps from the seafloor and forms a lake of poison beneath the waters. We were fishing for crystal when it passed over us, and we knew something great was occurring." He fought to get the words out of his narrow mouth, breaking the taboo.

"Too far, too long ago," Orethia declared, dismissing him.

"I saw two, once," said the Greatclaw woman, her head brushing the curved shell ceiling as she stood. "I saw them dance about each other in the water, slow as slow. I watched forever."

"Where?" the Ant demanded, and the huge woman shrugged with a scrape of armour.

"A distant place. I never went back there."

"Have none of you anything for me?" Orethia snapped. "Are you all so forsaken by the very things you venerate?"

"Who can tell where the gods will swim?" one of the Polypoi murmured, and the other two nodded their purple-black heads, their short hair twisting and twining.

Why don't they kill her? But Nemoctes could feel it too. Was it some magic she had, or some Art that let her cast her mind against all of them and bend them to her will? Or was it the Seagods themselves, reaching out through fathoms and leagues to bring this woman to meet them?

"I know." It was one of the Deepclaw, a round-shouldered woman wearing a harness of sharkskin studded with blue stones. "I will tell you where you must go. No sense knowing where the Gods *were*. But there is a place they come to, sometimes, often. There is a great struggle they are drawn to, sometimes. Wait long enough there, and they may come to you."

Abruptly, Nemoctes knew what she meant. Indeed the knowledge seemed suddenly at large in the room, freed by the Deepclaw's words. And why not? Why wouldn't the gods go there? Why should they only care about matters on a human scale?

"Tell me," Orethia breathed, and the Deepclaw told her. When she turned her cool gaze on him, Nemoctes nodded.

"I can take you there."

"Can I ask a question?"

The small voice was Carabin's. Orethia was sleeping, and Nemoctes had thought to stay awake while the ship was quiet, to enjoy some ersatz solitude and the sole occupancy of his vessel's mind.

The Collegiate girl was not weathering the journey well, he thought. There was an unhealthy greyish cast to her skin, a hollowness about the eyes. At his nod, she bit her lip and hesitated, as though waiting for her words to order themselves.

At last she came out with, "We can't be the only humans looking for Seagods."

The subject had been more than thoroughly covered in past conversations, so he just frowned at her.

"I mean," she went on, "surely they have a people already."

"A kinden, you mean?" and, at her quick nod, "Why?"

"Because they're there," she said simply. "And you Sea-people, you use everything. I understand your world now. It's a desert, with just a few points of life. So you sieve everything fine: nothing goes to waste with you. So if there is a great beast out there, a powerful beast, then someone would find a way to ride it, to live in it, to serve it, even..."

She had always been Orethia's shadow, with little to her save that nonsense talk about gold, but now he re-evaluated her. She had been so quiet that he had not heard the workings of her mind all this time.

"I have always thought they must do," he confirmed, "and by the same logic. But I've never seen them. I can't imagine them. I know Pelagists who claim... but we're notorious liars, all of us, especially about what we've seen in the far deep places. So is that what *she* wants? She wants to join the Seagod-kinden somehow? Or, no..." Because that didn't sound much like Orethia. "She wants to be their Edmir – their ruler," he clarified at Carabin's look. "Of course she does."

"I don't know," the Beetle woman said. "Maybe she will fight them. Maybe she doesn't want to share the Seagods with anyone."

They slept twice more before they came to the place the Deepclaw had spoken of. Orethia was fretful, twitchy, pacing the confined spaces of the nautilus shell as though looking for a way out. One night she came to Nemoctes, the two of them making war as much as love, struggling and twining until she overbore him and pinned him beneath her. Afterwards, he could only think of lonely, miserable Carabin crouched somewhere not far out of arm's reach, crippled by propriety and desperately trying to unhear them.

But then the senses of his beast were telling him all the changes of the sea: the cold water meeting the warm, the rich currents swarming with life, and he informed his passengers, "We're here."

Out there, the sea floor fell away into the abyss, the water column of the freezing dark ascending to meet the richness of the sun-touched surface. In that interstitial place of meeting, a great deal of life was possible. They hung in the water at the furthest extent of the sun's reach, surrounded by a thick greyness that shimmered with fish and shrimp, with a multitude of tiny living things, and dead things filtering down from above, and all the greater creatures that devoured them.

All this he saw through the eyes of his mount, and perhaps Orethia saw the same, but Carabin was blind. "What is this place?"

"This is where the giants hunt," Nemoctes told her softly. "This is where they make war."

"Show me," Orethia stated, and he blinked at her. She had been speaking to her companion, though.

"Is it safe?" Carabin whispered. "There are giants…"

"We have come this far. Nothing in the sea is *safe*," the Ant told her sharply. "I will see it with my own eyes."

She meant their conveyance, Nemoctes understood: the mechanical swimmer that the nautilus had carried all this way. Suicide, surely, to trust to fragile metal out there; to be a speck in the eye of the largest monsters in the sea. Except, if those monsters turned such eyes on them, would the shell of the nautilus offer any more protection?

And perhaps Orethia's madness was catching, because after he had escorted them, cauled, to their barque, he joined them inside it, crammed shoulder to shoulder, so that his own frail human eyes could see the wonders of that place.

The motion of the submersible worked on his stomach instantly, along with the artificial reek of the inside of it. Carabin was couched at the front, directing the machine's progress in ways that were more opaque than magic could ever be. The vessel seemed to move off readily enough, jerking and flailing its way through the water. Past Carabin's rounded shoulders, thick windows gave out onto the gloom of the undersea, and the lamps of the craft attracted whorls and spirals of shoaling fish.

"I take it these aren't your giants?" the Beetle asked. Being in her pilot's seat seemed to have restored some confidence.

"This is a place of life, when time and tide are right," Nemoctes told her. "As you said, such places are far between, and so they bring…" But the world outside had anticipated him: even as he spoke, his words became unnecessary.

Something coursed past their narrow view, a sharp-tipped body five times the length of their little machine, and then a streaming length of arms and tentacles trailing like pale ribbons that seemed to go on and on. Nemoctes had a split-second's glimpse of a round eye larger than their windows, gazing implacably out onto the world.

"Lights," hissed Orethia, jabbing a finger at the glass. Out in the murk there were flashes and ripples of brief luminescence: green, blue, purple.

"It is their speech," Nemoctes said, and then another vast squid rippled past them, slowing to take a better look at this little lit object that had invaded its world.

Carabin made a hoarse noise. "Are they – will they eat us?"

"No. They are not the danger here."

"That's – that's far from reassuring, Master Nemoctes."

"Where are the Seagods?" Orethia demanded.

"They may come here sometimes. Did you think they would be lined up waiting for you?" Nemoctes demanded. From her furious stare, he guessed she had.

"They come to eat these things?" Carabin pressed. She had let their machine coast, its mechanisms silent, and the squid passed silently back and forth like great pale shadows.

Something fell past their view like a grey cliff. For a moment, perspective was impossible. It was as long as the squid but, where they were ephemeral, it seemed composed of infinite mass and strength. The side of it was mottled and creased and rugged, studded with rogue barnacles and seaworms. Then Carabin was frantically backing them, pulling away and then pulling away, and still the appalling rock-like flank was all they could see.

And then the jaws with their great ranks of curved teeth, in which a desperate, fragmenting squid was caught, shredded and cut at and gulped down into the murderous, hungry interior of the monster. And presiding over it all with a calm tyranny was an eye: not the vacant lantern of a fish, not the calm, wide orb of a squid or the comforting facets of a crab, but an eye that seemed almost human in its regard. An eye capable of all humanity's comprehensions, all its cruelties.

The leviathan seemed to stare at them for a moment, to peer in at their very windows, and then it was gone with a powerful shudder of its flukes, passing into the lightless gloom.

"Tell me," said Carabin in a shaky voice, "does *that* have a kinden?" But she knew the answer, really. Such a monster could never have a people. There had been nothing in that mad, hating eye that admitted of any compact with the people observing it.

"The great menfish," Nemoctes pronounced. "There are smaller, in the shallows, but these depths are the hunting grounds of the most monstrous of them. Some say they were human once, transformed in those shapes by..." He shrugged: no use talking of magics to these Apt women when he himself could not believe the tale. "Some say they are still human inside, buried within that weight of flesh, always hungry, tormented by the horror of what they are. Or they are just big air-breathing fish."

"Will *that* eat us?" Carabin breathed.

"No, but it might kill us anyway." The blind hate in that little eye stayed with them all for a long time.

They returned to the nautilus, and Nemoctes busied himself in exercising his Art, replenishing their air and tending to some accreation projects he had stowed away. He could hear Orethia pacing and fidgeting, and sometimes slapping the curved walls: *so close, so close,* and yet still there were no gods moving in the waters around them. He almost expected her to cry out, "Don't they know who I am?" That self-centred monomania of hers, her utter disregard for any part of the world that would not serve her needs, it should have been repulsive; it should have made her ugly and terrifying. Instead, it had taken her beyond such petty considerations. She was such a self-made, self-reliant creature that Nemoctes could not stave off a helpless admiration. She and her purpose had grown to fit each other perfectly, like snail and shell.

Carabin was a different matter. Carabin thought she was going to die, he could see it in her face. When the gods came, if they came, Orethia would demand to be taken out into the sea of monsters again, and Carabin plainly viewed that as suicide.

And yet she would go. She could no more refuse Orethia than could the rest of the world.

Than the Seagods could, it seemed, for Nemoctes was woken out of an uneasy sleep soon after by the urgent clamour of his beast's mind. *They are here.*

Orethia already knew. She was kicking Carabin awake, and the anticipation on her face made her something more and less than human, honed to a single edge.

In the mind of the nautilus, the shadow of the Seagod coursed, vast and slow as it rose from the depths towards the distant sun. Coming to feed, or to record the fall of giants? Or to meet one hubris-ridden Land-kinden? Nemoctes felt a stirring in his stomach, a shift of primal emotions, just at the knowledge that such a beast was near. *Flee!* it told him, *Or fall on your face and hope it lets you live.*

But Orethia stood tall; perhaps she had never bowed her head to anything, on land or sea. "Get to your seat, pilot," she snapped. "It's coming. It's here now. This is what we've been waiting for."

That was a manifest lie: there was no *we* in the Ant woman's mind. Nemoctes decided then and there that she had always and forever been an *I*, alone and unique in the world.

Carabin turned to him, a beseeching look on her face. She wanted him there with them, when they cast their Seagod-shaped metal speck into the vastness of the sea. What good she thought he could have done, he could not say. Perhaps she did not want to be alone with Orethia, at the end.

But he shook his head. To stand so before the gods of the sea, in that company, was more than he could bear.

He saw them through the undignified scrabbling and clinging and floundering that got them from his domain, through the cold water and into their craft. From there, the Landswomen were on their own. He retreated to the nested chambers of his own living vessel.

His instincts were telling him to flee; so was his beast. He was out of Orethia's grasp while the open water separated them. He closed his eyes and tried to find traces of her mind in his, but in truth he had never believed that she had an Art to twist the minds of people. She didn't need it. That was simply *her*, the essential nature of her personality.

He had met many people of diverse kinden in his time: all the human bounty that the sea had to offer, and some few from the land. She was right, though. In all the world there was no other like her.

So he did not abandon the Land-kinden, but shadowed them as their little metal god-craft rowed itself out into the water column like an offering.

Through the nautilus's eyes he saw the squid trail past the metal god's lights, each a long pale flash of life, and then gone into the darkness in a ragged ripple of limbs. He tried to picture one opening its toothed embrace for that little morsel, mistaking the work of hands for something more palatable. But the great squid did not attack people. They were peaceful and they were wise, an artist's inspiration and a kinden's dream.

But out there in the unbounded vastness of the water there were huge, violent bodies that held darker thoughts: not a Seagod but the great manfish that was enemies to all. The nautilus felt the coming of the beast long before. Abruptly it was bucking under Nemoctes' control, feeling the approach of death. An invisible shiver spread through the water as the leviathan extended its Art outwards, seeking prey without the need for those tiny, human eyes.

Swim! Nemoctes thought, his mind on that little metal bauble out in the waters. He had no way of making them hear him, though, and he knew that Orethia's mind would be on one thing only. She would be reaching with her own Art, seeking the mind of the Seagod that lurked beyond her sight.

He had a sense only of something vast, the wash of its hunting Art blinding him to it, but the nautilus was wiser than he and flung itself away through the water, jetting with its siphon. The manfish was briefly all his ocean world, a wall of wrinkled grey flesh scything the water. *It's not going for them; it's coming for me.*

He met minds with his beast then, seeing the ponderous shape turn and fluke back for him, those murderous jaws agape. Manfish like this subsisted on the great squids, but what was a nautilus save for a squid in coiled mail? Or perhaps it was not food the manfish sought, but just a chance to indulge the hatred its eye had been so full of.

Nemoctes let the nautilus flee, his human intellect steering its instincts. Again the manfish passed close by, missing by the width of its own jaws and sending him spinning in its wake. Again the nautilus spouted away, not swift in the chase, but dancing with a ponderous grace as it kept out of the sweep of those teeth. How long, before the manfish needed to rise to the surface for air? Too long, Nemoctes thought. *I should never have come here; this was a fool's quest, and I wasn't even the fool.*

Then something tiny passed across the eye of the leviathan and he saw a little cloud in the water, like the death-moments of a squid. Not ink but blood, though: the Landswomen's submersible had struck out at the manfish with some weapon. That they had harmed it at all was miraculous. Certainly they had not done any lasting hurt, but they had its attention. It saw them; perhaps it even understood what it saw.

A thunderous flick of its tail sent Nemoctes rocking madly away as the leviathan's gaping maw swallowed the ocean.

Nemoctes wrenched his mount around, desperate to see, to record their last moments. Then the Leviathan bucked away, twisting in the water, locked in battle with a new contender: not one of the great squids, that could have done no more than write a few scars on that thick hide. The bloated grey body of the monster had been seized in the jointed grip of the Seagod.

The water was flurrying with shed blood; Nemoctes glimpsed it unevenly: saw-edged pincers scissoring deep into that dense flesh, a great humped back of ridged segments clasped to the leviathan's spine; mandibles at their busy work. What shocked him was that the manfish was the greater, vaster even than god. Mere size would not save it, though. As squid on fish, as the manfish on the greater squid, so the god of the depths fed on leviathan.

Nemoctes was hunting for the submersible, then, sending his companion bobbing through blood-acrid waters. How much air did they have? Had they even survived the fray? He had no understanding of their craft or what stresses it could endure. It could hardly be as adamant as the woman who commanded it.

And it had come back for him, despite all. Although, he would admit, that seemed more Carabin's actions than Orethia's.

When he found them, he was too late. They were hanging in the air before the vast and compound gaze of the Seagod.

The corpse of the leviathan had been discarded. Pieces of it still whirled and spun in the water, but the uneaten bulk was on its long descent to the seafloor, to become an island of new life in the cold, dark reaches of death. The Seagod had forgotten its prey, it seemed. All of that colossal attention was focused on the little metal image of its divinity.

And somewhere within that frail shell was Orethia, straining her Art, seeking to touch the mind of god.

Now Nemoctes saw the Seagod in all its glory, as it swum a lazy circle around the submersible. He saw it plain through his beast's eyes: the bluntly streamlined head, flanked by eyes with a thousand lenses, a hood for the bristling surgeon's tools of its mandibles; the folded pincers and lesser legs, all the way down to the flat paddle of its tail that sent it gliding so effortlessly through the water. His heart felt like it would break for the fear and majesty of the thing. He was utterly, utterly glad that it cared nothing at all for him. And yet Orethia had sought it, had come all this way solely for this. He had never felt further from her worldview than right then.

Through borrowed eyes, he saw that mote tumbling slowly before it, that pale and artificial imitation. Carabin had wrought well, to craft the form of a beast she knew only through Orethia's words, but how inadequate it seemed now. Just enough, perhaps, to spark interest in a vast, inhuman brain.

And now I go, but Nemoctes did not go. Was nobility of spirit the quality that chained him to this scene? He had been accused of it before, but that was amongst settled and civilized people. He was beyond all their mores and practices now. Perhaps it was the curiosity that Aradocles had levelled at him. Perhaps he just had to know how this would end.

And he guided his mount nearer, against its strongly held desires. He transgressed on the presence of the Seagod. It filled the senses of his beast; it filled his mind with its vast presence as it narrowed its lazy circling in on the submersible. As the Seagod passed him, he felt the shadow of its claws fall over him, close enough that it could have reached out and taken his vessel like a toy. The armoured length of its body and tail spun him about in the water as it passed. In all the reaches of all the seas of the world, any place would have been safer and saner, but still he nudged his recalcitrant companion on.

And at last the slow-beating legs of the Seagod were backing, arresting the glide of its momentum until it was still in the water, impossibly still, with the little metal barque before it. What was going on within that craft right then? Surely Carabin had been dragged from the controls to stop her fleeing her fate. Perhaps she had even been killed. Nemoctes could not imagine some small thing like the murder of her friend standing between Orethia and her desires.

He imagined her, proud and defiant, staring through the windows of the ship at that great dark shadow, the gloom that the filtered sunlight could not touch. He imagined her reaching out her Art to touch that breadth of mind. Would she command, or was this the sole and lonely moment she would admit to humility? What would she ask of the Seagod, in that private and unknown communion?

And he knew at last what he felt about her. He felt proud for her, one human to another, that she had come so far, and dared so much; that she had at least attempted this mad scheme of hers. Perhaps there had never truly been a Seagod-kinden; perhaps there was one now.

And he was close, so close, and neither machine nor god paid any heed to his gently drifting craft, and that was all to the good.

He saw the claw move, just one serrated pincer unfolding from beneath the creature's carapace, a forked shadow in the water. The sight struck him with a deep fear; what must the women in the submersible think, seeing that it was coming for them?

He felt the pincer close about its metal prey as though a shockwave had gone through the water: all in his head, yet very real to him. He was fighting the terror of his mount now, even as he fought down his own. *Closer*, he insisted, *Closer!* and then, *Orethia?* Because she might be there, might be sharing the frantic brain of the nautilus with him still. She might be calling for help, even now.

But there was only the beast and him. Orethia had found what she wanted now, and even with her fragile man-made shell groaning and protesting around her, she would not spare a thought for Nemoctes. She had achieved the end that she was means to.

The Seagod moved slightly in the waters, its oar-legs sweeping, casting itself lazily backwards. The vessel remained in the clutch of its claw, but there was no tell-tale explosion of air to show the hull yielding.

The vast tail rippled once, a single perfect curve of segments down to that flat paddle terminus, and then Seagod was departing, moving gracefully away from the feeble sun towards the cold depths.

Orethia: had she succeeded? Had she failed? What bond had sprung up between woman and arthropod? What boundaries had she transgressed? The thoughts were whirled past him and away, because there was something tumbling in the water where the machine had been.

Carabin. Not murdered after all, whatever she had experienced in those last moments had led her to prefer death by water to being taken where the Seagod was going. Or perhaps Orethia had told her to save herself; perhaps Orethia had told her Nemoctes was coming; perhaps the Ant had thrust her out of the craft herself.

She would never say. Of what had passed within the submersible, she would speak not one word. Some events were made to be secret, lost to story.

Nemoctes urged his beast forwards, seeing in its eye her struggles, clothing strangling attempts to swim that would have been futile anyway. The nautilus's tentacles closed about her in a sudden net – how much more terrifying must that have been than simple drowning? – and it thrust her through the portal in its shell. When Nemoctes drew her past the inner door she was sodden and still, but she jack-knifed up a moment later, vomiting out water, coughing and hacking and fighting him off.

For a long time, as the nautilus took them away from where the giants fought, she hid herself in one of the small chambers of its shell, and Nemoctes left her to her thoughts. Only later did she come out, still draped in sagging, soaking clothes she had not dared remove. But it was warm within Nemoctes' domain, and the gap left by the removal of Orethia gave them space to be themselves, rather than just appendages of the Ant's greater purpose.

"I will take you to Hermatyre," he told her. "From there, you will meet easily enough with those the Edmir has authorised to treat with the Land-kinden – with your people."

She watched him cautiously. He had expected her to ask him to put her ashore himself, but she just nodded, accepting what was offered. Given her past associations, he would have said she was a woman who should be questioning her lot in life more.

He tried to speak of Orethia, of the Seagod. Later, so did she. They found that they couldn't. Nothing lay that way but questions neither could answer. Only when they were at dock at Hermatyre, floating amongst the simple pen-shaped vessels of the Onychoi, jostled by the mounts of the Dark-kinden, did Carabin open to him.

"She might have had an hour of air in there," the Collegiate woman said. She stood at the water's edge, the vaulted coral of Hermatyre's structure coiling above her. Her clothes were still creased and heavy with damp.

Nemoctes, at the nautilus's opening, nodded.

"Or, if it just took her deeper..." Carabin's eyes were haunted, "I know you did that thing with the pressure, with your Art, but without you, the hull wouldn't have stood it. She'd have been crushed."

"Unless." Because Nemoctes had been thinking about all this just as much as she had.

"Unless what?"

"Unless there are Seagod-kinden. Unless it was taking her somewhere. Unless."

"You think that –?"

He shrugged, shaking off the question. "Nobody can say. Perhaps she's their Edmir, now. Or their pet. Perhaps in a year's time, or ten years, I'll walk into Shellgrave or some place like that, and she'll be there. Perhaps she'll become part of the stories they tell, out in the depths. Or not." He shrugged. "I don't imagine you'll be staying around to find out."

"No!" She had a hand to her mouth instantly, not meaning to sound so horrified. But the sentiment was out there and Nemoctes understood.

"You'd better have this, then." He reached back and pulled out the rough slab he had been working on. "It's not much, but you said..."

She blinked at the dull, yellowish lump, took it from him and lurched with the unexpected weight. "This is...?"

"You said you needed gold. It's gold."

Her expression said that this was madder than hunting Seagods. "You can't just... You can make gold?"

"It's in the sea. It's just about drawing it out, bringing it together." He remembered something from past discussions about the Land-kinden. "Probably you shouldn't tell people where you got it."

"Yes, I can see that." She shook her head, bewildered. "Will you – are you coming ashore – is this even ashore? – to meet with your Speaker, your chief or whatever?"

"Probably he wants me to," Nemoctes told her. "Probably he wants me to tell him everything that happened, like a good spy. But I don't feel like it, and I'm no subject of his. So I'll be going, now."

When he turned, he half expected her to ask him if he would be looking for Orethia. He wouldn't be. Of course he wouldn't be. That would be a fool's errand.

And yet, putting Hermatyre behind him, the thought kept its hooks in his mind, and would not be dismissed. *Somewhere out there... somewhere in the far depths where even Pelagists fear to tread, there is a cold, pale woman who speaks with the gods...*

About the Authors

John Gwynne writes epic fantasy. He is the author of the Faithful and the Fallen quartet and is working on a new trilogy titled Of Blood and Bone. Book one, *A Time of Dread*, is published, book two is finished and going through edits and he is hard at work on the final instalment. John is married with four children and a handful of dogs. When not writing, John can be found making his wife endless cups of tea, being an all-round slave to his daughter or standing in a shieldwall on the South Downs, with his sons in the wall beside him. He is a Viking re-enactor and lover of all-things Norse and Celtic. He also likes dogs a lot. He is represented by Julie Crisp. http://www.juliecrisp.co.uk

Frances Hardinge spent her childhood in a sequence of small, sinister English villages, then went on to study English at Oxford. While working as a technical author, Frances was persuaded by a good friend to submit her first children's novel, *Fly by Night*, to Macmillan. She has now written eight books for children and young adults. *Cuckoo Song* won the Robert Holdstock award at the British Fantasy Awards, and *The Lie Tree* was declared Costa Book of the Year 2015. Her most recent book is *A Skinful of Shadows*. Frances is seldom seen without her hat and is addicted to volcanoes.

Born of hardy East London teaching stock, **Joff Leader** is a writer, voice actor, and musician, who lives wherever Her Majesty's Armed Forces has posted his husband this year. He likes his Sci-Fi and Fantasy fiction like he likes his coffee: in a broad variety of flavours, categories, and styles, each preferably with a pretentious foreign sounding name.

Tom Lloyd is the author of ten fantasy novels including *The Stormcaller* and *Stranger of Tempest*. He never received the memo about suitable jobs for writers and consequently has never been a kitchen-hand, hospital porter, pigeon hunter or secret agent, but has worked in publishing since graduating. He lives in Oxford, isn't one of those authors who gives a damn about the history of the font used in his books and only believes in forms of exercise that allow him to hit something. Visit him online at http://www.tomlloyd.co.uk or twitter @tomlloydwrites

Keris McDonald is a UK-based writer of genre stories – a showing in Ellen Datlow's *Best Horror of the Year Vol.7* was a proud moment – who is currently dipping her toes in the writing of horror RPG scenarios for tabletop games companies. Most of her time is, however, spent under the name 'Janine Ashbless,' writing dark fantasy erotica and hot romantic adventure. Her most recent novel is *The Prison of the Angels* (Sinful Press), third in her Book of the Watchers trilogy about fallen angels, religious conspiracy and a war against Heaven. www.janineashbless.com

Juliet E. McKenna is a British fantasy author. Loving history, myth and other worlds since she first learned to read, she has written fifteen epic fantasy novels, starting with *The Thief's Gamble* which began The Tales of Einarinn. She writes diverse shorter fiction, from stories for themed anthologies to forays into dark fantasy and steampunk. Exploring new digital opportunities, she's re-issued her early backlist as ebooks as well as publishing original short story collections and most recently, the modern fantasy *The Green Man's Heir*. Visit julietemckenna.com or follow @JulietEMcKenna on Twitter.

Peter Newman sometimes pretends to be a butler for the Hugo and Alfie Award winning Tea and Jeopardy podcast, which he co-writes. His first book, *The Vagrant*, was shortlisted for a British Fantasy Award, and won the David Gemmell Morningstar Award in 2016. He has also written for Fantasy MMO Albion Online and is a Wild Cards writer. His latest book, *The Deathless*, is the first in a new trilogy.

Justina Robson was born in Yorkshire, England in 1968. She sold her first novel in 1999 which also won the 2000 *amazon.co.uk* Writers' Bursary Award. She has been a student (1992) and a teacher (2002, 2006) at The Arvon Foundation, in the UK, (a centre for the development and promotion of creative writing). She was a student at Clarion West in 1996. Her books have been shortlisted for most major genre awards. In 2004, Justina was a judge for the Arthur C Clarke Award. Her novels and stories range widely over SF and Fantasy, often combining the two and often featuring AIs and machines who aren't exactly what they seem. She is also the proud author of *The Covenant of Primus* (2013) – the Hasbro-authorised history and 'bible' of *The Transformers*.

David Tallerman is the author of the recently released crime thriller *The Bad Neighbour*, ongoing YA fantasy series The Black River Chronicles, the Tales of Easie Damasco trilogy, and the novella *Patchwerk*. His comics work includes the absurdist steampunk graphic novel *Endangered Weapon B: Mechanimal Science*, with Bob Molesworth, and his short fiction has appeared in around eighty markets, including *Clarkesworld*, *Nightmare*, *Alfred Hitchcock Mystery Magazine* and *Lightspeed*. A number of his best dark fantasy and horror stories were gathered together in his debut collection *The Sign in the Moonlight and Other Stories*.

Adrian Tchaikovsky is the author of the acclaimed 10-book Shadows of the Apt series starting with *Empire in Black and Gold* published by Tor UK. His other works for Tor UK include standalone novels *Guns of the Dawn* and *Children of Time* (which won the Arthur C. Clarke award in 2016) and the new series Echoes of the Fall starting with *The Tiger and the Wolf* (which won the Robert Holdstock award in 2017). His work has also been nominated for the David Gemmell Legend Award and the Starburst Brave New Words Award. He lives in Leeds in the UK and his hobbies include entomology and board and role-playing games.

TALES OF THE APT

Adrian Tchaikovsky

Tales of the Apt is a companion series to the best-selling decalogy *Shadows of the Apt* (Tor UK) by 2016 Arthur C. Clarke Award winning author Adrian Tchaikovsky.

Tales gathers together short stories from disparate places and supplements them with a wealth of new material written especially for the series. Together, they combine to provide a different perspective, an alternative history that parallels and unfolds alongside the familiar one, filling in the gaps and revealing intriguing backstories for established characters. A must read for any fan of the *Shadows of the Apt* books, where epic fantasy meets steampunk and so much more.

"The whole Shadows of the Apt series has been one of the most original creations in modern fantasy"
— *Upcoming4.me*

"Tchaikovsky makes a good and enjoyable mix between a medieval-looking world and the presence of technology" — *Starburst Magazine*

Spoils of War
A Time for Grief
For Love of Distant Shores

Available now from NewCon Press: www.newconpress.co.uk

Cover art by Ben Baldwin

NewCon Press Novella Set 4: Strange Tales

Gary Gibson – Ghost Frequencies

Susan MacDonald knows she's close to perfecting a revolutionary new form of instantaneous communication, but unless she makes a breakthrough soon her project will be shut down. Do the odd sounds – snatches of random conversation and even music – that are hampering her experiments represent the presence of 'ghosts' as some claim, deliberate sabotage as suggested by others, or is there a more sinister explanation?

Adam Roberts – The Lake Boy

Cynthia lives in Cumbria, where none suspect her blemished past. Then a ghostly scar-faced boy starts to appear to her and strange lights manifest over Blaswater. What of the astromomer Mr Sales, who comes to study the lights but disappears, presumed drowned, only to be found wandering naked days later with a fanciful tale of being 'hopped' into the sky and held within a brass-walled room? What of married mother of two Eliza, who sets Cynthia's heart so aflutter?

Hal Duncan – The Land of Somewhere Safe

The Land of Somewhere Safe: where things go when you think, "I must put this somewhere safe," and then can never find them again. The Scruffians: street waifs Fixed by the Stamp to provide immortal slave labour. But now they've nicked the Stamp and burned down the Institute that housed it, preventing any more of their number being exploited. Hounded by occultish Nazi spies and demons, they leave the Blitz behind in search of somewhere safe to stow it…

IMMANION PRESS

Purveyors of Speculative Fiction

Venus Burning: Realms by Tanith Lee

Tanith Lee wrote 15 stories for the acclaimed *Realms of Fantasy* magazine. This book collects all the stories in one volume for the first time, some of which only ever appeared in the magazine so will be new to some of Tanith's fans. These tales are among her best work, in which she takes myth and fairy tale tropes and turns them on their heads. Lush and lyrical, deep and literary, Tanith Lee created fresh poignant tales from familiar archetypes.
ISBN 978-1-907737-88-6, £11.99, $17.50 pbk

A Raven Bound with Lilies by Storm Constantine

The Wraeththu have captivated readers for three decades. This anthology of 15 tales collects all the published Wraeththu short stories into one volume, and also includes extra material, including the author's first explorations of the androgynous race. The tales range from the 'creation story' *Paragenesis*, through the bloody, brutal rise of the earliest tribes, and on into a future, where strange mutations are starting to emerge from hidden corners of the earth.
ISBN: 978-1-907737-80-0 £11.99, $15.50 pbk

The Lightbearer by Alan Richardson

Michael Horsett parachutes into Occupied France before the D-Day Invasion. Dropped in the wrong place, badly injured, he falls prey to two Thelemist women who have awaited the Hawk God's coming, attracts a group of First World War veterans who rally to what they imagine is his cause, is hunted by a troop of German Field Police, and has a climactic encounter with a mutilated priest who believes that Lucifer Incarnate has arrived…*The Lightbearer* is a unique gnostic thriller, dealing with the themes of Light and Darkness, Good and Evil, Matter and Spirit. ISBN 9781907737763 £11.99 $18.99

All these and more on our web site
Immanion Press
www.immanion-press.com
info@immanion-press.com

Lightning Source UK Ltd.
Milton Keynes UK
UKHW040638161218
334103UK00001B/123/P